Let It Ride

Let It Ride

Samuel F. Pickering, Jr.

University of Missouri Press

Columbia and London

5 4 3 2 1   95 94 93 92 91

Library of Congress Cataloging-in-Publication Data

Pickering, Samuel F., 1941–
    Let it ride / Samuel F. Pickering, Jr.
       p.   cm.
    ISBN 0–8262–0801–0 (alk. paper)
    I. Title.
    AC8.P664   1991
    081—dc20   91-4176
                                                               CIP

∞™This paper meets the requirements of the
American National Standard for Permanence of Paper
for Printed Library Materials, Z39.48, 1984.

Designer: Elizabeth K. Fett
Typesetter: Connell-Zeko Type & Graphics
Printer: Thomson-Shore, Inc.
Binder: Thomson-Shore, Inc.
Typeface: Goudy Oldstyle

The author and publisher gratefully acknowledge the following
publications in which essays in this volume first appeared:
*Artful Dodge, Chattahoochee Review, New England Review, Schoolbook,
Southern Review, Southwest Review, Virginia Quarterly Review.*

For Nashville

Contents

Let It Ride

Speakeasy

Waiting for me each August when Vicki and the children and I return to Storrs from Nova Scotia is a bag of mail. Because I had been identified as the inspiration for the John Keating character in the movie *Dead Poets Society*, this summer the mail was more colorful than usual. From Florida a cousin sent a clipping from his local paper. Under "Names and Faces" appeared three people: Dan Quayle to the left, Billy Graham to the right, and in the middle, me. "Praise God, teaching, and the Republican Party," Vicki said when she looked at the pictures. From Indiana a man wrote and described the death of his only son from leukemia, after which he concluded, "May the good Lord continue to bless you and yours and wrap his arms around each of you and give you good health!" A woman who baby-sat me when I was young said that her children saw her "in a different light" after learning that she knew me. "Their old dull predictable Mother and Grandmother knew somebody of importance," she wrote; "I want to thank you for the pedestal they put me on, if only for a brief time." From Missouri a boy sent cards to be autographed for Judy, Jason, and Kelly. After asking my favorite hobbies, he ended, saying, "I hope that you are living your life to its fullest and are enjoying personal prosperity."

Living life to the fullest—seizing the day and gathering rosebuds, as John Keating put it in *Dead Poets Society*—is all right for children, most of whom know little about flowers, blooms or blight. Keating's

1

prescription for living, however, would not do for me. I am too old to live anywhere near the fullest; and if I tried to seize but an hour, I would be swept away by a cardiovascular storm, carried off to that land where there is no night or day, only eternity, and where all the roses are white lilies. Still, as I held the mail, I thought that someone, if not the Lord, had wrapped his arms around my family, giving Vicki and the children good health. For that and for the letters themselves I was thankful. Although they occasionally upset me, the letters enriched the day, and reading them resembled reading a collection of stories, not a collection contrived to educate or reflect social need, but an honest collection, filled with voices, humane and true. Of course not all my correspondents were genial or even pleasant. Not realizing that "personal prosperity" had eluded generations of Pickerings and assuming that I had financial connections with *Dead Poets Society* and as a result had a bundle of cash in hand, they sent letters bristling with chaffy anger. From Canada "The Poorest—Humblest—Divine Magistrate King of All Mankind," or, as he also called himself, "The Supreme Ruler of the Sacred Planet Earth," sent a four-page, photocopied letter. "O You Intellectually and Morally Dishonest Thug of Humanity," the Ruler began mildly before working himself into the warm spirit of criticism and accusing me of being a degenerated, dehumanized product of "alcoholics, prostitutes, whores, homosexuals, lesbians, satans, sinners, and power-hungry criminals." Eventually the Ruler demanded that I hand over all my worldly goods to him to be distributed "amongst the poorest of this Sacred Planet Spaceship Earth."

The day after reading the mail I walked to my favorite August spot in Storrs: the rough land surrounding Unnamed Pond, just off Route 195 near the campus police station. As I walked I forgot not only the mail but also my talk for convocation. Earlier in the summer the university had asked me to give the traditional speech welcoming freshmen and setting the mood for the new school year. Being invited to give the talk disturbed me. Last year's speaker had won a Nobel prize, and I was asked to speak, not because I had achieved anything significant, but because of my identification with *Dead Poets Society*. Convocation was two weeks away, and feeling fraudulent and a little depressed, I had not written a word. By distracting me from myself, a few hours at the pond would restore my spirits. Like a bumblebee in a spring garden, my pencil, I hoped, would then lumber across pages, gathering words like pollen. As I walked around the pond, I quickly strolled beyond mood, and the flowers rumpled together in my mind like a comfortable crazy quilt of colors and names. Black-eyed Susan; daisy fleabane; horseweed bushy and green; dried shafts of red dock; vervain; thistle, seeds floating on the air in icy slivers; pilewort; willow herb; and then joe-pye weed, wild carrot pushing through the blossoms, white against purple and making me think of Victorian wallpaper and long, dark halls. About the flowers butterflies pitched and waved—whites and sulphurs, dark Eastern swallowtails, and then monarchs and viceroys, orange napkins shredded into wings at a child's birthday party. Over everything hung dragonflies, old-fashioned and bright as candy canes.

Instead of hours, I spent days at the pond, eating blackberries and unripe fox grapes for lunch and chewing mint and the leaves of lance-leaved goldenrod. The longer I stayed the more I saw and the less I worried about convocation. Life around the pond was short. Stuck between the petals of sunflowers were the dried husks of bees, looking like small, hairy clumps of mud. One morning a robber fly heaved heavily by, wavering under the weight of a white butterfly. After blooming, the blossoms of wild carrot folded upward and then curved in on themselves, forming domed clumps resembling tall, gray wigs. Small insects hid from predators in the carrot; the wigs, though, were not completely safe—in many crab spiders crouched open-armed. On goldenrod lurked orange and black ambush bugs, their front legs seemingly as thick as weightlifters' forearms. Herds of luminous orange aphids fed on milkweed. The caterpillars of monarch butterflies eat milkweed also, in the process absorbing toxins from the leaves and making themselves "distasteful" to many predators. As the bright color of the caterpillars supposedly warned birds off, so, too, perhaps, the color of the aphids frightened predators away—or so I thought until I saw a small parasitic wasp inserting its eggs into the aphids.

The struggle to live never ended. One day I found some gray and white caterpillars curled on the tops of leaves and disguised as bird droppings. When I showed them to Eliza, my four year old, she pushed two or three about with her index finger and then said, "Daddy, maybe we are all caterpillars crawling on leaves." Eliza's response startled me, and I wanted to mull it over, so I suggested we walk down the hill past the dairy barn to the creamery and get ice-cream cones. On the way, I think I may have had one or two interesting thoughts, but now I have forgotten them. What I remember is the ice cream. Eliza had Oreo and I had strawberry cheesecake, and the girl who waited on us gave Eliza more than she gave me. That night at home I wrote my convocation speech in four and a half hours, and although thoughts of soldier beetles and Carolina grasshoppers may have stopped my pencil once or twice, I didn't fritter away a moment in doubt.

At the pond one day I saw a honeybee so busy digging pollen out of wild mint that he flew into the web of a black and yellow argiope. Although the bee fluttered and turned desperately, he was caught fast. Like the bee I, too, had tumbled into a web, not that of a spider, though, but that of publicity. No matter how I twisted, publicity would spin words about my life, packaging me for consumption. The university advertised my speech, hanging posters in all its buildings and placing sandwich boards along Route 195 at the entrances to the campus, inviting people to "Meet Sam Pickering, the teacher who inspired 'Dead Poets Society.'" In the past attendance at convocation had been low, and the publicity reassured me, for one of my greatest fears was that no one or maybe only twenty-two people would come. I shouldn't have worried; fourteen or fifteen hundred people attended convocation, the largest number ever. My talk itself was old-fashioned, drawing sustenance, I want to think, from the land around Unnamed Pond. I talked about community, first that in Storrs at the university and then that of the past, present, and future. I urged students to wander intellectually and physically. "Cultivate your curiosity," I said, "and develop interests which will enrich your long living." I told them to go to the pond near the police station where the goldenrod was blooming and the milkweed bugs misbehaving. My talk was sappy and rambling, cluttered with stories about the children and our humorous little doings and then words like *responsibility, decency, duty, modesty,* and *compassion.* I said nothing original or profound and trotted out old swaybacked advice, generalities which I thought had cushioned the paths I trod. "Seize the chance to broaden your sympathies and understanding here," I said; "escape the self. Learn about the past so you can understand the present and perhaps have some small influence on a future. Learn not so you become weakly tolerant. But learn so you can grow beyond abstract toleration and become that better thing: the kind and helpful person, the decent son or daughter, the gentle and loving mother or father. I want you to become intelligent enough to say 'I was wrong.' I want you to become big enough to say 'I'm sorry.' "

At the end of my talk the audience stood and applauded—a convention of the occasion, I assumed, for I had never gone to convocation before. I felt wonderfully relieved. After attending a brief reception in the basement of the auditorium, I could bury *Dead Poets Society*. In the future my speeches would be domestic, not public; around the kitchen table, not from a stage; about picking up toys and behavior on the school bus, not about sensibility and community. I was mistaken. In the basement a line of students waited for me to autograph their programs for the convocation. Although I felt foolish, I signed all the programs. Better, I thought, for me to do something silly than embarrass innocent children. In the four months since convocation I have signed my name hundreds of times: on books, programs, notebooks, dollar bills, and shirtsleeves. When a young woman asked me to sign a napkin and I told her that I had never autographed a napkin before, she asked me to write, "This is the first napkin I have ever signed." I did as she directed. My discomfort at autographing programs and napkins is but a small thing, and rather than make another person feel foolish, I suffer my own foolishness gladly.

Publicity changes a person, making the public me, at least, more accommodating. At the reception television reporters interviewed me for the local news. The form of the newscast determines the questions. Because stations could devote only seconds to the convocation, the reporters focused not on idea but on personality. Never having been interviewed for television before, I was naive and at first talked about teaching, insisting that I was an ordinary instructor, simply one among many successful teachers at the university. On being asked for the fourth time, however, what made me stand out, I suddenly realized the reporters wanted colorful fiction, not dull truth. "Oh, hell," I thought; "if it's character they want, they can have it." I wasn't sure I stood out in a crowd, I began, but I got bored easily and sometimes did things to pass the time. "This past summer in Nova Scotia," I recounted, "I bought my eight-year-old son, Francis, a new bathing suit. To pay for the suit I waited in a line. To entertain myself I put the bathing suit on my head, pulling it down tightly over my ears. At first, people in the line glanced furtively at me and the trunks and then quickly looked away. Because the line was long, however, they could not escape curiosity. Finally a woman in front of me turned around and said, almost resentfully and in exasperation, 'Do you always wear your bathing suit on your head?' 'Of course,' I answered, puffing up, 'of course, where do you expect me to wear it? On my behind?'" In telling the story to the reporters I am afraid that when I said *behind* I looked like a toad, pushing my head forward, dropping my chin, and saying the word so that the *hind* rolled about the room and bounced off the walls in a deep, resonant echo. That night my behind, not the convocation, was news. Indeed I sometimes think my bottom the most famous in Connecticut. Throughout the fall and early winter the clip of the convocation interview has been used as filler when the Celtics don't play or the weatherman isn't able to dish up a rich broth of tropical depressions, tornadoes, and hurricanes.

That was my only appearance on television. Soon after the convocation, channel 3 in Hartford asked me to appear on a show called "Live at Five." In between essays and too tired for a walk, I agreed to appear. Things, however, did not work out. I do not drive much, and I got lost in traffic, ending in the Ramada Hotel on East River Drive. When I called the station and said I was returning to Storrs unless someone fetched me, the producer sent a photographer for me. Initially the station seemed almost as rough as the land around Unnamed Pond, and I enjoyed wandering about. The main room was broken into small cubicles; blue dividers separated desks; behind the desks stood red chairs. Telephones rang like crickets, and print machines clacked and chattered like willets disturbed on a nest. On a shelf over a producer's desk was a stack of books: *Super Joy, How to Put the Love Back into Making Love, Win the Food Fight, Don't Blame Mother,* and *You Only Get Married for the First Time Once.* Like the honks of geese, shouts suddenly rang out: "Cut the bullshit," "Give me ten seconds of the cops going in," and "I just called the neurosurgery department. Who's the brain doc?" When I introduced myself to an announcer and asked her name, she exclaimed, "You don't know me! You must be kidding!" I rarely watch television, not because I disapprove of it, but because I prefer to spend my free hours playing with the children or roaming over the university farm. Still, I felt guilty, and if I could have fashioned a covering lie and assured the woman I knew her well and intimately, I would have done so. The time at the station was interesting, and when a tennis match ran longer than expected and "bumped" me off the air, I wasn't bothered. Still, despite several calls I have refused to return. One glimpse of the station was enough; the great golden digger wasp dead in a cream pitcher on my desk simply interests me more than television.

In part, I have avoided television because most shows celebrate character at the expense of idea or even truth. Of course news articles usually do the same. As in television, structure or format determines content. In five hundred or a thousand words, ranging deeply or probing complexity is almost impossible. To be successful an article must attract readers, and drawing readers to a piece about an unknown like me forces the writer to rely on the catchy phrase or colorful tale, verbal equivalents of the bathing suit on the head. After convocation several reporters interviewed me by telephone. For fifty minutes I talked to a reporter from Memphis about reading and teaching. When his article appeared, it was mostly seasoning, the pepper and salt of my offhand remarks, my saying, for example, that the last time I was in Memphis the day was so hot that alligators crawled out of the Mississippi River and were sizzling in the streets. In another conversation, when a writer, envisioning me, I suppose, as a fat, well-basted Tom turkey, asked, "Mr. Pickering, what is it that gets your teaching juices simmering," I told the truth. The good class, I said, often had little to do with students or even the material read. The weather, learning that a friend didn't have cancer, a witty letter, affection domestic—such things influenced classes more than books. Yesterday I taught well, I explained, because of breakfast. At breakfast the family was grumpy, so grumpy that Eliza climbed down out of her high chair and, coming over to me, put her arms around me and said, "Everybody is so mean to you Daddy that I am going to give you a big kiss." The truth, I am afraid, turned the reporter's creative juices to cold, packaged lard, and in the article he did not mention the kiss. Instead he wrote about my standing on desks and in waste cans, things I did twenty-five years ago when hormones spun through me like high-pressure centers.

I did not see *Dead Poets Society* until Thanksgiving. When it came to Willimantic in May, the children had chicken pox, and by the time they recovered the movie had moved on. Shortly afterward we, too, left, going to our farm in Nova Scotia. On returning in August I put off seeing the movie until after convocation. I thought it might influence my talk, making me speak like John Keating. After convocation classes began, and small responsibilities cluttered my hours until the Thanksgiving holiday. Not long after the holiday a producer for the Canadian Broadcasting Corporation telephoned, explaining that he heard I was the model for John Keating. When I told him I had just seen the movie, he was excited and set up an interview for two days later. Supposedly the interview would last an hour, and the arrangements were elaborate. While I talked on the telephone, a freelance technician recorded my conversation in the house. Later the technician's tape and that of the studio in Toronto would be spliced to create the illusion of intimacy. Alas, having seen the movie I was weary of illusion. I didn't put a bathing suit on my head; I said what I really thought, and the interview lasted twenty minutes. Robin Williams, I said, was more restrained and a great deal more sensible than I was twenty-five years ago. Still, I declared, I recognized bits of myself and liked the movie. I liked it because it was a movie, not a work of art, not one of those Swedish or Hungarian films that binds tension to heart and stomach and makes one sigh for Metamucil. When I left the theater, I said, I felt good about life and myself. I didn't mention my "part" in the movie to anyone at the theater. I wanted to, though, and considered telling the man who took up tickets. But I thought better of that, and instead bought a three-dollar tub of buttered popcorn. I almost shed a tear or two at the end, but the scenes in which the Society met in a cave frightened Eliza, so for the last half of the movie I bounced her on my lap. I told the announcer that the movie and the celebrity, such as it was, had not influenced my little doings. In October, however, I said, my eighty-one-year-old father fell, and that had affected my life. I wanted to take care of him, I explained, but wasn't sure how. Builders looked at my house and made suggestions. One morning I put the house on the market; that afternoon I took it off. Bringing Father up from Tennessee would not be easy on him, so, I said, I had talked to schools in the South about jobs. When compared to the effect of Father's fall, I summed up and ended the interview, the effect of the movie upon my life and feelings was negligible.

The newspaper accounts of the convocation smacked of the celebratory ritual of the occasion and were so kind and generous that friends on the faculty wrote their own reports. "Rumor has it," the Associated Press supposedly wrote, referring to the husky, the mascot of the university, "that Sam Pickering is going to dress up in the dog suit at football games." "Convocation at the University of Connecticut," stated UPI, "traditionally a small gathering characterized by tweed jackets, shuffling feet, and hacking coughs of professional pipe-smokers, was transformed yesterday by the presence of a media superstar, displayed with the aid of modern technology to a dazzled audience of attentive adolescents. Professor 'Sam' Pickering, who recently burst upon the world as the academic model for the character portrayed by Robin Williams in the movie 'Dead Poets Society,' singlehandedly brought the convocation ceremony out of the doldrums and into the TV spotlight."

Because of convocation two collections of my essays made the best-seller list for September at the university bookstore. After *The Night of the Mary Kay Commandos* and *Yukon Ho!*, one of my books was the third best-seller, while behind something called *Apocalypse*, the other was fifth. The number of books sold was small. In November, I called the university presses of Iowa and Georgia to find out how the publicity surrounding *Dead Poets Society* influenced sales. From the first of July through the end of October, Iowa sold forty-seven copies of *May Days*; during the same period Georgia sold forty-three copies of *The Right Distance*, for a total sale at both presses of ninety books, ten of which I bought. Although convocation did not increase the sales of my books appreciably, the publicity affected my mail. After reading newspaper accounts of the ceremony, scores of former students wrote me. The letters flattered me. Like deathbed scenes in early children's books in which the sun inevitably rose and music was always heard, the letters were similar, so similar that the movie seems to have set off a general appreciative response. If Keating had been a scoundrel, not only would I have not spoken at convocation, but I suspect I would have received letters from students damning me and then blaming all their failures after college on me. Still, Keating was a hero, and in the letters so was I. "Thanks for treating us like people— not the inconveniences or dullards we seemed to be to others," a man wrote from Pennsylvania. "Not a week goes by that I don't think of how you inspired me and how," a high-school teacher wrote, "I can inspire my students."

Although I cannot separate one year from the next, much less one young boy or girl from another, the students remembered my classes clearly. "I have better recall of your lectures," a newspaper reporter wrote, "than the story I wrote yesterday." Another student remembered the day on which Francis was born, "when *Jane Eyre*," she said, "took on mythical proportions." "One time I wrote a poem for your class and apologized for it," a woman recalled. "You wrote back a note that I've always kept. Do your best, you said, and say no more. This advice has made all the difference to me over the years." The letters both touched and disturbed me; in truth I hoped they reflected not reality so much as convention. If I thought that I really influenced the lives of students, I might stop teaching. I am not a big enough person for such responsibility. Happily not all the letters were tributes; unintentionally some were funny and kept me from taking my correspondence and myself too seriously. "I am a former student of yours (class of 1982)," a man wrote; "I've recently written a poem and was wondering whether you might be willing to critique it, and help me with the punctuation, i.e. where commas should be placed."

Although I received letters from diverse people—Tom who drove the UPS truck when we first moved to Hillside Circle, and then an old girlfriend who ended her letter, "From one who has loved you for a long time and has known that a seed of greatness lay within"—most of my mail came from students and then teachers. Unlike students who thanked me for inspiring and giving them good advice, teachers wrote for advice and inspiration. A teacher from Massachusetts described her lessons, then asked typically, "Are these writing assignments really meaningful or are they just stupid? Is it meaningful to have a high school sophomore write a character sketch of someone who has influenced her? Is it right to have them write four- and five-paragraph essays on a short story or novel they've read?" From New Jersey a teacher sent the reading list for her high school's English department and asked me to revise it, so "it would be relevant and mean something to the students." Receiving a reply, I decided, meant more than particular suggestions, and so while I wrote long answers to such letters I tiptoed around revising reading lists and judging assignments. Many letters came from tired or, as they labeled themselves, "burned-out" teachers. Having lost energy and sometimes optimism, they wrote hoping I could supply some magical intellectual or spiritual elixir that would enable them to recapture their early years of splendor in the classroom. In responding to these letters I felt myself on surer ground. No longer was I an energetic movie character. I had aged, and so I wrote, telling them that they were not burned out, just older. "You are no longer twenty-six and free from worry," I said, "you now have children, sick friends, aging parents, and probably a broken lawn mower. You understand more than you ever did and the more that you understand has made you gloomy." Cure-alls are for the foolish and the naive, and so I offered them none. I did, however, urge them to take walks, to wander through books and across landscapes, to find their own Unnamed Pond. Amid the goldenrod and the milkweed, Shakespeare and petri dishes, they might, I wrote, be able to put things into some satisfactory but probably undefinable prospective.

I thought convocation would end my "celebrity." I was wrong. Because the talk was successful, publicity increased. Instead of fading gray and out of sight like asters in November, I bloomed, not however as the green model for a character in a movie, but as an orangy, autumnal, commonsensical voice. Immediately after convocation, groups began importuning me to speak. Not only that, they offered fees, almost always giving me what I asked. At first I charged four or five hundred dollars. Now I have settled on a thousand dollars and my traveling expenses, an amount, frankly, that strikes me as akin to robbery, something I tell people who approach me to speak. Of course I don't charge local and charitable organizations. Not surprisingly, I have not escaped the movie. In October, I spoke to an alumni group at Worcester State College. Although my topic was the personal essay, the man introducing me mentioned *Dead Poets Society*, saying I was "the epitome of a great teacher." At the reception after the lecture a woman turned to me and said, "You have changed my life." Taken aback, all I could think to say was, "For the better, I hope." "I was working for an insurance company, trying to make megabucks; then I saw *Dead Poets Society*," she explained; "soon after, I quit the company and came back here to school to get a teaching certificate. You only live once," she continued, pausing before adding a questioning "right?" "Right," I answered, "good for you."

Like the letters I received in August, the talks broadened my ac-

quaintance and enriched my days. In November an older woman who
heard me speak telephoned, and for over an hour we talked about the
death of her only son. In December, a woman introduced herself with
a vita, writing "BS '80, MBA '84, TBI '87 (Traumatic Brain Injury)."
She said that writing was a "healthy form of rehabilitative therapy"
and asked me to become a pen pal. Along with the sad and the serious, speeches have brought the light and the comic. From Tennessee
a man sent a postcard depicting the home of country music singer
Loretta Lynn in Hurricane Mills. Along with the card he enclosed
an article from the *Chattanooga Times*, the headline to which read,
"Woman seeking direction in life lost for two weeks in woods." Printed in red and blue on white paper, a letter arrived last week from an
eagle scout in New York. For four years, the scout wrote, he had led
the students and faculty at his high school "in reciting the Pledge of
Allegiance each morning over the public address system." He was
inviting me, the scout continued, to participate in his Patriotic Pledge
Program, consisting of "prominent Americans introducing themselves
and reciting the Pledge of Allegiance on cassette tape. The partici-
pants are also encouraged," he added, "to briefly comment on Amer-
ica's freedoms and/or opportunities in the introduction as well."
Among the people whom the scout had already recorded were "The
Fonz" Henry Winkler; Casey Kassem, the top-forty radio announcer;
Malcolm Forbes; Annette Funicello, alumna of the Mickey Mouse
Club; Dan Rather; Alex Haley, author of *Roots*; the astronaut "Deke"
Slayton; and from the Howdy Doody Show, Buffalo Bob Smith. John
Keating, not me, belonged on the list. To forestall discussion of my
political views in an interview I once said that I was a Communist
Republican, a statement which like many of my offhand remarks appeared in print. Whatever I am, however, Communist, Methodist,
Republican, dervish, chiropractor, or teacher, I don't wear my patriotism publicly. "Unfortunately," I answered the scout, "my voice is
raspy and anyone who listened to me would be sure to decamp for
countries more musical. My recitation would undermine patriotism,
and so," I said, "for the good of the nation I must decline your kind
and flattering offer."

While interest in my speaking increased, interest in my teaching
and association with *Dead Poets Society* did not fade completely. In
September a member of a public relations firm in New York asked if
his company might represent me. I declined the offer. In October, a

woman interviewed me for the *Sewanee News*, the alumni publication
of my old college. In November, the article appeared under the headline "Teacher of the Year." Since the *News* gave her six columns, the
writer had the leisure to be thoughtful and the article was good. In it I
sounded like myself, criticizing the emphasis upon self in our society
and then explaining that I drifted into teaching. "I'd have been happy
doing something else," I said. "I would have been happy as a banker;
by nature I'm not the sort to be unhappy." In November a writer
attended two of my classes. I don't teach in the building that houses
the English department; instead I teach across the campus in the agricultural school. I have a bad disk in my neck, and the walk to class
relaxes my neck and lessens the pain. Not only that, but I also like the
idea of teaching in the agricultural school. The sweet aroma of ma-
nure helps keep mind, nose, and literary criticism in the fleshly world
of the actual. The writer, however, did not know the reasons for my
teaching in the agricultural school, and after attending the lectures
he called a department secretary. "Mr. Pickering," he said, "teaches
awfully far away from your part of the campus. Has the English department banished him because he is so boisterous and unruly?" "Boisterous and unruly," the secretary responded; "why he's not boisterous
and unruly; at least he's not when he takes his medication."

To a degree I have been responsible for my continued identification with *Dead Poets Society*. Before convocation and shortly after I
started roaming around Unnamed Pond, I wrote a brief essay about
the movie and my "celebrity" as a way of putting the experience behind me. Almost immediately the *Hartford Courant* bought the essay;
unfortunately the piece was not published until December 24. Appearing just when I thought curiosity about the movie and me had
died, the essay stirred interest anew. Happily, though, people respond
to the same story differently, reaching different conclusions and being moved in various, sometimes odd, ways. In answer to a query from
a school superintendent I noted in the essay that I was not an educational theorist but simply someone who happened to teach, "a guy
with a nice wife, three small children, an aging father, and a six-year-
old Plymouth." At nine o'clock in the morning on the twenty-sixth,
the telephone rang. On the line was Benny Cardinello from Gem
Chevrolet in Willimantic. He had read my "wonderful" article, he
explained, adding, "and Mr. Pickering, do I have a deal for you."

In talks and answers to letters I tried to capture the spirit of the convocation talk and be generous and compassionate. Being always thoughtful was difficult, and at the end of September a new character, Josh, began appearing in my essays, pushing aside the sentimental country people who had bumbled through my writings for five years. "Babykins, the King has arrived," Josh said, "and it's time to pitch the saccharine and kill the sweetiepies. To stay healthy and survive the foolishness a man has got to have a fatty streak of meanness in his character. Sugar and spice might do for the kids at convocation, but they won't do for a writer." Josh was fifty years old and a disappointed idealist. "Hell," he told me, "it took forty-five years of hard work for me to become a liberal, and then it only lasted seven minutes." "Still," he mused, "that's about twice as long as a good . . ." And here I stopped him because I sensed that he was going to speak crudely and use a word that I never intend to write. Unlike me Josh often talks about intimate doings. One day he burst into my office, interrupting me in the middle of a letter to a former student discouraged by graduate school. "Do I really want to devote an entire life and passion to wringing meaning out of two lines, one line, or even one word," she wrote, "and not even wringing out something but mangling, mutilating, torturing the word enough to mean what my thesis paper or my doctoral dissertation or my article says it means?" Reassuring the girl was difficult, and I welcomed Josh's interruption. "Have you noticed that every shyster in the university claims he's an expert?" he said; "well, I am going to dip into the honey myself. I have decided to become a consultan." "Consultant," I answered; "don't you mean consultant?" "Hell, no, jackass, I mean consultan," he exclaimed. "Oh," I said; "well how much will you get a day?" "As much as I want," he said, looking long at me before turning and leaving the office to me and the girl blushing unseen in the dry air of graduate school.

When Josh first showed up, he made relatively harmless remarks, asking me, I remember, why skinny people always had heavy relationships. Later, though, as winter approached, and I spoke more often and received more mail, he became increasingly abrasive. When the state decided to place a minimum-security prison in Mansfield, Josh called it a "human toxic waste dump." As town officials knew what pollutants were dumped in the landfill, so he said, they should know what vile waste was stored in the prison. The prisoners were not there, he told me, for taking candy from babies. They were hard cases, villains who had plea-bargained the brutality out of their crimes. Because I did not want the prison either, Josh's remarks did not bother me, although later I told a friend that I thought Josh "lacked compassion." Josh went too far, however, when he showed up at my house one morning at eight o'clock, clutching a student newspaper in his hands. Printed in the paper was a list of support groups on campus, some thirty or forty. "Great God Almighty," Josh exclaimed, "there are so many support groups on this campus that almost everybody must belong to one. Anybody who doesn't is obviously a fruitcake and had better head for the psychiatrist." The statement was prologue to his real subject. "Here," he said, pointing to an advertisement on a back page; "here's one that gets me in the gut." In a big square was a notice announcing a meeting of a support group for people suffering from eating disorders: "anorexia, bulimia, and compulsive eating." "Dammit, old buddy," he said, "let's have a banquet for these folks. Of course we'd have to set out pots for people with Bulgaria." "Bulimia," I interrupted; "it's bulimia." "Bulgaria," he answered; "I call them as I hear them." And here he pronounced *Bulgaria* in an unsavory fashion, first bellowing *Bul*, then letting *garia* roll off in a long gag, ending in an exhausting and exhaling short *a*. "And, of course," he said, although I tried not to listen, "we'd admit anorexics at a reduced rate, charging them, say, only a fourth of the price of regular admission. If you are worried about losing your cookies on the deal," he continued, "we'll make it up on compulsive eaters. A compulsive eater," he said, "is a first-rate trencherman, and when he is in his stride can go through five or six meals at a grazing."

As soon as Josh left, I walked to Unnamed Pond. For the next week, whenever I had free hours I went to the pond, and for two months Josh disappeared. If he had returned to mind during this time, I wouldn't have talked to him and probably would not even have noticed him. Amid the weeds of late fall I was content and too busy to listen to his barbed ranklings. About the pond, days were cool and pastel, mornings flowing from gray through silver then breaking into soothing patches of red, orange, white, and blue. I spent afternoons sitting deep in reed grass, the soft heads cottony above me and the sheaved khaki stalks rustling in the wind, the stir natural and not forced by publicity. Home to the children I brought rough-fruited cinquefoil, evening primrose, mullein, elegant spikes of verbain, the

red stems of goldenrod, motherwort, yellow rocket, and then armfuls
of mountain mint. Bunched together the gray heads seemed hard,
but under a little pressure they shredded into fragrance, clean and decent. Frequently Eliza accompanied me to the pond. In brambles and
low in alders we found birds' nests, often lined with mud and down. In
stalks of sunflowers insects laid egg capsules, and minute orange worms
slept the fall away. Once we opened the thick stem of pokeweed. The
inside had frozen then thawed into separate yellow circles of fiber,
resembling bananas sliced regular and round. The centers of the circles were thin and translucent, and when they were held up against
the sun, they resembled wedding bands. "Daddy, what is God?" Eliza
asked, as we looked up through the pokeweed at the clouds. "Is he a
face in the sky?" "Yes," I answered, satisfying Eliza and myself, too.

   Josh avoided me until last Monday. I was driving back to Storrs
from Woodbridge, a trip of an hour and a half. I had spoken to teachers at Amity Regional High School. Although I don't think I got
them to think "a bit more creatively" as the principal instructed, the
talk went well. When I finished, a woman my age came up and said,
"You look like all the boys I dated in college." Just before getting on
the Merritt Parkway, I stopped at a bakery and bought a chocolate
cake for Vicki and the children and then for me a sweet roll to eat on
the way home. When I returned to the car, Josh was sitting inside.
"Old buddy," he said as I got in, "long time no see." The trip was
tense; traffic was heavy and people drove fast and foolishly because
the weatherman predicted a snowstorm. Josh did not make the trip
pleasant as he spent the time talking about the English department.
He had thought, he told me, of a new head for the department, Man-
uel Noriega. Not only did he have administrative experience, but he
was Hispanic. Even better, Professor Noriega was a victim of imperi-
alism. At first, Josh explained when I looked puzzled, the green dollars and gray men in blue suits helped the professor rule. In the process, though, Josh sighed, the professor became so addicted to Yankee
luxury that he practically lost his soul. "What is admirable in a senior
vice-president at Bankers' Trust," Josh said, "won't do for a branch
manager in the banana provinces." Now the professor was hapless
jailbait, the sort of person likely to be interviewed on public radio and
get the university lots of good publicity, "like," Josh added, "your
convocation speech." As far as the professor's "fitting in" was con-

cerned, Josh noted that he liked opera and pornography, both of which were perennially popular in English departments. "I'd recommend him to the dean tomorrow," Josh said as we approached Storrs, "except for one glaring flaw in his character. If he couldn't hold out against the American army, that ragtail and bobend bunch of dropouts and teenagers, any longer than he did in Panama, he wouldn't stand a ghost of a chance against those crafty bastards in the English department."

When I let Josh out at Four Corners, he said he would get in touch the next day. Shortly afterward the snowstorm swept into eastern Connecticut. For dessert Vicki covered the cake with vanilla ice cream. At eleven that night I put on my boots and heavy coat and trudged out into the storm. I was gone for three hours, roaming through the woods behind Horsebarn Hill, following Kessel Creek as it turned under ridges and ran down toward the Fenton River. The light in the woods was blue and white; the air was fresh, and I followed animal tracks. Deer tracks ran in lines over the slopes, and although I didn't see any deer, I often heard them running away from me, their hooves crunching in the deep snow. The next morning Eliza and I built a snowman and a snowwoman in the front yard. We used corncobs for noses and hickory nuts for eyes. For a mustache we stuck the long reddish-black seedpod from a honey locust across the man's face. On the woman we used bunches of dried asters and mountain mint for hair and clusters of seeds from mapleleaf viburnum for earrings. We also put a bosom on the woman, something which caused much tittering among Francis's and Edward's friends on the school bus that afternoon. As could be expected, I didn't hear from Josh, and so long as I wander field and meadow chances are I won't hear from him.

Josh labeled my speeches "oral journalism." Since convocation I have been a prolific lecturer. I have talked because people asked me, and being asked to do something is nice. I have also spoken because I am paid. I'm not growing wealthy, however, and I told an acquaintance, "If you see me driving a new Plymouth in the spring, then you will know I have made it into the big time." I have also spoken because the talks allow me to visit family and neglected friends. In December, I spent a hectic week in Nashville, Tennessee. In five days I appeared on a panel, lectured four times, and attended three receptions, two dinners, and a luncheon. The talks enabled me to visit

Father, and at the end of the week he and I flew back to Storrs for Christmas. My first engagement was at Vanderbilt, where I was on a panel with Tom Schulman, my former student and the writer of *Dead Poets Society*. Seeing Tom was a pleasure, for he had grown into a generous and talented man. The panel, too, was fun. The crowd was large, and the auditorium in which the panel was scheduled filled quickly; to accommodate the overflow, Vanderbilt opened two rooms with closed-circuit television. Many of my childhood friends came, and I labored to be honest. On being asked why I wrote, I said that as a college professor I did not have to work hard. Consequently, I wrote essays out of guilt and for the sake of appearances. I simply didn't want people to think me a layabout. Later in the week I was the after-dinner speaker at a meeting of the alumni association of Montgomery Bell Academy, my old high school. Five hundred people attended the talk; the next night twelve hundred more heard me make the gradua-tion address at the winter commencement at Belmont College.

Writing a talk does not take long, and I worry that speaking could stamp slovenly habits of mind and work into my character. If in three hours I can write a speech that I can "sell" for a thousand dollars, why devote weeks to writing essays for literary magazines which pay only ten dollars a page? Moreover, because an audience does not have the leisure to analyze the spoken word, as readers do the written, a speaker need not be precise or even particularly careful of word choice. The wash from a comic story generally sweeps criticism and recollection of shoddy reasoning out of an audience's mind. Even worse, speaking is intoxicating. Much as an audience is rarely able to weigh and judge a good speaker's thought, so the speaker himself has difficulty dissect-ing compliment. Rereading reduces flattering letters to conventions and in so doing protects the recipient from taking their praise too seriously. After a lecture a speaker is often too weary to be critical, and instead of analyzing compliments and putting them into sensible perspective, he lets them sweep warmly over and perhaps into him. Without conscious assent he may come to believe, as silly as it reads on paper, that he is "truly a Socratic teacher with a compelling and magnetic personality and mind."

Among my reasons for going to Nashville was the possibility of teaching at Vanderbilt. For some time the Vanderbilt English depart-ment had not filled an endowed professorship. In October I applied for the post, probably for the wrong reason—not because I was un-happy in Storrs or wanted to teach at Vanderbilt, but because my father's health was failing. I did not think him strong enough men-tally or physically to move to Connecticut. If I taught at Vanderbilt, he would not have to leave his world and I could care for him. With-out consulting the English department, prominent alumni had urged me to consider the chair. Sensitive about their prerogatives, English departments forever raise little matters to big principle, and after the alumni suggested my candidacy to the administration I was nervous about my reception in the English department. I should not have worried. There was no reception. The day after the panel I spoke to English majors at Vanderbilt. Following the lecture the students served dinner. Several faculty members attended the meal, and although I stayed at the dinner for two hours talking to students and signing books, and napkins, no teacher introduced himself to me. Waiting for me on my return to Connecticut was a letter from the head of the department dismissing me out of hand. Besides "scholarly eminence," "extensive and sophisticated experience in the direction of graduate work" was, he wrote, "expected of our endowed professors." "Captain Kangaroo," Vicki said when I showed her the letter; "they think you are Captain Kangaroo, climbing on desks and out of windows. Your academic career is finished, big boy; fall on your hands and knees and thank God they wouldn't have you." "But," I said, "the half-dozen books, the hundred and thirty or so articles, my running the graduate program here—didn't that make any difference?" "Damn," she said, "you are slow. Get Josh to explain it to you. Those pissants couldn't care less about that stuff. Anyone who has received as much publicity as you have has got to be a fraud. Be satisfied with the money you made." Vicki was right; there were checks on the icebox door for twenty-four hundred and fifty dollars. The problem was I had spent over half of it: a hundred dollars for a Christmas present for Rosie, Father's maid, and one hundred and forty-seven dollars for two Christ-mas presents for Vicki, a print of cedar waxwings and an artsy char-treuse plate, both presents being stuff from which attics are furnished. While in Nashville I also spent two hundred and fifty dollars on inci-dentals, much of it going for good food for Father: rib roasts, Aus-tralian wines, key lime pies. The big expense, however, was eight hun-dred and thirty-two dollars for clothes. I had not bought a pair of gray flannel pants or a new suit in fourteen years. The lapels on my jackets were thinner than inchworms, and once I cinched my trousers together I looked like a milkweed pod in the fall, swollen and ready to burst. If I was going to continue to speak, I needed better clothes, so I bought a suit, a blue blazer, and two pairs of gray slacks.

I have already worn the clothes several times. Although publicity may have ruined my name as an academic, my reputation as a speaker flourishes. During the next four months, I am addressing a state library association, lecturing at four colleges, talking to a group of people with multiple sclerosis, and speaking at conventions in Arkansas and Illinois. I have been invited to deliver two commencement talks, one at a junior college, the other at the local high school. This past week I received invitations to give keynote addresses at two meetings, the first focusing on child abuse and the second on planning for higher education in the 1990s. Although I know nothing about either subject, conference organizers were unconcerned. We want you, one wrote, "because you sound like a real-life, thoughtful person and not an 'expert.'" Not only can experts not understand other experts, but they are bored by them. People come to me, I think, seeking not new ideas or approaches, but common sense and hope. That frightens me, both for myself and for others. To say the wrong thing about Charles Dickens in class is a matter of little consequence. To say the wrong thing about child abuse could influence lives. I also worry that as more people convince themselves, as one man put it, that there is a "special aura about you," I might delude myself and lose contact with the rough land around Unnamed Pond and that humbling, rougher land within. I hope that won't happen. Maybe it won't if the little things I talk about don't blow loosely about in the sky but draw their nourishment from the dark, wormy soil of family and tale. Just a few minutes ago when I was writing this piece and taking my thought and self too seriously, Eliza came into the room. Words had not come easily, and as I struggled to express myself, I ran my left hand back and forth through my hair. "Daddy," Eliza said, frowning and putting her hands on her hips, elbows stuck out just like her mother, "Daddy, promise me every day you will comb your hair down. I comb mine down. Why should you leave yours up?"

Real

"Daddy," Edward said at breakfast this morning, "was God real when the dinosaurs were real?" "Absolutely," I said, "no question about it. God created the dinosaurs." The reply satisfied Edward, but it, alas, did not satisfy me. Little in my life seemed absolute or, for that matter, real, not even breakfast itself. Gone from my days were eggs freshened by bug and worm, tomatoes from the garden, and corn pone fried in bacon grease and hot from the skillet. In front of me was a pale tablet of extra-strength Ascriptin, containing "50% more Aspirin plus Maalox," and two gels, a round one twice as big as a BB containing three milligrams of garlic oil in a base of soybean oil but equivalent to fifteen hundred milligrams of fresh garlic, and then a long gel resembling a yellow miniature dirigible, filled with a thousand milligrams of concentrated fish oil, extracted from, the label informed me, the marine lipid. Covering my cereal, an all-natural granola, were wheat germ and brewer's yeast, the whole awash in skim milk. Steaming in the mug to my right was not boiled coffee, lumps of thick cream floating about the top like white islands, but caffeine-free tea. "Yes, Edward," I repeated, "God was real then, and he's real now. He made the dinosaurs, and he makes everything, except what I eat for breakfast each morning."

"And how," Mother said in one of the last conversations I had with her, "and how are those little Yankee boys?" "Yankee boys," I

21

said; "Mama, they're my babies. They're not Yankees." "Do they say 'yeah'?" Mother asked. "Yes ma'am," I answered. "Then," Mother said, ending the discussion, "they're Yankees." Mother was right. Born in Connecticut, my children are not southern. Although they will eat corn pone, they have never tasted a beaten biscuit or heard of spoon bread or Sally Lunn. Of course I haven't eaten Sally Lunn in years and don't remember the taste of spoon bread. The last time I was in Nashville, Father took me to lunch at the Belle Meade Club. I ate from the breakfast buffet, not, though, selecting any of the traditional southern dishes of grits, hickory-smoked ham, or redeye gravy with biscuits. Instead I chose belgian waffles, covering them with raspberries and sweetened whipped cream.

The waffles were good, but lunch made me feel like a stranger, and so that afternoon, in hopes of recapturing both place and belonging, I walked over the grounds of Belle Meade Mansion. Thinking taste might nurture association redolent with savory memory, I chewed boxwood leaves, much as I did as a boy when I spent summers on my grandfather's farm in Virginia. The leaves, unfortunately, had lost their bite and brought no thoughts to mind, no images of the sagging floor of a country store or of trumpet vines wrapped red around wooden fences. Eventually I spit out the boxwood and walked not to gain entrance to the past but for exercise, to escape the effects of eating too much in the present. The big sugar maples were in bloom, and robins were on their eggs, tail feathers sticking up and out of nests like the long handles on ladles. On sycamores the fruits were softly green and hairy; later they would turn hard and colorless and lose their hair. For an hour I identified trees and hunted birds' nests, but then I grew tired and, thinking of Connecticut, went to the Museum Shop and bought presents for Vicki and the children.

The South no longer seemed a real part of my life, and almost desperately I recorded fact and tale. When Father told me that he operated the scoreboard at Vanderbilt football games for two years in the 1920s, I wrote it down. As if I were staying an inevitable break with things southern and familial, I took notes throughout my visit. On Sunday the doorman does not start work at the Belle Meade Tower, where Father owns a condominium, until ten o'clock. Outside the main entrance is a directory listing people living in the Tower and a small device resembling a telephone with numbers printed on raised squares. To gain admittance to the building on Sunday morning, visitors press the apartment number of the person whom they have come to see. My father, for example, lives in apartment 31; to visit him, a person presses 3 and then 1. Pressing the number rings the telephone in that apartment and enables the visitor to speak to the person inside. To let the caller in, the person inside pushes 8 on his telephone, and downstairs the front door opens automatically. Father had never used the system, and curious about its workings, he asked me to go downstairs one afternoon so we could test it. Initially all went smoothly. I pressed Father's number; the telephone rang, and he answered it. But then when he pressed 8, nothing happened. Three times we tried, and three times we failed. After the last attempt the doorman let me in. Looking sheepish, Father met me in the kitchen upstairs. "I pressed 8," he said, "and I pressed it hard. But I didn't press it on the telephone. I pressed it on the remote control for the television." I went back downstairs, and the fourth time we tried the door the television was silent, and the system worked flawlessly.

Because the South is not part of my life and I am, to some extent, a placeless person, family is important to me. In an attempt to build something solid, I record stories about Father and the children, imagining each anecdote a rock, together the stories forming a narrative, running like a wall through wood and over hill, in places tumbled and covered by moss and brier, but yet real and heavy, the mark of me and my place. Not only do I record anecdotes about my immediate family, but I also collect matter about the name *Pickering*. On the table beside my bed is a Bible box, made from walnut and yellow poplar with black locust and holly inlay. After reading my essays people often telephone or write me about the doings of other Pickerings. I put the information I receive into the Bible box. "Just outside Jonesboro, Arkansas, heading west on Bypass 63," a man wrote recently, "my eyes were assaulted by a large billboard sign, the text of which is printed above." At the top of the page is a blue rectangle, black letters in the middle reading "PICKERING TERMITE & PEST." The next item in the Bible box is a piece of scratch paper on which is written "Samuel Pickering, born 1732, Newington, Connecticut, died 1797, Greenland, New Hampshire." The local dermatologist discovered this Pickering lurking on a limb of his wife's family tree and thought he might be one of my ancestors. Below the scratch paper is a letter. In

February a minister wrote me from Pennsylvania, enclosing a picture of the Pickering House in Salem, Massachusetts, gables rising above it like points on a compass. A Pickering built the house in 1651, and the family has occupied it ever since. The minister grew up in the house; the most famous Pickering who lived there, he said, was Timothy Pickering, quartermaster of the Revolutionary Army and later secretary of state. "Although big in supply," Tim came out of the war, the minister wrote, a "poor man, so that's good." Beneath the minister's letter is a postcard, also from Pennsylvania and informing me that just west of Bryn Mawr was Pickering Creek, named after one George Pickering.

The presents I brought back from Tennessee for Vicki and the children were not successful. For the boys I bought Civil War souvenir army caps, one blue and Union, the other gray and Confederate. Although I selected the largest size in the Museum Shop, the caps were too small for the boys, and from the front of the Confederate cap someone had removed the decoration of crossed rifles, something I didn't notice in Tennessee. Temporarily successful was Eliza's gift, a clear plastic purse shaped like a slice of watermelon and with seeds and fruit painted black and red on the outside. Unfortunately Eliza stuffed the purse full of coins from her piggy bank, and the rind split, spilling pennies over the kitchen floor. For Vicki I bought a big book on southern food and then a six-"pak" of Goo Goo Supremes "with Pecans," a candy manufactured in Nashville. "Well," Vicki said when she opened the presents, "you have done it again. You've given me candy I won't eat and a book I won't read." Vicki rarely likes the presents I bring home from trips, and her reaction did not surprise me. Still, I thought the book and candy improvements on the college sweatshirts I brought her from Sewanee, Northeast Louisiana, and the University of North Carolina at Charlotte. In part Vicki's reaction did not bother me because the presents were almost as unreal as my breakfast. The book described foods, many of which were disappearing and which, in any case, Vicki would never cook in Connecticut. Even worse, turning the uniforms of the Civil War into souvenirs destroyed history, treating the armies as if they had been baseball teams; the cannonballs, popcorn; and the blood, thin, pale beer. Instead of a slice of watermelon from a museum shop Eliza should have had a real purse, made from leather and stitched tightly together, a purse strong enough to carry a heavy weight of pennies and place.

At a time when watermelons turn into purses instead of food, it is not surprising that people behave oddly, living lives of gesture more than deed. Matters of no consequence occupy my thoughts. For example, I dislike strangers using my Christian name, and for years I fumed over receptionists in doctors' offices and waitresses in restaurants asking my first name. Since winter, however, I have been getting my name back. Now whenever a clerk asks my first name, I provide an absurd one, vaguely unpleasant, difficult to say, and almost impossible to spell. In late February, Vicki, the children, and I ate dinner in Nature's Way, a small vegetarian restaurant in Willimantic. The menu is written on a blackboard; the cashier takes orders, and when the food is ready, she calls out one's name. In Nature's Way the cashier is stridently familiar, insisting on shouting first names, or at least she was until February. I don't know what she does now, but I suspect that in my case *Pickering* will be used. When the cashier asked my name in February, I answered "Rynapeepee." "What?" she said. "Rynapeepee," I responded, raising my voice. "Let me spell that for you," I continued, "R-Y-N-A-P-E-E-P-E-E, Rynapeepee, a family name from the old country. Don't," I warned, "get it mixed up with the other." "What other?" she asked. "Rynapoopoo," I answered, turning and walking back to my seat. Later when the cashier called "Rynapeepee," Vicki said she felt like crawling under the table. Before bed that night she made me promise never to use *Rynapeepee* again. If I didn't promise, she said, she would never eat in Nature's Way again. I promised. In truth I hadn't intended to use *Rynapeepee* again. If I ever go back to Nature's Way, I am going to use something worse, a name like *Largobehind* or *Bigabuttukes*.

Whatever name I use Vicki won't crawl under the table. She is not really bothered by my behavior. This summer in Nova Scotia I planned to write an essay called "Night Thoughts." So that I could wander our farm in the dark, I bought a Justrite Electric Head Lantern from Forestry Suppliers in Jackson, Mississippi. Worn in the middle of the forehead, the lantern is attached to an elastic band that circles the head much like the sweatbands tennis players wear. When the lantern arrived, I was eager to try it, and so that night, after Vicki fell asleep, I crept out of bed, took off my pajamas, and strapped on the light. Turning it on, I stalked around to Vicki's side of the bed, making "hooing" sounds and, I must admit, thinking I looked impressive in a rather primitive sort of way. My appearance, I am afraid, did not impress Vicki. After my third or so "hoo" she opened her left, upper eye and, after running it up and down me for a moment, rolled away, saying, "Your wattage is low. You need a bigger bulb."

Vicki is from New Jersey, where, so far as I can tell, people don't eat cornbread or hang hams in the basement for a year or two before eating them. Not only that, people there don't seem to think so much about the past as I do, and instead get on with making money. Whatever the truth about New Jersey, thoughts about dinosaurs and God don't unduly distract Vicki, and she handles most practical matters pertaining to our lives—until this spring, for example, doing all the banking. Then, worn down by the children, she sent me out for money, telling me it was time I learned to use the bank or Barney card, as it is labeled, and the automatic teller machine. She wrote instructions, and I took them with me to the machine near the university bookstore. I followed the instructions carefully and returned with fifty dollars. I kept the instructions and used them ten days later when Vicki was again too tired to do the banking. After two successes I was ready for independence, and the next time Vicki asked me to go to the machine I left the instructions at home. At first things went well. I inserted the card right side up, typed in our secret code, and pressed buttons for the transactions: Withdrawal and From Checking. Then I typed in the amount of money I wanted, $65.00, being especially careful to insert the decimal point between the five and the first of the two zeros. "What a snap, I should be a venture capitalist," I thought, straightening and smiling at the man behind me before reaching out to get my money. Unfortunately the money did not appear. Instead the machine buzzed. "Oops wrong code" flashed across a green screen, and my card popped out. "Darn," I said to myself, "I'm sure I typed in the right number." Then turning to the man behind, I said, "Just a second. The machine seems to be on the fritz, and I have to do this again." He looked at his watch and nodded, and I inserted my card and went through the procedure once more. This time when "Oops" appeared on the screen, I was positive the fault lay in the machine, not me. Still, I decided to try again, not at the same place, though, but at the other window around the side of the building. No one was in line, and so I took an extraordinary amount of time, reading the instructions twice and checking every move. When I finished, the teller clicked icily. "Your Card Is Retained" appeared on the screen, and a thick plastic shield rolled out of the machine, snapping down in front of the window like bulletproof glass. I was so angry that if I had had a gun I would have shot the machine. Instead I stalked off to the office and telephoned Vicki. "Was our secret code 8281?" I asked. "Yes," Vicki answered, "what's the matter?" "What's the matter?" I answered; "I'll tell you what's the matter. That damn machine ate my card. Wait until I get a hold of those bastards at Connecticut Bank and Trust, the sons of bitches." For a second or two the line was quiet, and I could tell Vicki was thinking. Finally she spoke. "What card did you use?" she asked. "Visa, what the hell card do you think I used?" I answered and then stopped. Ten days later I received a new Visa card in the mail. I stuck it in my wallet and haven't used it or the Barney card since. "People, I like to deal with people," I told Vicki; "machines aren't real. They are for misfits who can't get along with people. No one who owns an iron skillet or keeps a can of bacon grease beside the stove would ever use one of those machines." "My God," Vicki responded, "you're a real dinosaur."

Not being able to use the teller machine embarrassed as well as angered me, and before going home to the children, I decided to brighten my mood by visiting a bit in the English department. Changing mood is not always easy, though, and feeling more critical than amiable, I read rather than talked, and read not books or magazines but doors. In gloomy moments, despite assertive chatter about "the mission of the humanities," I think teaching English accomplishes little, at best keeping a group of modestly intelligent people so occupied with self and other things frivolous that they stay out of trouble. Certainly literary criticism often has no more to do with truth than legal decision does with justice. As interpretation has made law less a matter of substance than of word, so literary critics deny the reality of texts and raise wordy constructs, silly and fabulously vain, purses shaped like slices of watermelon, bulging with deep thought, the play money of university life. On the office doors of members of the English department were pictures of a gallery of heroes, most literary, but some not: Proust, Virginia Woolf, Mike Dukakis, Gandhi, Charlotte Brontë, Norman Thomas, Dickens, Frederick Douglas, Van Gogh with his ear chopped off, and Babe Ruth. Pasted on several doors were bumper stickers, one reading "Support Your Local Rhetorician," another advertising the "National Cowboy Hall of Fame" in Oklahoma City. Beside the stickers were newspaper clippings, many frail and yellow and most political, describing little wars in small countries. Cartoons framed peace signs, the best of the cartoons showing a professor standing in front of a class and saying as he shut the book in his hands, "But enough about John Milton. Let's talk about me."

The doors and clippings soon rippled over each other in a dislocating stream. Near a poster for *The Guardian*, an "Independent Radical Newsweekly" devoted to providing "You" with "The Whole Story," was a red and white advertisement for a "Trick Lobster," proclaiming, "It Jumps. It Squeaks." Taped to the wall beside the next door was a photocopy of the first page of a tale entitled "Twitch City." Down the hall "SEND HELP" stood out in black letters on an orange background, while on the wall just beyond a headline from a newspaper announced, "Study Isolates Traits of Chronically Excessively Boring People." I was in the real Land of Make Believe, not the imaginary one, although that was present too. On one door was a three-by-three-foot poster depicting the landscape of nursery rhyme and fairy tale. Little Bo-Peep looked for her sheep in a gully while Tom the piper's son ran along a road, a pig under his arm. Nearby Little Boy Blue dozed on a haystack while his cow foundered in the corn. Humpty Dumpty sat laughing on a rock wall; the little black hen laid eggs for gentlemen, ten round white eggs; Old Mother Hubbard fed her dog a bone; Jack and Jill rolled down a hill, and Mary watered her garden, hollyhocks and petunias, not silver bells and cockleshells. High in the distance was Bluebeard's Castle; shining in the mountains above was the Emerald City; while over everything scowled the moon, obviously irritated by the cow's surprising familiarity.

I wondered if the doors of people in other departments resembled those of English teachers, and so early the next morning I went to the Life Sciences building. Getting to the doors themselves took a while, however, for the halls did not run straight and bare. Instead they resembled paths in a forest, so cluttered with things they seemed to turn, twisting not through space but through association and idea. Hanging along the wall on the first floor were paintings of mush-

rooms: Violet Cort; Shaggy Mane; Dyrad's Saddle; Two Color Bo-
letus, reddish brown berets with thick creamy linings; Brick Top;
Sticky Gray Trich; and Destroying Angel, gleaming and frighteningly
white. Atop a cabinet was a crab trap, a bucket-shaped mesh of blue
wire. In a corner leaned a log, five feet long, a hand wide, and covered
with lumpy mounds of dried fungus. On the third floor were glass
cases containing stuffed wildlife, mostly birds and animals. The sides
of the cases were clean, but the tops were dusty, and on one case I
wrote *Vicki* in tall letters. Later I rubbed the letters out with the side of
my right hand, wiping the dirt off on my trousers, not something of
which Vicki would have approved. Most of the animals in the cases
were local: red squirrels, eastern chipmunks, beaver, mink, river ot-
ters, and star-nosed moles. In a small case was a striped skunk with a
litter of five tubular kits, eyes shut and a white design shaped like a
wooden clothespin on their backs. In some cases were reptiles: a hog-
nose snake on its back; spotted salamanders, the orange dots along
their sides too bright and resembling the metallic paint used on model
airplanes; and then snapping turtles looking content and strangely
benevolent in death. Many cases contained birds, the smallest resembling frayed pieces of cord, the dye in their fibers washed pale by time.
A few of the larger birds retained some dignity, the hawks and owls
staring from behind the glass stony and unblinking in the light. Two
cases contained birds' eggs, conventionally enough those of the robin,
woodcock, crow, flycatcher, and grasshopper sparrow, but also, oddly,
those of the emu, flamingo, and ostrich. Originally the cases probably displayed only wildlife native to Connecticut, but then, as some
of the exhibits collapsed into dust and wire, they were replaced almost randomly, it seems; one case, for example, contained an eight-
foot Pacific sailfish, paint and plaster chipped but still so blue that it
seemed the stuff of a pizza restaurant, fit companion for pepperoni
and flashing neon signs advertising Miller Lite. In another case was a
box containing a selection of bills from the broad-billed swordfish;
printed on one bill, each letter precise and geometrical, was "taken
off Nantucket, Mass. July, 1964."

On doors in the Life Sciences building were posters, for the most
part of animals: bats with friendly red faces hanging from lush, green
trees; white and yellow orchids covered with purple spots; the Philip-
pine eagle looking startled, feathers sticking up around his head like

sparklers. On one poster were pictures of forty-six Amazon parrots, "vanishing because of large-scale destruction of forests and capture for pets." I looked at the parrots trying to puzzle out differences between them. Both the Spectacled Amazon and the Sonoran Spectacled Amazon had red circles around their eyes and patches of white and blue above their beaks. The blue, however, was darker and thicker on the Sonoran than on the Spectacled Amazon. On many doors were bumper stickers, urging support not for cowboy museums but for environmental groups: the Sierra Club, Nature Conservancy, World Wildlife Fund, and Connecticut Ornithological Association. I looked through several open doors into offices; in one office was a tank containing an octopus in preservative, the glowing brown liquid resembling Scotch.

Warnings of various kinds were posted in the English department. Generally speaking, English teachers seem to be against racism, capitalism, nuclear war, and being male. In addition one or two oppose bad grammar, posting specimens of poor usage from local newspapers. "Windham No. 1 singles player Marjorie Brown," a caption under a picture read, "returns a forehead volley Wednesday." "You'll have to know if you want a canoe for a flat water lake, for light water use, or for serious whitewater canoeing," a paragraph explained; "usually it's a combination of both." The warnings on the doors of the Life Sciences building were more immediate, provoking not smiles or yawning agreement, but fear. "Biohazard Virus Laboratories Restricted Area" stood out in black. On several doors were yellow signs with pink circles in the centers and around them three blades like parts of a fan, warning people against radioactivity. Painted on one door was "Caution Radioactive Materials. No Smoking. No Drinking. No Eating. No Mouth Pipetting." Although no warning was attached, I swung wide in the hall, looping around the door labeled "Parasitology." Out of ignorance, however, I did not avoid the pathology building just down the street, at least not until I reached the second floor and a poster labeled "Pathology of Poultry." In bright color the poster depicted diseases and parasites of chickens: cholera, typhoid, tapeworms, and then roundworms, wrapped about the small intestines like grapevines around forsythia. While aspergillosis turns the lungs dark and lumpy, making them resemble black cherry Jell-O with balls of cream cheese buried in it, coccidiosis turns intestines a gay Valentine's Day red, and gumboro makes the bursa of fabricus swell two or three times its normal size, taking away, from me, certainly, all hankerings for grapefruit. The poster also took away my appetite for doors, and I started down the stairs out of the building. Near the entrance, though, I saw a sign with an arrow pointing toward the basement and reading "Post Mortem Office Below." Just where such a place ought to be, I thought, and down I went. After winding past the furnace and bundles of gray pipe, I reached the door to the office. On it was a sign, white letters stamped on brown plastic. "Post Mortem Admissions Office," it stated; "Hours 8:30–12:00; 1:00–4:30. Please Walk In." My hand started toward the doorknob, but then I stopped. "Not today," I thought, and hurried upstairs, out into the yellow sunlight and the fresh, clean air.

In Nashville, Father described people he knew as a boy in Carthage, Tennessee. After Beasley Nickerson retired from the bank, he roomed with his daughter Hattie Mae and her husband in their home on Jefferson Street. Although Hattie Mae cooked, washed, and cleaned, Beasley moved in more for her sake than his. Lafayette Fisher, her husband, was charming but feckless, and often when the mortgage or insurance came due, he found himself embarrassed. At such times Beasley stepped forward and paid the bills. The Nickersons, however, were notoriously long-lived, and toward the end of his life, Beasley slipped and spent much of his time walking about Carthage, roaming streets and a world that only he understood. No harm came to him, however, as people watched out for him, inevitably taking him home to Hattie Mae just before dinner. Late one afternoon Lafayette found him outside Hawkins's store on Spring Street. He led him home, and as they walked, they talked about old times in Carthage, Beasley's memory seeming keen and clear. When they reached the little gate on the sidewalk beside their house on Jefferson, Beasley turned to Lafayette and said, "I certainly enjoyed walking with you, but this is where I live. I'd invite you in for dinner, but I don't know if my daughter would approve."

As I walked home from the pathology building and remembered Father's story, I thought about where I lived. The time had come, I decided, to wander about Storrs. Maybe I could stride through observation into place, sloughing off disturbing thoughts about the real. I began roaming and observing that afternoon. In the backyard I saw a brown creeper; in the dell bloodroot bloomed, yellow and white. As I walked down Eastwood, I saw pussytoes then a polypod fern spilling like water out of a rock. I remembered Bill the groundhog. He hadn't appeared in the yard, and I wondered if he was still alive. Perhaps, I thought, he had been run over by a car, just like Suzy, the rabbit. The day darkened and did not lighten until I moved beyond houses and cars, automatic bank machines and gels filled with garlic. I crossed the South Eagleville Road and started into the marsh, stretching west along the road from the Mansfield Apartments toward Maple Road. Beyond the marsh lay a ridge of oak and pine, then Tift Pond. Before entering the marsh I crossed a border area, a place where people dumped trash almost as if they were building a wall between themselves and the marsh. On one side were bumper stickers, belgian waffles, and electric head lanterns; on the other were grits, skunk cabbage, old Pickerings, wood anemones, and God—or so I wanted to think.

In between stretched a barrier of garbage: a dull, silver-coated beer keg; two boxes for Domino's Pizza, the large size; a five-gallon container for PR–26-D "Asphalt Emulsion Tack Coats"; three Kelly-Springfield Roadmark tires, the bottoms smooth with no trace of treads; coffee cups from Papa Gino's, Dairy Mart, Friendly, Store 24, and the Sugar Shack; bags for potato chips, onion, barbecue, all-natural, and rippled; light bulbs; beer cans, all returnable; milk cartons; a bag for a grinder from Subway; Christmas trees; and a twenty-one-inch bicycle with the front wheel missing. Leaning against a tree was a sofa, springs and stuffing sticking through a brown and green cover. Next to the sofa a Frigidaire stove lay on its side, wires torn loose and burners on the ground behind, the whole resembling a skull, white and empty.

I forced a way through the trash and then began pushing through the marsh. Soon, though, I slowed, making myself look down at the immediate rather than up and off into the distance. In April leaves were still buds on the trees, and sunlight rained into the marsh, hurrying wildflowers into bloom and fertility. Later in the year leaves would block out the light; blossoms would fall away, and the marsh would be darker and quieter. For the moment, though, color and movement washed together across the ground with the sunlight. Flowers from red maples had fallen into a stream and been caught in an arm of rocks. As the current flowed past, the water spun the blossoms into a red wheel, foam rising white in the center and around the edge. On the rocks themselves marsh marigolds bloomed; beyond were the dark, almost shellacked horns of skunk cabbage, patches of purple violets, and ferns pushing through the ground, small, hairy, green scrolls. From rocks under the water mica flickered, sometimes silver, but other times coppery and golden. In the hollow of a tree was a chickadee's nest from last summer, lined with rabbit fur and still soft. Beneath the bark of a dead oak black lines of fungus spread like fans over cocoons and the glittering tracks of slugs and through a community of red ants, dusty beetles, centipedes, and minute spiders, gray stripes marking their abdomens like wrinkles. On logs in the shallows of Tift Pond painted turtles sunned themselves, so close they seemed beads strung together.

Although I spent days roaming marsh and wood, I was not quite able to walk through time to ambrosia and sweet divinity. Around the pond I found broken bottles and empty beer cans. One day at the foot of a tree I found a dead crow. Wrapped about his feet and binding his legs together were two bundles of plastic string, one silver, the other black. The crow died hard; his legs stretched behind him like those of a diver entering the water, and one of his wings pushed up over his head while the other thrust to the side, clawing at the air and creating a sense of desperate motion. The crow had been on the ground all winter; its skin was leathery, and the carcass had been picked clean by ants and carrion beetles, the long spine looking almost washed and the skull resembling a gall on a branch, a sudden swelling, smooth and brown. I brought the crow home and showed it to Vicki and the children, after which I hung it on a nail in the garage. The next morning I swam at the university pool. Before swimming one signs in, writing down his name and social security number. In the past I signed in meekly and conventionally. This day, though, I omitted my Christian name, writing just *Pickering*, after which I wrote *REX* in big letters. Now the lifeguards call me King, and I don't even write *Pickering* on the sheet, just *REX*. If someone were to ask why I do it, I wouldn't be able to explain. I would only mumble confusedly about dinosaurs and a dead crow.

In the marsh beyond the barrier of trash, however, thoughts don't have to be pressed into words. On Mother's Day, Vicki, the children, and I walked down through the woods behind the old Kessel house at the edge of the university farm. We heard ovenbirds and saw scarlet tanagers. At the edge of the dam in the woods a northern waterthrush bobbed up and down; below the dam purple trillium bloomed. Beside a road through a fallow field winter cress ran in long yellow lines; in the field dandelions stood a foot tall, their blossoms bigger, it seemed, than buckets. After the walk we went to the Cup of Sun, and Vicki and the children ate blueberry coffee cake while I ate breakfast, a good breakfast, too: a banana nut muffin, eggs over lightly, bean sprouts, coffee, and hash browns cooked with garlic, onions, and green peppers. As we ate, Eliza, my four-year-old Yankee girl, turned toward me and said, "Daddy, I wonder what man I'm going to marry for my wife." Storrs isn't Nashville. The community of children, parents, and grandparents that I knew as a child in Tennessee doesn't exist here, and arranging a good marriage for Eliza will be difficult, so I said, "Honey, that's a long way off. Maybe when you're a grown woman, you won't want to marry." Eliza's mouth dropped in alarm; looking hurt, she shouted, "I want to. I want to. I want to have babies." "Don't you worry," I said, suddenly frightened and reaching over and wrapping my arms around her, binding myself to her like bark about a tree, "you'll marry a nice man and have lots of babies, real Pickering babies, fat Yankee babies—so help me God."

Night Thoughts

"Hey, guys," Eliza, my four year old, said to her brothers as we drove up the shore road past abandoned farms at Chegoggin, "guys, when we die, we'll start a new life. That'll be the dead life." Beside the road barns slumped inward, the roofs bowing down then rolling out like the shoulders of tired men. In the fields alder had rooted, and in the distance spruce rose black against the sky. "The dead life has already started here," I thought, "but this is nice, just the place for a graveyard, family plots swollen like loaves of bread and tombstones orange with lichens." As we drove, I thought about Kill-sin Pemble, a character I created for my essays. Here I would bury him and all his daughters: Fly-fornication, More-fruits, Weep-not, Stand-fast-on-high, and little Calvaretta, the child of his old age. As a young man Kill-sin climbed the stovepipe in the tabernacle at Darling Lake, damning the flesh, the smoke and pain rising from his burning hands smelling sweeter, he said, than the flames of Judgment Day. As he aged, though, he grew weak and, reconciled to the world, doted on Calvaretta. When she died from influenza at nine, Kill-sin hardened for a last time, on this dark day raging against the god who tore his child away. "She is gone, my little girl," he carved on her gravestone; "Never more on earth to dwell. / And for the grief I bear. / My soul will burn in hell."

If Chegoggin had been gullied and angular, I would not have thought about Kill-sin, for the lay of the land often determines the

35

pitch and flow of my mood and ideas. We were driving back to our farm at Beaver River after spending the afternoon at Cape Forchu, a spur of land running out to rock and the Yarmouth Light. There I climbed over the heavy stone to wait for the Bluenose to arrive from Bar Harbor. At the quick edge of land, my thoughts pointed, and after the ferry passed, gulls trailing it like confetti, I gathered the children and, organizing the landscape into cause and effect, marched them through beach pea, little hop clover, hemp nettle, foxtail, and black mustard. Only at "Vole City" as I followed runs through the deep grass did the plane geometry of my lessons soften into wonder and appreciation, and I let the children drift back to the shore to collect sea jewels, colored bits of glass ground round and misty by the roll of tide and rock.

That night I wandered the woods surrounding a peat bog on our farm. In the dark, paths made by day become almost unrecognizable and the familiar becomes strange, short distances stretching into mystery. Because I could barely see, imagination brightened the night, and I stayed outside five hours. At the edge of Ma's Property, behind an apple tree and hidden by bay and a fallen tamarack, I found an abandoned car. The next morning the children and I returned to it, searching first for skeletons and gold and then for parts for their robots, slabs of wood covered with nails, screws, doorknobs, almost anything found in barn and backhouse. The car was a Volvo, something I have long wanted but cannot afford. A sedan sold by Twin City Motors in Halifax, the car had been battered out of model. The side windows had been smashed; the seats removed; and the tires stripped off. Rubber mats, wires, springs, and blue hunks of metal lay scattered on the ground, while small white mushrooms grew up through the air vents below the windshield and a black spruce rooted in bark and fallen leaves on the roof. "We are going to leave the car here," I told the children, "but when we return to Connecticut, you can tell your friends that we have a Volvo. Tell them that it is so special we keep it at our summer home, preferring to beat around Storrs in the old Plymouth."

This summer I spent many nights roaming the dark, searching not for Volvos and pirate treasure but for ideas and fragments of understanding. In past summers I explored the farm, learning wildflowers and naming the land: Strawberry Dip, Quaking Bog, Bear Hole. As soon, though, as dusk darkened out of shadow, I returned to the house, to dinner and a kitchen table overflowing with swiss chard, buttermilk biscuits, halibut, and rhubarb pie. Afterward I read to the children in the study. Days, though, are more than light and books, and in May, I decided to explore the dark, imagining myself stirring through nights under skies cloudy as splatterware bowls and turning through smells and emotions as clean as pitch on a damp wind. I saw myself startled by a nighthawk, the white bands on its wings slicing through the mist over the Gulf of Maine like a man cutting silhouettes at a state fair. I bought a head lantern. Placed in the middle of the forehead, the lantern was attached to an elastic band that circled the head. From the side of the lantern a thin black cord ran down to a red battery case. Designed to be hooked over a belt or stuffed into a trouser pocket, the case was waterproof and held four batteries.

Immediately after buying the lantern I was eager to try it out and impatient to leave Connecticut for Nova Scotia and the night. Patterns of living and thinking, though, are not easily broken. Once we arrived in Nova Scotia, the night became immediate, not simply something to imagine in the cool of the day. Once the night was close, it seemed foreign, almost a distant country, the customs of which frightened me because they were unknown. Instead of pushing outside into the new, I did what I had always done in Nova Scotia. I wandered the house in hopes of finding something inside to draw me away from the night. As words often mold experience into reality by influencing how one sees life, so the search shaped my first week in Nova Scotia. On the second floor, in the Scotch Room, I found a box containing speeches made by Vicki's great-grandfather, George Dudley Jones. "Before I go out into the night," I told Vicki, putting the box down on the kitchen table, "I'm going to read these speeches. Maybe I will learn something about our children. We have always said we didn't know where they came from. Besides," I added, "digging into the past isn't much different from wandering around at night."

As often happens, what started as diversion turned into interest. Much as my love for wildflowers rooted and spread the more I learned about them, so my admiration for George Jones grew the more I read. Born in Newport, Ohio, he did not attend college but read law while working in an office in Columbus. He was an astute scholar, so much so that one of the railway magnates, family tale recounts, offered him a lucrative position. Thinking that law should serve people, not commerce, he turned the offer down and for fifty years went his own way, making a modest living but building a reputation for integrity, storing assets not in banks or trusts, but in that greater vault beyond the corruption of moth and avarice.

In the box were forty-three speeches, some eight hundred and seventy-five pages, the first speech being delivered in the 1870s, the last in the Ohio Senate in the 1920s. Both typed and handwritten, the speeches were on various papers: formal stationery; legal pads fourteen inches long and eight and a half wide; and thirteen-by-eight-inch notebooks, the pages occasionally divided to measure six and a half by eight inches. Often Jones wrote on headed paper, sometimes that of O. E. D. Barron, the treasurer of Franklin County, Ohio, or that of George S. Marshall, the city solicitor. Often, though, he used stationery from his and his brother's law firm, Jones & Jones, at 137 South High Street in Columbus. After the turn of the century he wrote on paper furnished to members of the Ohio House of Representatives and then later the State Senate in which he represented Columbus, the tenth district. In the upper left corner of this last stationery was a round emblem depicting the sun, twenty-four rays bursting from behind it like petals on a flower. Beneath the sun stretched a line of sharp hills; at their feet were sheaves of wheat, swollen and so top-heavy they resembled tired mushrooms.

A frequent attender of chautauquas, Jones was active in local political and philosophical societies, speaking at the Broad Street Lyceum in Columbus, lecturing to the Epworth League, and then in 1897 delivering the Washington's Birthday Address at Hilliards, Ohio, before the Booth Club, a Democratic political group. For his wife, who was secretary of the local chapter of the Women's Foreign Missionary Society in 1878, he wrote a speech discussing the place of women in society. In 1916 as president of the Columbus branch of the National Association for the Advancement of Colored People, he urged blacks to insist upon their rights. Although he often spoke about particular legislative matters such as the League of Nations and capital punishment, in this latter case introducing a bill in the Ohio Assembly to abolish it, he enjoyed lecturing on historical and broad rather than specific social matters, on topics such as "The Religious Instinct," "Socialism," "The Higher Criticism," "The Crusades," "Hannibal,"

"Joan of Arc," and "The Evolution of Religious Thought in America." Jones's thought itself did not alter much over the years, although his political affiliation changed. As a young man he followed his father into the Republican party, proud of the role it played in abolishing slavery and blotting out the "dangerous doctrine of states' rights." In the 1890s he left the Republican party, saying it neglected "the rights of the great industrial and producing masses of the country," and becoming for a short time at the end of the century chairman of the Silver Republican party of Ohio, campaigning for the restoration of silver in hopes of wresting the monetary system out of the hands of "great syndicated wealth" and returning it to the people. Early the next decade he was a Democrat and a successful candidate for office. Behind the political affiliations, however, Jones was constant, and if asked to affix a philosophical rather than a political label to his views, he would, I think, have called them socialist and then simply American.

The more speeches I read, the more I liked Jones. He was optimistic, believing that evolution and scientific discovery were bringing a better, more unified world. Evolution, he wrote, was "but a less ecclesiastical name for the thing we call God and to which letters we no longer attach the coarse qualities of personality and gender." In unfolding the laws of physical life, science, he believed, "revealed a purpose in the creative mind sufficiently large to embrace all things, all places and conditions, even Time and Eternity, the Heavens and the Earth." Science, he thought, would free man from the fetters that bound him in slavish devotion to the dead past. Jones read Emerson, and from Emerson absorbed the belief that behind the seeming chaos of life lay unity, not abstract or metaphysical but real, an organic power and an immanence binding men to men and man to nature. In the past, he thought, superstition, creeds, and nationalism fragmented peoples, bringing blood and destruction. Dante's *Inferno*, he wrote, mirrored the superstition of the dying past and offered little "moral value" to the present. "Devils and Hells can't teach us anything. The hopes of harps and crowns, the fear of unquenchable fire can't make us better," he wrote; "the problem is not one of worlds or bodies or places, of future heavens or future hells, but of the essential value and beauty of the life which now is." Jesus, he declared, was great, not because he was a descendant of the house of David, but "because he was an honest, conscientious, simple, radical, courageous man," an idealist "who had to do with nothing but the affairs of everyday life, whether in the physical or the spiritual world." Much of what passed for wisdom, Jones stated, was only a "smooth trick." The greatest wisdom of the world, he wrote, was not found in sophisticated arguments, and he urged his listeners to distrust complexity, arguing that the substance of the spiritual life and the spiritual world was found in simplicity. To this end he occasionally compared life in the city to that in the country, the fret of the first confusing and corrupting, the simplicity of the second healing and teaching. The most impressive scene he ever saw, he recounted, was a country funeral, the sun shining through a clear sky "in his full splendor," and nature impressing itself upon him like "the visualized presence of God." In the city, in contrast, nature was absent, and since property was more respected than life, people devoted more attention to fire alarms than to funeral bells.

In the city people paid more regard to law or the surface of things than to the spirit, and Jones warned members of the Broad Street Sunday School against teaching theology to children. Instead, he said, children should study the life of Christ and the Ten Commandments and learn to see beyond mere story to the life beneath. Studiously nondoctrinaire, Jones admired the Quakers, thinking their recognition of "God in all men in all places and at all times" the basis both of toleration and of responsibility. In contrast he attacked the pilgrim fathers, narrow "self-serving saints" so blinded by doctrine they staggered into blood, damning the Quakers' inner light as "the stinking vapor of Hell."

Religious persecutions, Jones thought, were a thing of the past, for religion had now yielded first place in the social framework to science, and no scientist would ever "burn the religionist at the stake or hang him upon the gibbet." Man was still set against man, however, and government had not yet achieved its primary excuse for being: the establishment of "liberty and equality." In great part, commerce, Jones believed, was responsible. "The competitive system of economics which has thrived in our free democracy as it could no where else perhaps has carried the commerce and industry of our country far from their natural and proper moorings out into a wide and stormy sea. There is no limit," he declared, "to the acquisition or ambition

of man under such a system. The rights of man are not an element
entering into this fierce and bloody system. How to get the most for
the least is the watchword of our industrial and commercial system."
Competition led to exploitation and undermined "fellowship," all,
Jones stated, "that makes human life endurable or even possible in
an organized state of society." Because socialism emphasized unity
and the general good, it attracted Jones. Without negating individual
rights, a philosophic socialism free from dogma would, he thought,
dull the sharp, inhuman edge of competition. For Jones equality and
brotherhood were not distant ideals fit for future generations, but
principles governing daily life. Thus he supported the League of Nations, attacked capital punishment, and led the local chapter of the
NAACP. Whatever narrowed the vision and sympathies of people he
criticized: religious doctrine, unions and trusts, racial and sexual dis-
crimination, nationalism, partisan politics, extreme wealth and social classes, the law, and then literature, all those *Infernos* blighting
spirits and "born in the disordered conscience of dark ages."

Jones believed that men often became their occupations, their
minds assuming the character of objects around them, the shepherd,
for example, becoming pensive, his thoughts turning and flowing like
the hills across which his flock grazed. In a commercial economy
occupations were often unnatural, based not on the real needs of humans but on luxurious artificial desires. Even worse occupations so
narrowed men that they lost their humanity, becoming unthinking
tools. "Take from the average soldier," he wrote as an example, "his
bright uniform, his standard of bright colors, the blowing of the horns,
and all the other spectacular appendages of war, and we have left, as a
rule, a moral deformity." Molded by occupation the soldier so con-
formed to this world that he was almost incapable of being "transformed," of entertaining ideals and recognizing links between the
soul of man and the universal soul of life itself.

"Our great and glorious masterpiece," the French essayist Mon-
taigne wrote, "is to live appropriately." To my mind, Jones lived appropriately, fashioning not a masterpiece, for he would have thought
the word swollen and inappropriate, but a decent, decorous life. His
ardent generosity and compassion, his democracy, appealed to me,
brightening not simply July nights in Nova Scotia but the gloom that
settles around me whenever I look closely at my world, at nations

celebrating self at the expense of community and elevating greed and consumption to virtues, poisoning not simply mind and body but the very earth. Jones's speeches filled me first with admiration and then with feelings of inadequacy. For fifty years he preached fellowship, his strength raised on the muscular conviction that society and man were evolving "from lower to higher ideals." Bringing order out of confusion, science, he thought, was revealing "organic power" and creating possibilities for "a less contentious and more mutual life." Would that I had Jones's faith, indeed his imagination. For me evolution implies only change, not betterment, and instead of being devoted to truth and beauty, science seems committed to nothing higher than enriching its practitioners, be they individuals or Jones's "great syndicated wealth." If man did his task in "honest faith," Jones said, the hobgoblins of life would vanish. If I wrote essays in honest faith, not hobgoblins but readers would vanish. The best I could do, I decided, was to beam Jones's thought into an essay, in hopes that someone, most probably my children, would pause over a word or two and think "yes, that's the way life ought to be." And then, of course, I could strive for unity, not Jones's high organic unity, but a lower unity. Putting on my head lantern I could roam the dark, discovering links between night and day, times, I thought, like nations, metaphoric light years apart.

Only in exceptional people, however, are philosophic commitments long-lived. Despite my intentions, five days passed between my finishing the speeches and the first explorations of the night. During that time I busied myself with small things, examining the oddments I found stuffed in among the speeches: a six-inch ruler "For the Lady's Work Basket" advertising Columbus Lace Cleaning Works on 49 Greenlawn Avenue, and then a bill from the Roberts Plumbing Company charging $10.13 for replacing a "Bol" on June 1, 1916. Also in the box was a calling card with Jones's picture on it, stating that he was the Democratic candidate for state senator and listing the election date, November 7, 1916. Stuck in the middle of a speech was a broadside urging people to vote for Woodrow Wilson for president. "A Vote Against Wilson Is," the card declared, "a Vote for Wall Street. For Industrial Oppression. For More Power for the Few. For Less Power for the Many. For Government By and For Special Privilege. For Militarism: Jingoism: War." The card also stated that a vote against Wilson supported lower wages and longer working hours, but these lines Jones marked out. On the reverse side the card stressed that Wilson had kept the nation at peace. "Do YOU," the card asked, "want yourself to be made cannon fodder to conquer Mexico for the benefit of Wall Street?"

During these five days I walked around Beaver River and Port Maitland, renewing acquaintances and having imaginary conversations with characters I created for earlier essays. Otis Blankinchip, Bertha Shifney told me at Gawdry's Store, had gotten a dog, a yellow stray with a broken tail. "Otis named it Worby," she said, "and thinks the world of him. The other night Worby howled something fierce, but when Otis went outside he didn't see anything. The next morning, though, when Otis picked my paper up for me, he was, he told me, struck with amazement. 'I knowed it,' he said, 'Worby ain't no fool. He don't bark for nothing. Right there on the front page of the paper it said that Pealand Timberlake died in Halifax. He hadn't lived here in Port Maitland for eight or nine years, since Worby was a puppy. Imagine Worby knowing old Pealand.' "

My first walks at night seemed longer than they actually were. For a time the dark changed my perception of distance. I knew our farm well, and when I wasn't able to see far ahead of myself, even with the headlamp burning, I imagined how my way looked in the light. In so doing I envisioned familiar landmarks, in the process so anticipating them that I brought them closer than they really were. As a consequence landmarks were almost always farther from me than I expected them to be, thus making distances at night seem greater than those in the day. On my first walks the dark seemed a heavy curtain, fixed and opaque. As a result my imagination was active; not distracted into thought by lively detail, it colored the night with fears, not, though, of brutish men or savage animals, but of revengeful plants, roots turning under my path and long vines waving over my head like green fingers. Some years ago Japanese knotweed sprouted along the north side of our barn. Ten feet tall and growing in thick, leafy, bamboolike clumps, it initially seemed an attractive windbreak. In summers the children pushed into it and, crushing the stems, made paths and fashioned huts, some with living rooms, others with dungeons. In winter, though, the stems dried and collapsing inward stacked against each other, forming great sheaves of tinder. Nervous about fire, I had the knotweed mowed late in May, and when we arrived in June, I started digging the roots. Using an iron bar I levered up great orange bundles, damp and heavy as hams. To prevent the knotweed from growing again I dumped the roots beneath black spruce, deep in the woods and out of the sunshine, after which I covered them with tree limbs, the needles as tight as wool. A week later the knotweed sprouted; by the time I began my nightly explorations, the stems were two feet high and growing through the dark and my imagination.

Plants affect me more than they do other members of my family. Brushing my hands across the big oaks in Storrs comforts me—much, I suppose, as a room full of old leather books must comfort a literary person. I feel uneasy when I dig dandelions out of the yard, and I won't let Vicki toss tired houseplants into the woods. Instead I plant them in the dell. More often than not they die, but at least I think I haven't been cruel and by giving them a chance to live have "done the decent thing." The man who mowed around our barn was not able to reach all the knotweed. Some had sprouted in among the roses near the door to the barn. After arriving in Nova Scotia, I pushed the roses aside and pulled out the knotweed. To do so I didn't wear gloves at first, in part because I had forgotten where I left them last summer and was too lazy to search for them, but also because I sensed that the roses would know that what I was doing was good for them and they would not harm me. For a while they didn't prick me, and for a while knotweed frightened me on my walks, but then, just as I inevitably scraped my forearm on a thorn and started wearing gloves, so night ceased being a curtain and in the clarity of the dark my fears dried and withered.

Besides being dislocating, my first rambles were discouraging. I hoped that the uncommon time of my explorations would lead to uncommon thoughts or, if not that, at least to new understandings. I hoped that for the first time the stars would mean something to me. Their high immensity, though, lay beyond my comprehension, much as Jones's organic unity was, ultimately, beyond my grasp. To bring the stars closer to earth and mind I learned their names. Although the names of many old woodland and meadow deities are still green, those of the constellations are dead, Sagittarius and Pegasus hobbled deep in the cold, far from inspiration and association. When a new moon reminded me of a slice of cantaloupe, I turned constellations into vegetables, Boötes becoming squash, Cygnus celery, and Hercules a giant cabbage. Not made immediate, however, by use—navigation or worship—the heavens were too far away to domesticate, and no matter the metaphors I churned through the clouds, my garden didn't bear fruit. Instead of stars I thought more about planes flying over the farm. So many passed overhead that they seemed bound together, a strand of tinsel twinkling from dusk until dawn. Inside the planes people sat side by side in long rows. While they poured wine from little bottles and pulled adventure novels from overnight cases, they, I imagined, dreamed of better places, white houses on blue islands, and then maybe a place like my Nova Scotia, pasture roses on the night wind and the summer's last lightning bugs yellow under the alders.

I expected to surprise animals at night, but I didn't. In fact I saw animals only during the day—red squirrels throughout the day, and then one morning and again another afternoon a short-tailed weasel or ermine looping through soft brown arches and in and out of sight along the stone wall at the back of the side meadow. One afternoon I discovered a porcupine climbing a spruce by the wall. Although I did not see any more porcupines, by the end of the summer I found a web of porcupine trails in the woods, leading from dens to favorite trees. Scattered under the trees were droppings and quills, small cream-colored quills with minute barbs at the ends. Although I had never seen one before, I saw more shrews than any other animal. Late in the afternoon of our second day, I saw a masked shrew foraging under the clothesline. Shrews are active at dusk, and I learned how to discover them. Going into the spruce woods, I sat silently in rooty and mossy arbors and more often than not eventually saw a shrew scuffling rapidly along a favorite trail, darting into small holes under roots to search for insects, and then disappearing on an underground path, only to reappear momentarily a foot or so away. As I age, ambition seems silly, and the virtues I most admire are modesty and humility. Little moments beyond success and envy grow more significant, Eliza's hugging me and saying, "Daddy, I love you. It will break my heart when you die." Similarly, small creatures attract me more than large. Films about the massive animals of African plain and forest bore me, and at dusk in the woods of Nova Scotia I was wondrously happy, a little game hunter following shrews in search of beetles and slugs.

From my first few night walks I returned with random impressions.

In the dark, for example, the ferns that rose in great tufts through-out the woods vanished, while trees grew in stature. No longer did dead trees slump loosely against each other. Instead they appeared solid, their limbs threads pulled tightly, almost magically, through a fibrous piece of silver-and-black needlepoint. Along the bluff over-looking the Gulf of Maine all flowers except daisies disappeared, and these fell out of dimension, practically out of color. Instead of rising fresh from the ground, they sank, resembling flat cutouts pasted on dark gray construction paper. On Route 1 cars swept through the night, making me think not of the cold damp air blowing across the fields but of plants, particularly the chair-maker's rush. The cars blossomed along the road then disappeared in a moment, much, I thought, as the rush's brown nutlets suddenly pushed through the stem and then jutting heavily out to the side appeared precariously attached, a spikelet of seeds on tar, wheels spinning on a slender green spear.

The distance between cars and plants is too great to be spanned by metaphor, and I realized my impressions of night were distorted and untrue. Instead of shortening my walks, I lengthened them. The more I explored, the greater the possibility of discovering patterns, or if not patterns at least links between random impressions, links that did not smack of crankcases and the bookishly mechanical. In hopes that days cluttered with observation would balance the empty nights and keep me from becoming discouraged, I investigated the small pond at the low end of George's Field. No bigger than a farmhouse kitchen, the pond had once been a watering hole for cattle. After the cattle disappeared, alders grew up around the pond, and dirt washed down from George's Field and silted up the eastern edge. From the west, acids leached in from a bog, and the water was still and brown. Under the surface was an unknown world, a kind of night, I imagined, while above the surface all was day. Hunting insects, warblers twisted like ornaments through the alders, black and whites, yellows, and then yellowthroats, rakish with a mask of black feathers over their eyes. On the ground above the waterline grew rushes, while shafts of pick-erelweed stood thick in the silt near George's Field. On the opposite side of the pond, water milfoil spread under the surface, always with two or three large green frogs splayed out on it like sunbathers dozing on rafts in a swimming pool. Occasionally butterflies flew through the alders, sometimes orange fritillaries, but mostly black and white admirals pitching awkwardly about like scraps of paper in a wind. On sticks and plants around the pond damselflies laid eggs, their bodies curving into blue half-circles. Over the pond hung heavy dragonflies, sparkling in the light, early in July big green and blue darners, and then, later, smaller skimmers, first browns and yellows, then reds.

For $49.95 I bought an "aquatic net" to explore the pond. The net had a five-foot hardwood handle at the end of which was a thick bag shaped like a capital D, the flat side of the D being a foot long. With the net I swept across the bottom of the pond then up through the milfoil. After bringing the net to the surface I emptied it into a flat aluminum cake pan with sides three or so inches high. The pan was good-sized, large enough to bake snacks and seconds for a big kindergarten class. Although the pond, like night, appeared still, the surface calm was deceptive. Below in the dark, life and death were linked, the lives of small creatures beginning and ending in a moment, the whole process somehow spinning beyond the individual and out of time, at least out of any time I could comprehend. To feed on small swarming insects, tadpoles came out of hiding in the heat of the day, their heavy heads gray lumps beneath the surface and their tails trailing down into the gloom beneath. In pursuit of tadpoles water tigers paddled under the surface. The larvae of large diving beetles, the tigers were almost three inches long. Down the center of their backs a yellow stripe ran straight as a desert highway, and on either side black fell away to gray like the dirty shoulders of a road. Unlike tadpoles the tigers swung down from the surface like sickles, their heads resembling a child's thumbnail with hooks turning around the edges to meet in the front. Behind the head were six legs which they used almost like oars to row through the water, and then curving up and behind and breaking the water was the tail through which they sucked in air. I caught many tadpoles and water tigers. As soon as I dumped them in the cake pan, the tigers set out after the tadpoles. Once I freed a big tadpole from a water tiger. The tadpole quickly twisted away in the pond, but I suspect he eventually died, for the tigers' hooks or mandibles are hollow, and once they seize victims, the tigers pump poisons and digestive juices into them. Unlike the tiger, the adult diving beetle must chew its way into prey. In the net I caught several large diving beetles. Although they had smoky gray, almost alcoholic eyes and a yellow stripe circling their bodies, the beetles

resembled brazil nuts, flattened then smoothed out and polished. I
also caught whirligig beetles, back swimmers, and dragonfly larvae.
Although they were voracious and efficient predators, these last
seemed friendly to me, the silly cocker spaniels of the pond. I also
liked the salamanders, gills circling up and behind their heads like
ruffs, making me think of sixteenth-century fops, then wenches and
codpieces, doxies and conycatchers.

George Jones's favorite writer was Ralph Waldo Emerson, the essayist and philosopher. In speeches Jones often cited Emerson, declaring that when the "inward eye" opened to the unity of things life
became a feast. After I explored the pond, my days and nights became
linked, not by a sublime organic unity, but by that lesser thing, approach. On my first walks my attention had wandered, the deep drum
of fishing boats, for example, almost always pulling me toward the
Gulf of Maine, the next moment the bark of a fox turning me inland
toward the stone wall behind Ma's Property. Under a spruce close to
the wall was a swarm of yellow jackets. Nearby ran an animal path. I
knew it was only a matter of time until a fox dug up the nest and ate
the larvae, and I wanted to catch him digging. Because it was small
and confined, the pond focused my attention. After exploring the
pond, I shortened my walks. Instead of roaming shore and field indis-
criminately, following the barks of foxes and the lights of fishing boats,
I concentrated on the woods behind Ma's Property. Although I did not
stop roaming over the farm, I spent more time in one place, stretched
out on and then crawling along a strip of ground where the woods
sloped toward a bog and peat moss began rising under black spruce in
thick mounds.

Ways of observation, like those of thought, are difficult to change,
and at first I saw only familiar territory, the ground rolling not as itself
but like the uplands of eastern Connecticut. To my right was Horsebarn Hill; to my left Wolf Rock; behind the ridge ahead I imagined
Unnamed Pond and instead of moss, red tips filled with spores, a long
field of green corn, the stalks thick and close, and above the corn
crows, black wrinkles in the blue sky. Slowly, however, the crows drifted
out of mind, and I began to see, initially the obvious: white moths
swirling about my head lantern; the burrows of small creatures, the
openings to some no bigger around than my little finger, others almost as large as my fist; and then mushrooms, covered with slugs,

most of the slugs orange but a few big ones brown and gray. At night slugs crawled up from hiding places under the moss and fed upon plants. A favorite food was Canada mayflower, and by July the slugs had stripped the plants on the forest floor, reducing leaves to veins. After hours on the ground I returned to the house and occasionally discovered the remains of slugs not on but under my trousers, orange splotches marking the spots where they had been crushed. Although slugs stripped the leaves, they did not eat the berries of the mayflower. Remaining attached to the stem, the berries were round and speck-led, resembling glassy bulbous parts of *Gone with the Wind* lamps. By August bunchberries were bright red, and whenever I found them, I ate them. At times I seemed to graze through nights, eating bunch-berries in the woods, beach peas on the shore, and near the barn pulling up and munching on new shoots of Japanese knotweed.

The longer I stayed in the woods the more comfortable I became, slipping not into idea, though, but mood. The moss was soft, and sometimes I dozed. Once or twice I found myself hoping I would die and my body would not be discovered. Then, I mused, I would be-come part of the woods itself, the rich stuff of other life. I crawled under ferns and, looking up, saw moths staring down at me, their eyes pinched and silvery. I smelled partridgeberry blossoms, the fragrance resembling almonds and reminding me of marzipan candy. I dug be-neath the moss, finding ground beetles, worms, centipedes, and then salamanders, once a fat spotted salamander, its big yellow splotches bright as moons, but usually red-backed salamanders, clutches of eggs nearby, small salamanders inside twisting slowly about creamy yolks. Although few birds were visible in the woods, even in the day, feath-ers clung to the roots of fallen trees. Animal droppings were every-where, and I opened them searching for seeds. Whenever I identified a seed, I felt proud. I considered tasting the droppings, but I refrained, despite knowing the textures would be grainy and the flavors oaty at worst. By doing something people usually didn't admit to thinking about, I imagined that I would push through limitation to discovery. Despite believing Jones right in preferring the communal to the indi-vidual good, I sometimes longed to distinguish myself, in the process turning observation away from the world and toward the self, narrow-ing appreciation.

Such moments did not last long, however, for the woods held an infinity of distractions. When I saw a red mite climbing the orange cup of fly agaric, I forgot what I was thinking. I almost lost my notebook on a cold morning when I found a big mound of moss radiating heat, the mound's center a mass of white fungus. On leaving the woods I carried the habit of observation and a capacity for distraction with me. Late one night after hanging damp trousers on the mantel behind the woodstove, I went into the pantry to get a peach. Much as I had never observed the night, so I had never really looked at the pantry, despite, I realized, passing through it a dozen or more times a day for many summers. Against the back wall was a new Hitachi washing machine, reminding me of our weekly routine. Monday was washing day, when the machine was pulled away from the wall into the middle of the pantry and attached to faucets on the sink. During the week soiled clothes accumulated in the long front hall: nearest the kitchen a pile of trousers, mostly blue jeans; next to them, light-colored clothes, shirts, shorts, pajamas; in a green, armless chair, on top of sheets cleaned by South West Laundry in Yarmouth and wrapped in brown paper, were white socks, underpants, and dish towels; and last, almost under the chair, dark socks and work shirts. In the pantry beside the washing machine was a General Electric Deluxe refrigerator; some forty years old, it was defrosted every Thursday. Friday was shopping day, while on Sunday I emptied the ashes out of the stove.

The pantry was cluttered. Nailed over the back door was an ox-shoe; reed baskets hung from the beams; under the sink was a large ironstone jar, filled with potatoes and made by Medalta Potteries in Medicine Hat, Alberta. Screwed into a shelf was a rusty pencil sharpener. Next to it sat two gravy boats. Decorated in the blue willow pattern, the first rested low on the shelf, its bottom wide and stable. With greenish flowers swirling up sides scalloped into scuppers, the second boat rode too high for the unstable seas of children's dinners. All sorts of things filled the shelves: glass milk bottles, a sack of mousetraps, an oil lamp under a paper bag. In a corner of the pantry was a broken Hoover Electric Suction Sweeper, the motor on top squat and the size of a big Christmas pudding. Leaning against it was a wooden carpet sweeper, "Bissell's 'Cyco' Ball-Bearing Boudoir" stamped on the side in gold and its wheels resembling those of a steam engine, two big wheels with a little one sandwiched between. Like the woods the pantry was a jumble of distractions. What held my attention for the longest time, however, was a round brass-bound gauge screwed into the wall above the refrigerator. Six and a half inches wide and standing out from the wall two inches, the gauge had been removed from an old fire engine. Around the face of the gauge ran numbers measuring pressure, the gauge recording a top figure of one hundred and forty pounds. At the bottom of the gauge in a decorative script resembling thin swirls of smoke was the manufacturer's name: "American Steam Gauge Co." Printed under the name of the manufacturer was the date of patent, February 3, 1852, and then "T. W. Lane's improvement," this patented on February 22, 1859. In the center of the gauge was a sketch of a horse-drawn fire engine. Toward the rear of the engine the boiler rose like a huge samovar. In the front, resembling a silvery balloon trying to rise from the ground, was the compressed-air chamber. Like a heavy worm a thick hose curled from the front of the engine back to the side and, forming a half-circle around the boiler, hung over a tall back wheel.

Because the children were asleep when I explored the woods at night, I took them for walks in the day, showing them my discoveries: Volvos and the dug-out papery nests of yellow jackets. At breakfast I told stories about the creatures I saw, giving them names similar to those in the children's books of Thornton Burgess. Hurrying about the woods were Busy Baskins, the mother shrew, and her baby girl, Bertha. Little Tommy Telltruth, the young mouse, spent vacations with his grandmother, old Mrs. Pantry. Always shopping in her orange apron, Mrs. Worry Worm, the robin, rarely stopped in the woods to chat. In contrast Chittery, the squirrel, was forever gossiping, much to the displeasure of Gray Beard, the daddy longlegs. A retired school superintendent, Gray Beard was stuffy and ceremonious, although once a week he attended the meeting of the Cicada Club and screeched as loudly as anyone there. At the meetings he sat next to Whiney, the mosquito, a deferential friend from childhood, and talked with Bloom, the slug, a portly banker and social climber who patronized the arts but whose shiny dress betrayed his ambitions, exposing him to the ridicule of those not quite so respectable. Occasionally I met Blue Billy, the Canada jay, in the woods. Billy was a good friend of Field, the crow, and Chips, the wood frog. Often these three skipped school and played hide-and-go-seek. Chips was a good player. When he sat still, he resembled a small rock and was hard to find, not so hard, though, as Secret Sally, the salamander, who always won the game when she played. Sally did not play often, however. A good student and a responsible girl, she spent most of her after-school time baby-sitting her brothers and sisters or curled up in her mossy bed reading a book, this summer the same books I read the children, *Anne of Green Gables* and Ursula Le Guin's *Earthsea* trilogy.

In a speech on the Latin dramatists Jones declared that the immature mind sought the concrete and was incapable of appreciating the abstract. Despite my admiration for Jones, my explorations led only to the concrete. The greatest dangers to the small inhabitants of the woods, I told the children, were specific not abstract: the big foot of Mr. Man and the long nose of his friend Dog. Since we did not own a pet, we could not do much about the long nose, but we could, I said, watch where we stepped. When we played our sort of hide-and-go-seek, searching for treasures under the moss and finding Sally in the nursery with her brothers and sisters, we could close the door gently—reverently I would have said if I could have been certain the children would have understood. As Chegoggin influenced mood and shaped fiction, so the long nights on the farm softened me. In wandering the dark I did not discover an organic power behind night and day. Still, I reached the point where I wanted to believe, along with Vicki's great-grandfather, that "the simplest things in life are the most profound."

Representative

"Neil," I said, shivering under a pile of blankets, "I have been bitten by the flu, not the political bug." "Sam, all I know is what I read," he answered. "The *Hartford Courant* says that among 'those now being mentioned' as Republican candidates in the 'Second Congressional District' is 'University of Connecticut Professor Samuel F. Pickering, Jr., of Storrs, the model for Robin Williams's character in the movie *Dead Poets Society.'*" "Neil, I will talk to you later. I'm going to be sick," I said, adding as I put down the telephone, "I don't care what the paper says. It's wrong." For two days I languished in and out of fever. Although I was occasionally so irrational that I imagined my new book becoming a bestseller, I did not dream at all about politics. Not only had I never met a real politician, but I knew few Republicans. In the last election the Republican lost the Second Congressional District by sixty thousand votes, and even if the party was having trouble chasing a sacrificial lamb out of the fold, I couldn't imagine them nipping at the heels of an unknown, a black sheep who usually voted Democratic and said so.

Politics was rarely discussed in my family. "The right people do not run for office," Mother once said; "they are appointed." For Father political matters were the ephemeral stuff of story, not life. When he was a boy in Carthage, Tennessee, state Democrats gathered for a week every August at the Grand Hotel in Red Boiling Springs. There

53

they picked candidates for offices, plotted legislative strategies, divided
tax revenues, and parceled out rights-of-way for highways. The Grand
was old, and Mr. Hawes, the owner, did not keep it clean. Going to
Red Boiling Springs was a tradition, however, one of the few the Democrats had, and they didn't consider changing towns or hotels. Besides, Father said, politicians were comfortable with dirt; flies, though,
he added, were a different matter. A few legislators from big towns
like Nashville and Memphis were bothered by the fat red-eyed flesh
flies that buzzed through the hotel like builders swarming over meaty
contracts for state construction. One morning as he was shaving,
Coker Knox, who represented a smooth, silky district west of
Nashville, turned to Squirrel Tomkins and said, "I just can't stand to
use the bathroom; the flies get all over me." "That's nothing," replied
Squirrel, who was from Hardeman County just above the Mississippi
line; "If you'll come up here at lunch or when dinner's being served,
you won't find a single fly in the bathroom, and you'll be able to tend
to your affairs in comfort."

For most of the year the Grand was practically empty, and when
the Democrats held their yearly meeting, Mr. Hawes had to beat across
Macon County looking for help, down to Gum Springs through Union
Camp and Freewill and then up and over Goad Ridge to Shakerag
Hollow. Although the people he hired were the salt of the earth, they
were more accustomed to plain home fare than to the highly sea-
soned doings of the "Solons" at the Grand. Late one afternoon as he
was returning to his room after drinking waters at the springs, Coker
Knox, so the tale went, thought he heard the dinner bell ring. Seeing
a hotel employee sweeping the walk out to the road, Coker approached
him and asked, "Is that the second bell?" "No sir, Mr. President," the
man said, straightening then leaning over his broom to think a bit,
"no sir, that's the second ringing of the first bell. We ain't got no
second bell in this hotel."

Dividing the spoils of office went quickly as dessert, and once the
platter was clean, the politicians set about the serious business of
having fun. Toward the end of the meeting each year "The Mighty
Haag" circus came through Red Boiling Springs. With two old ele-
phants trailing behind four horse-drawn wagons, the circus wasn't
spectacular. Its tent, though, provided the boys with an arena for antics. Each year some innocent young Methodist surprised the party

bosses and got elected to the legislature. That August when he came to Red Boiling Springs, he was invited to referee a badger fight—an invitation which he was told was really an initiation into the party and which he could not refuse if he were ambitious. The badger fight was held under the circus tent. Tied to a stake driven into the ground was an old dog, rough and bony and with long, yellow teeth. Nearby was a large wooden box; sticking out from under it was a thick rope, at the end of which was, supposedly, the badger. The legislator's job was to hold the rope and control the badger so the dog wasn't killed right away. As soon as the box was lifted, the legislator was to jerk the rope toward himself and pull the badger into the fray. The preliminaries to the fight took some time, and while the young man held the rope and two circus employees sat atop the box to keep the badger from digging free, the audience bet on how long the dog would last. Finally, however, the tent grew quiet, and then Haag himself appeared, dressed in red and gold and carrying his trumpet, looking as if he were marching to Waterloo. He blew a long fanfare—sounding, Father said, like a cross between a cattle call and the *William Tell* Overture—after which the two men lifted the box and the dupe jerked the rope, pulling toward himself not a badger but a chamber pot.

Although much drinking went on at the Grand, politicians were urged to avoid drink before the final dinner. Local preachers were invited to the dinner to bless the party, and although public relations had not yet become a science, party leaders thought they ought to make a good impression upon the clergy. To this end they scheduled the dinner for three o'clock in the afternoon, so the preachers, some of whom had long drives ahead of them, the politicians explained, would not be out after dark. In private they told the truth, noting that by three o'clock serious legislators were usually just starting to drink and were not yet tumbling in the need of prayer. Much as the preachers' lessons for saving souls fell on deaf ears, so the leaders cast their plans on rocky soil, and a good many Democrats floated into the dinner buoyed aloft by drink and speaking in tongues. One year when Squirrel Tomkins was the front-runner in the race for lieutenant governor, he brought a jug with him. By dessert he was dancing on tables, and by the time the Reverend Hackett rose to give the final blessing, Squirrel had taken off his trousers and was standing on his head, waving his legs in the air. "Oh, Tomkins," Coker Knox said, looking at

him with chagrin, "you have danced away the lieutenant governor-
ship." Squirrel smiled and, kicking hard, tossed a shoe over the lec-
tern, just missing Reverend Hackett, and said, "Squirrel don't care."

Squirrel's attitude has always seemed sensible to me, and after
laughing once or twice with Neil about the article in the *Courant*, I
forgot politics. Then one night a week later a member of the Republican state committee telephoned me. Would I, he asked, consider running for Congress. On my answering no, he replied that he expected
such a response, adding, "That's why some people want to talk to
you." For a moment I thought about kicking a shoe through the air.
But then, reflecting that I wrote essays and thinking a piece on politics might be fun, I agreed to a meeting, though, I stressed, "running
for office was far from my mind." We set a date near the first of February, ten days off. "Well," Vicki said when I told her, "if they read your
books it's good-bye meeting." "There is little chance of that," I responded, saying that people in politics usually didn't read. Besides, I
added, my sales had been so low that even if someone wanted to glance
at one of my books he would have a devilish time finding a copy. And
as for my life, I added, looking, wistfully off, I am afraid, into the
distance, "ever since marrying you I have been a good boy, damn near
a saint." "Huh," Vicki grunted, "what about that picture you got in
the mail the other day?"

On my desk was a photograph taken in Switzerland twenty-six
years ago. In the picture a boy lay on his back, shirt pulled up to his
chest. From his belly button sprouted a bouquet of alpine flowers:
yellow, purple, and pink trumpets. "Alas, dear Ellen," I wrote after
receiving the picture, "the hounds of winter are biting at the summer's traces. Where flowers once bloomed, weeds now thrive: goose-
foot, plantain, barbed teasel, and thin strings of knotted, gray dod-
der." In the past I had misbehaved with little girls, but not, alas, very
often. Once while playing with three girls I broke a bone. But then
we were all four years old, and the game was ring-around-the-rosy.
When we fell down, they tumbled on top of me and snapped my
collarbone. Insofar as boys were concerned I hadn't even bruised a
fingernail. One night twenty-five years ago I slept in a double bed
with another student. We met on a train, traveling from London to
Vienna. We arrived in Vienna late at night. The cheap hotels were
fully booked, and the agent at the station could find only one decent,

free room. I was exhausted and slept like one of the dead. The next morning, however, I got a single room. What bothered me most, though, about shenanigans with boys and girls was not anything I had done, but what Josh, a rough character who wandered through my writings, might say. Josh has little patience for platitudes: political, pious, or sexual. "Dammit," he said recently, bursting into my office; "I'm tired of people accusing me of being prejudiced whenever I argue with them. Hell, I am going to come out of the living room and declare that I am homosexual. Then when people differ with me, I'll accuse them of homophobia." "But Josh," I said, "you're married with three children and, so far as I know, have never had a homosexual experience. Somebody is bound to point that out." "By God, I hope so," Josh answered; "if she does I will accuse her of stereotyping. Who is she to say what I am. Limiting cultural diversity in such a manner is the most invidious form of harassment imaginable." Some other time I might have listened patiently to Josh, but I didn't want to have anything to do with him until after my meeting with the Republican committee. "Out," I said; "out of my office. What you are saying is political dynamite."

That afternoon *Writing Home*, a newsletter written for parents of students attending the University of Connecticut, was published. A sketch of me appeared in the newsletter. The author stated that I refused to go on television, noting that my only appearance on television occurred in 1969 at halftime of the Princeton-Rutgers football game, celebrating one hundred years of college football. "Clad in a blue blazer and red striped pants and fueled by a couple of whiskey sours," I, the newsletter reported, "marched behind the band carrying a punch bowl." The article was almost accurate. Although the punch bowl has slipped from memory, I did march—though, in truth, I was fueled by more than a couple of whiskey sours. Two little nips would not have gotten me out of my seat, much less past midfield. And I marched, not alone, but with a companion, herself a field of flowers, not a posy of wilted alpine blossoms, but bluebonnets and larkspur fresh in the sun. Although the red trousers still hang in an attic closet, and I think I could fit into them without much pushing and twisting, I have not worn them in fifteen years. On bright football Saturdays, Vicki and the children and I roam the university farm. High on Horsebarn Hill we push through the long scratchy rows of corn, stumbling upon groundhogs and then watching red-shouldered hawks as they wheel over the Eastern Uplands. After walking for two or three hours we go to the dairy bar for ice-cream cones: pistachio, fudge royal, blueberry cheesecake, lime sherbet, and mint chocolate chip. Whiskey sours have lost their sweetness, and rarely do I even drink a glass of wine. Only once this summer did Vicki and I share a bottle, and that was on our farm in Nova Scotia, at dinner after I was asked to speak at convocation in the fall. We drank a bottle of Canadian wine, something called Baco Noir on sale for six dollars and ninety cents. "A superior, full-bodied, rich red wine, vinted from the distinguished Baco Noir grape," the label stated. After dinner, while Vicki washed the dishes, I led the children out into a peat bog. For the first time all summer I got turned around and lost. Edward and Eliza started to cry, but Francis had a whale of a time, imagining himself poor Ben Gunn, marooned on Treasure Island. Ten minutes later we were on the kitchen porch, singing "Fifteen men on a dead man's chest" and picking spruce twigs like laurel wreaths out of our hair.

"For those booze-swilling, cigar-chomping, ass-grabbing boys in the back rooms," Josh said later when I mentioned the evening in Nova Scotia, "drinking Baco Noir would be practically the same thing as stopping cold turkey and flopping onto the wagon. Not only are you overqualified for the job, but you are too good. Forget Congress and stick to playing jokes at the university. That's a higher calling." Although the humor of some people might be elevated, my jokes usually run to the earth, much like the groundhogs we startled on Horsebarn Hill. For signing letters the head of the English department has a rubber stamp with his signature pressed on it. Two months ago I saw the stamp on a secretary's desk. I removed it and an ink pad, and going into the lavatory stamped the head's name on some pieces of functional equipment found in men's but not women's bathrooms. At least I assume such things are not found in women's bathrooms, not having explored a woman's bathroom since the third grade and then making only a cursory, terrified inspection. I removed the signatures sometime later, after a friend showed them to the head and accused him of being both unclean and addicted to graffiti. "David," I said to the head afterward, "I got rid of your signatures, but I'm not going to tell you how I did it."

Although playfulness is often misunderstood, making the serious person seem frivolous, the jokes I played didn't bother me. More damaging to my campaign, as I now occasionally labeled it, was my shaky allegiance to the Republican party. I was the worst sort of party member, a Republican not because of zeal or principle but because of tradition, and inertia. Pickerings have been Republicans since the Civil War. In 1861 my great-grandfather left Ohio University to fight for the Union. After the war he settled in Tennessee, and we have remained Republicans ever since, not because we believe in partisan politics but because we disbelieve. Thinking one group liable to be as self-serving as another, we have never felt compelled to change parties, this despite voting for Squirrel Tomkins and supporting Democrats more often than Republicans. For my part I didn't vote for Mr. Bush in the last election. Indeed I have often referred to him and his running mate as Shrub and Partridge, though when days were sunny and country things were on my mind, I whistled and called the vice president Bob White. On most issues I wasn't sure where the Republican line ran. Wherever it twisted, though, I didn't follow. Instead of gun control, I'm for gun confiscation. Little would satisfy me more than violating the constitutional rights of gun owners. I would not vote for anyone who wanted to restrict abortion. As far as possible I want Eliza to control her life. She can determine whether or not she has children, not some primitive mullah chanting high abstractions from a tabernacle. Thinking developers enemies of the people, I am such an environmentalist that I ought to belong to a weed or flower party, not a political party. As I pondered what seemed my beliefs, I realized that I should not run for office. Deluding myself into believing that I was honest, I would speak injudiciously. Even worse I would probably enjoy making people angry. Although deciding that I was a poor candidate did not make me gleeful, for no one likes confronting his weaknesses, the realization brought relief, and I pushed political matters out of mind and got on with ordinary living.

Actually the *Dead Poets Society* awakened more than politicians, and at times ordinary living seemed extraordinary. One night a real-estate agent invited me to Hawaii to lecture other realtors on selling homes. The next morning the Air Force invited me to participate in a Civic Leaders' Tour and inspect military bases in Florida and Mississippi. A teacher from Tolland asked me to talk to one hundred and twenty-five first through sixth graders on writing. The local chapter of the Connecticut Alumni Association invited me to dinner. The senior citizens asked me to speak at their yearly banquet, and a professor in education urged me to spend an evening talking to suburban school superintendents. I had already agreed to many talks; my calendar was full, and so with the exceptions of the senior citizens and the school superintendents I refused the invitations, even the military tour and the trip to Hawaii. Two years ago I spoke to young writers in Mansfield, so I did not feel guilty about not talking in Tolland. I told the Alumni Association to contact me in the fall, explaining I had spoken too often in Storrs, in the library and in churches, adding that in June I would give commencement addresses at the local high school and at a junior college in Danielson. In the middle of the week a friend telephoned and offered me the headship of a private school with some nine hundred students from kindergarten through high school. The job and its perquisites tripled my university salary, providing house and utilities, car, private-school tuition for my children, and a salary of about eighty thousand a year, though this last, I understood, could be negotiated upward. In *Writing Home* I was quoted as saying, "I'm not interested in fame or money. You might as well not want the things you're not going to get." Words trap a person, forcing him to acknowledge what is important, and I turned down the headship.

That night I wrote a letter to the *Hartford Courant*. In part I refused the headship because I liked teaching at the University of Connecticut. The previous weekend the *Courant* printed a letter from a man who spent a semester teaching in our English department. In his letter the man described the poor condition of the Humanities Building, seeing its shape not simply as a "public shame" but as an emblem of general deterioration. Although some buildings at Connecticut needed repair, I answered the letter. I did so for my students. It would be sad, I thought, if critics of the university convinced students that their school and, by extension, they themselves were inferior. "Gosh," I wrote, I was sorry that our visitor found things so ramshackle in Storrs. The truth was that low-bid, functional buildings didn't function well. They required lots of maintenance and deteriorated quickly, sometimes turning those in them into functional people, gray and spiritless. Still, I wrote, I was happy in the old hulk at the University of Connecticut, even though I was one of those people who shared an office, something our visitor found particularly galling. Actually, I explained, I liked sharing an office. "For years Joe, my officemate, has laughed at me and kept me from swelling with self-importance. For a teacher pride is a danger. After writing a book or two, we sometimes get above ourselves and think we deserve the trappings of celebrity and recognition. We forget that we are, at best, servants of community and stewards of culture. We even forget how fine our jobs are. Every cultivated person in Connecticut ought to envy my job," I continued; "I spend days talking about books that thrill me. Nice young people look up to me and listen, even when they should not. Moreover, if the Humanities Building has aged into disrepair, my salary has remained sound, and I have time to write and play." Not everything at Connecticut, I said, was hunky-dory. I wrote that spending twenty-five million dollars on a basketball arena seemed "damned irresponsible." If that money had been used to put the essential plant to rights, I said, I suspected that our visitor would not have been so disturbed. Still, that was my particular hobbyhorse, one I had ridden through boredom and beyond. What bothered me more was the fear that our visitor's "gloom might become a dark litany and color the future. The University," I wrote, was not sad or shameful but good. "Some clocks in the Humanities Building may be broken, but many classes are electric. Across the campus the range of courses taught and the expertise and dedication of the teachers are astonishing. No matter the condition of a building we will make do and we will work for better things because, sappy as it sounds, we want the best for all our children." At the end of the letter I described a walk I took late one night in the snow, two or so weeks earlier. On the way home I climbed Horsebarn Hill. At the top I stopped. Below me the campus glowed yellow. I wrote that I couldn't see or think clearly, but the soft light made me feel good. I stayed, I said, "on the hill for a long time, eating snow, and identifying buildings, and thinking how lucky I was to be teaching English at the University of Connecticut."

I mailed the letter at the airport the next morning. I was flying to the College of Wooster in Ohio to speak to scholarship students. I was glad to escape, if only for a moment, from the Connecticut me that had become political and public. Of course I couldn't completely escape. The meeting with the Republicans was three days away, and politics was back on my mind. Boarding the plane ahead of me was a

woman reading a book entitled *Everyone Is Psychic*. I almost asked her
if I had a chance to win the Second Congressional District. Instead I
asked if she had "good vibrations" about the flight. She said she did,
and I boarded and slept all the way to Cleveland. That night I spoke.
The next morning I got up before dawn and explored the campus.
The gray squirrels were larger and redder than in Connecticut. A
flock of robins made its way across the grass, the birds' breasts bounc-
ing like fat orange balls. Beside the classroom buildings grew dogwood, while great oaks, chestnuts, and sycamores towered over the
commons, their limbs bulging like muscles and seeming almost to
support the rising day.

     Two nights later in the rain I drove to Norwich and met twelve or
so Republicans in a coffee-filled room at the Sheraton. The people
were nice. Not openly partisan, they were the sort of gentle folk one
would like for neighbors or relatives. No one blanched when I outlined my thoughts on abortion and development. They agreed when I
said the military budget should be slashed, and they laughed when I
said I got my economic ideas from the *Willimantic Chronicle*. They
asked whether Vicki would enjoy an election campaign. "No," I said;
"she is private and retiring, devoted to children and home, not interested in politics." She was, I added, "a pleasing person, one whom
most people like immediately." I did not tell the group that as I walked
out the door that night she said, "I don't approve of this meeting. I
hope you make a fool of yourself and get this jackassery out of your
system."

     When asked if I would like living in Washington, I replied that I
could not imagine raising children there. "Still," I continued, "that's
beyond even slender possibility. The incumbent has this district won."
Gingerly, the group asked about my past, wondering how spotted it
was. No bantlings or drugs, not even a traffic ticket lurked, I responded,
behind the years. "But," I said, and here I told the first lie of my
political career, "but I have lived with passion and long ago was the
lover of many women." I'm not sure why I told such a lie. Maybe the
writer in me provoked it. Much as I knew my future campaign would
be only an essay, so perhaps I wanted to shape a colorful and intriguing
past. Be that as it may, the group was too polite to linger over love,
and we pushed on to finances. How much would it cost to run, and
where would the money come from, I asked. After some debate the

group settled on an estimate "of somewhere between six and seven hundred thousand dollars." As for raising such funds, that was usually done by the candidate. "I have never asked anyone other than my mother for a penny," I said, "and I am too old and poor to start now." I told the group that I had no debts and would not risk my peace of mind and my children's futures for something as fleeting as politics. If I ran for office, I said, I would urge people to donate the moneys they might have contributed to my campaign to charity. That way, I explained, "when I got beat, I could at least say that I had accomplished something decent."

There may be "a tide in the affairs of men, which taken at the flood, leads on to fortune." All I know is that I clambered out of a gully and high above the wash felt relieved. The next morning I turned my attention back to summer and Nova Scotia, to little things more alluring and somehow more significant to me than politics. One morning late in August I saw a yellow jacket fly into a spiderweb hanging in the corner of a kitchen window. Almost immediately a small orb weaver rushed out from a retreat at the side of the window and fell down the web toward what it assumed was prey. The spider erred; the yellow jacket was not victim but hunter. As soon as the spider drew near, the yellow jacket curved its abdomen into a half-circle and stung the spider. The spider quivered; its legs curled up and then turned down and inward, much as the blossoms of wild carrot fold into small bushy cups in the fall. In a brisk, efficient manner, the yellow jacket seized the spider and, chewing rapidly through its thin, stalky middle, separated the abdomen from the cephalothorax, this being the upper portion of the spider containing its head and eight legs. The yellow jacket then flew away to its nest, carrying the abdomen as food for its larvae. The upper portion of the spider hung lightly in the web, the wound at what was once its middle gleaming and wetly orange, resembling the flesh of a bruised nectarine. Within minutes the yellow jacket or another from the nest was back. Often I had wondered why the spiders around the house hid during the day and came out of hiding only at dusk. As night approached, yellow jackets retired to their nests, and spiders were, I now saw, comparatively safe.

I followed the yellow jacket as it hovered over the porch and drifted to the side of the house, brushing through shrubs and beating against windows. The yellow jacket didn't see webs; instead it flew where webs ought to have been. Once in a web it tried to fool the spider out of hiding, initially fluttering its wings rapidly to feign panic then slowing them to simulate exhaustion. Suddenly I realized why spiders did not attack some moths caught in webs at night and instead allowed them to batter their ways to freedom, in the process destroying the webs. The vibrations the moths sent through the webs must have resembled those transmitted by predators. Out of instinct the spiders avoided the moths, preferring to give up a meal rather than risk becoming another's dinner.

From the bridal wreath under the bay window the yellow jacket flew across the side meadow to the bank of roses behind the well and around the barn. Pushing through the roses, the yellow jacket disappeared. As I looked for it, I noticed flies: gray, green, and then swarms of small gold flies. In the early sun the flies sparkled as they spun through the air. As I watched them I wondered why I never noticed them before. Had dreams about the large and distant obscured my vision and led me to neglect the small and the immediate? As I stood by the roses I saw a robber fly, bearded and bristled. Ferocious predators, robber flies often resemble the creatures they prey upon, much, I unaccountably thought, as the predators of man resemble men. Wearing trousers, shirts, and shoes, our predators speak our languages and are us until they pounce and drain life and beauty away. That morning my thoughts were not deep or original, but they were thoughts, not postures assumed because they were expedient or winning. My attention soon wandered from the flies, following broad whim, not the dictates of party or campaign. Through thorns and the swelling, heavy hips of the roses pushed spikes of long-leaved speedwell, cool and blue. Blooming pink at my feet was hemp nettle. At the edge of the meadow bittersweet nightshade twined through the roses, some of its fruit bright red droplets, others green. Out in the high, unmowed grass the dainty seedpods of willow herb split, pushing the long, winged seeds into the air and making me think of gulls riding the wind over the Gulf of Maine.

Just today I put pencils and paper and Nova Scotia aside. I walked down Eastwood and, crossing the South Eagleville Road, dropped down the slope into the marsh below. Sticking up through the ice were the horns of skunk cabbage, still green and tight. In holes in rotten trees I found two birds' nests, one filled with wood shavings, the other with moss. From the thin branches of shrubs and young trees drops of icy water hung in bumpy silver lines. I squatted down, and when I looked up toward the sky, sunlight broke through the drops, turning them yellow, then blue, then yellow again. My knees began to ache, and so I sat on the ground, the snow melting and seeping through my trousers. I wondered if politicians had time to do such things, and I was glad, ever so glad, that I was not running, just sitting.

Will It Never End

Long ago in the green land of childhood I read books about romance and saw movies in which lovers danced hours away in sweet amorous play. In my happy inexperience I believed true love was long and slow, crawling over time and flesh like Virginia creeper wrapping itself about a stump. One night, alas, taught me better. The air was humid and perspiration rolled off me, more, I am afraid, from mental than from physical exertion. To turn lust into romance, I ran through the presidents, the multiplication tables up to nine, and the world's longest rivers and biggest lakes—the Nile, Amazon, Yangtze, Mississippi, and then the Caspian Sea, followed by Lakes Superior, Victoria, Huron, and Michigan. I was just starting to conjugate Latin verbs when a voice rose muffled as if it came from the deepest gorge on earth—Hells Canyon on the Snake River, a place I had named, just after the multiplication tables, in fact. "Oh God," the voice cried in despair, "will it never end." Shortly thereafter it ended.

Many sensible years have passed since that hot night. Love, I now know, is not something to linger over but an item to fit into a schedule, behind or between ice-skating, soccer, swimming, piano lessons, ballet, rag ball, workshops in the Natural History Museum, and the next episode of *The Lord of the Rings*. Instead of the stuff of movies, doings intimate are a practical antidote for grumpiness. If romance, however, has become therapeutic, indeed a medicinal moment, reasonable in extent with a prescribed beginning and end, other matters wind interminably through days, impervious to the hoe and sharp-toothed clipper. Two and a half months ago the *Hartford Courant* wrote that I might become a candidate for Congress. Although I told people who asked that I could not afford a campaign, the rumor spread. Six weeks ago a writer from the *New London Day* telephoned during dinner and asked to interview me, explaining, "Everybody in New London is talking about your running for Congress." "I can't believe that the animals, the babies, and the children are talking about it, too," Eliza, my four year old, said when I returned to the table. "That's silly," Francis, who is eight, said turning to his mother, "Daddy doesn't know anything about politics."

Silly though the subject was, I agreed to the interview. Since summer and my identification as the model for John Keating in *Dead Poets Society*, I had enjoyed considerable attention, becoming, I am afraid, slightly addicted to publicity. The interview took place two days later in the living room. The columnist and I sipped coffee, ate blueberry and bran muffins, and talked about politics, family, and writing. The next Sunday, under the headline "Pickering Ponders Politics," the article appeared on the front page of the *Day*. The piece was good. "I only have one complaint," I wrote the author; "you write better than I do." "Sam Pickering, you may recall," the story began, "is the last national celebrity from the University of Connecticut who does not play basketball." The writer was thorough, describing not only the muffins we ate but my living room, even my haircut. Of this last he observed that I "had been to a very thorough barber earlier in the week," adding that I had "something of the young Jack Kerouac" in my look, "especially with the military trim around the ears and brush of dark hair across the brow." "Humbug," Vicki said, "Baden-Powell not Kerouac, boy scout not beatnik." I liked the article more than Vicki did. In truth I like most things written about me more than she does. What upset Vicki was the writer's mentioning my salary, fifty-four thousand dollars a year. "That is private," she said, "and should not be printed." "No," I answered; "I'm a state employee, and it's public record. Besides," I added, "although I am overpaid for what I do, the salary isn't high enough to make people jealous." "That's for damn sure," Vicki said, "people will now think they've overrated you. If you really were a good writer or teacher, they'll conclude, you'd make a bundle more."

Unlike Vicki, I am not bothered by what is written about me. The columnist in the *Day* was meticulously accurate, getting not only my salary right but also my clothes, noting that I wore a green checkered shirt, khaki trousers, "green socks and leather slippers." Usually writers get a lot wrong, something that strikes me as only, perhaps even happily, human. This fall a writer attended two classes of a course I taught in writing fiction. During one of the classes I discussed creating believable characters. The students in the class seemed almost unaware of human failing. As a result they created flat characters and wrote unconvincing stories. People, I said, conventionally enough, were often complex mixtures of strengths and weaknesses. Before they wrote more stories, I told the students, they should think about human failings. Good people, I said, were often weak. As illustration I created a character for them, a decent person but a person addicted to vulgar sensationalism. After every airplane crash this man read through the long list of victims. He hoped to find the name of someone he knew, not because he wished anyone ill, for in his daily living he was gentle and kind, but simply because he was bored and wanted to feel part of the news. Imagine how he reacted, I said, when he discovered that a friend was on the plane that crashed at Lockerbie, Scotland. For hours after the crash, he called mutual acquaintances, telling them about the death of their friend. The students understood the point I tried to make about human nature, and for the next class two or three wrote stories with deeper, richer characters in them. Unfortunately the writer got things slightly wrong. He confused me with the fictional character I created in class, and in his article wrote that I called people after the crash, experiencing "an extraordinary pleasure conveying bad news."

Happily most things wrong make me seem foolish rather than callous. Occasionally I am able to correct them before they go to press. For an essay in my last book I wrote, "droppings, human or otherwise, have never bothered me unduly." In setting the book up to be printed the typesetter changed the *e* on *me* to a *y*, so that the droppings did not bother "my unduly." What readers would have thought had the error slipped past me I dare not think. No matter the care I and writers take, though, errors will appear in my essays and in essays written about me. Slow-moving humorous tales will also appear in my writings. For a decade I have dallied with such stories, their characters clinging to mind and affection like Virginia creeper, their antics running through my books like tendrils forming adhesive disks at the tips whenever they touch a solid page. Many of the tales in my essays take place in Carthage, Tennessee, my father's hometown. For years Vester McBee worked for the Hampers who owned a heavy Victorian house on Main Street. Vester was born in the hills above Gladis, and although she lived in the flatlands down near the Caney Fork River, she remained a hill person, warmhearted and naive. When Orene Hamper went to Nashville to attend Ward-Belmont and then got engaged, bringing her sweetheart back to visit at Easter, all Carthage was curious. "Have you seen Miss Orene's fiancé?" Vester's friend Mavis asked her one day in Read's drugstore. "No," Vester answered, pausing to rub her chin, "no, it ain't been in the wash yet."

An old acquaintance, Vester has long wandered through my books. New characters occasionally join her, and although they are not so unsophisticated, they are cut from a similar fabric. While Vester's remarks cling to memory because they are simple, Josh's comments are memorable because he is outspoken. In the university world the faddish social commitment of the day is to "diversity." "Huh," Josh snorted at me the other morning after class, "diversity hasn't made the Middle East a vacation spot. Diversity leads to nationalism and blood." When I started to protest, he interrupted, exclaiming, "What the hell do you think is going to happen in eastern Europe if the Soviet Union breaks up? Diversity," he said, answering his own question, "diversity bringing sweetness and light to the Georgians, Armenians, Azerbaijanis, Uzbeks, and all the other nice tribes. What the world needs is similarity, not diversity. After two generations people should be required to change their names. Italians would become Scots; Scots, Poles; Poles, Spaniards; and Spaniards, Lithuanians. Soon ethnic slurs would disappear. Nobody would insult his own grandmother. The Irishman who was Turkish four generations ago certainly wouldn't insult the old Turk." When I tried to speak, Josh would not let me get a word in, saying, "I know what you are thinking. People celebrate their roots despite the fact that most families are as common as crabgrass. Well, getting them to change names won't be difficult. Right-thinking women have been changing their names for generations and have grown accustomed to it. Men, I admit, need an incentive. If the government offered them payments, though, men would go along. Most men would sell not simply their names but their wives and children for a song. Anyway, those who refused to give up their names could be forced to take unpleasant, unpronounceable, embarrassing names."

Unlike Josh, who visits me throughout the year, some of the characters in my essays are seasonal, appearing, for example, only in summer or fall. This spring, Baby Lane, the advice columnist in the *Carthage Courier*, received a letter from a distraught wife. "Baby," the woman wrote, "you got to tell me what to do. I've done come to the end of the rope with H. T., my husband. Not that H. T. isn't a good provider because he is. Not only that but he don't play around and does his duty whenever I ask him, if you get my meaning. But, Lord help me, H. T. eats bugs. Before we got married he only ate them once in a while but now he eats them every meal. In the last year I've seen him eat a dragonfly with spots on its wings as black as raisins and then, covered with onions and ketchup, a luna moth in a sandwich. One day this summer he ate a whole bowl of ladybugs in cream. For soup the very next night he boiled up a mess of june bugs, throwing in two green stinkbugs for seasoning. And then, Lord God, just the other morning he ate a spider as big as a peach. Its legs were black and white, and there were white specks like drops of paint all over its back. H. T. told me it was a Shamrock spider and that he was eating it in honor of St. Patrick's Day, even though it won't but the third of August. What am I to do? I am just beside myself. H. T. might eat a whole nest of worms next, and I just couldn't abide kissing him after that." "Dear Beside Yourself," Baby wrote back. "Honey, you got a husband that keeps his zipper up when he shouldn't and lets it down when he should. How many women do you reckon have men with such regular appetites? If I was you, I'd count my blessings before every meal, no matter what bugs was crawling on the table."

The letter to Baby was written in February. Every February about the time snowdrops appear, my thoughts turn to insects, first to the carpenter ants in the south wall of the bedroom and then to the odd bugs in the Life Sciences Building. Late one February afternoon the children and I went to see the dermestid beetles that the university uses to clean meat from dead animals. The beetles have a room to themselves, and when we showed up, they were busy working on the head of a deer. Around the corner and down the hall was a room stacked with aquariums containing sundry small creatures—tarantulas, for example, and curly-tailed lizards from Haiti. The children's favorites, though, were cockroaches from Madagascar. Orange and black and big as a large man's thumb, the roaches hissed when we approached them.

I'm not the only person whose thoughts warm and begin to crawl about in February. As the days grow longer, I receive more mail, much of it describing bygone days at the university, not so much life in classrooms as that on hillsides and down through woods. "My roamings," one man recalled, "took me to what we then called Turner's Meadows, a great expanse of grassland that was mowed perhaps once a year if at all. Pheasant and ducks were present and grouse and rabbits were on the hillside to the west. Deer were almost rare in those days. I had a border collie as a companion. She was a castoff of old Joe Prichard, the college shepherd. She was too fast for a good sheepdog and loved to chase cars along 'faculty row.'"

As February brought memories of wandering about the university to my correspondent's mind, so I begin to roam in February. I never go far, over the university farm and then to Wolf Rock. Vicki and the children and I stand at the top and look across woodland and marsh to Chestnut Hill and Martinhoe Farm. Greens have not begun to appear, and everything—the sky, the trees, even the air itself—seems gray. The walk always satisfies me. Vicki, however, is not so easily pleased. "Other families," she said this year, "go skiing in Vermont, and we go to Wolf Rock." February is hard on Vicki. Her birthday occurs early in the month, and we never go anywhere exotic, even on the day itself. Last year we ate pizza at Tony's on her birthday. This year we went to a potluck dinner, the Blue and Gold Cub Scout Banquet, and Vicki baked a casserole for eight.

If most Februaries, however, are similar, this one was different, marking not reassuring, albeit dull, continuance but an end. I grew up in Nashville, Tennessee. Although I have lived most of my life outside Tennessee, I have always thought of Nashville as home. Two or three times a year I visited Mother and Father there and saw or talked to old friends. Two years ago Mother died, and then this February, Father collapsed. No longer was he able to live on his own, and so in February I brought him to Connecticut, in the process shattering the ties not only of his lifetime but also of mine. Father was in the hospital when I arrived in Nashville, and I spent much time driving back and forth from his apartment. Knowing that my Nashville life would soon be past, I took sentimental journeys, going out of the way to pass through not simply the neighborhoods of my childhood but childhood itself. I quickly realized that my life in Nashville had practically been dismantled already. Richland Market had become a bank, and Dr. Schwartz's Drugstore was a unisex barbershop. Candyland had moved and changed its name to Vandyland. Still, I stopped there for lunch and had a double-chocolate soda. Afterward I walked down West End to Centennial Park to see the old trolley car that I crawled over as a child and that I showed the children just two years ago. The trolley had vanished, and with it went a scrapbook of memories. As I stood at the spot where the trolley had rested for forty-five years at least, I unaccountably thought of Mother and something she had done as a schoolgirl at St. Catherine's in Richmond, Virginia. Mother was a day student and after class drove home, carrying a carload of girls with her. Streetcar tracks ran down the middle of the road in front of St. Catherine's. Passing a slow car was easy, however; the road was wide, and if a person drove near the side of his lane, the cars behind could pass without even approaching the tracks. One afternoon, Mother recounted, "I got behind an old fool driving a beat-up jalopy. Every time I tried to pass he drifted to the left and pushed me against the tracks. Finally I decided to show the jackass. I pulled out and bounced over and along the tracks until I got alongside, then I shot back in front of him. I turned a little too soon, though, and the back bumper of my car hooked his front bumper. The moron blew his horn, and so I stepped on the gas and jerked his bumper right off. I sped off down the street and was still laughing when Father came home from the store that night and said, 'Katharine, have you ever heard of license plates? Even the worst sort of person can sometimes read one, especially when cars are hooked together.' "

Later that afternoon, after seeing Father, I drove out West End, past the spot where the Sulgrave Apartments once stood. For eight years I lived in the Sulgrave, exploring the alley behind, which ran parallel to Fairfax, and then climbing Love Circle and bringing back loads of sticky, yellow Osage oranges. Although the Sulgrave had disappeared, some of the stone wall that bordered West End remained. I used to sit on the wall and look at people and cars, always hoping that the fire trucks in the hall across the street would be called out to answer an alarm. One day, as Father sat with me, a man and his sweet-heart walked by, spooning, arm in arm. "Daddy," I said pointing, "look at that man's big ears. They sure are funny." The trouble, Father recounted later, was that the man's ears were big, and that he was too in love to have a sense of humor. From West End I drove to Belle Meade, to Iroquois Avenue where we moved after leaving the Sul-grave and where Mother and Father lived until three years ago. Our daffodils were up, but the toolshed and garage had been torn down. A trench cut across the backyard, and I wondered if the bones of my dachshunds had been uprooted: Pup Pup, Heinzie One, Two, and Three, and then Fritzie, born in the garage and for eighteen years my dog. I haven't had a pet since Fritzie died, but this fall I am going to get the children a dachshund. "Your old grandfather," I told them, "wants you to have a young dog."

In the middle of the week Father left the hospital and returned to his apartment. He told me what clothes to pack for Connecticut, and I shut his Tennessee life down: changing subscriptions, resigning mem-berships, and filling out medical form after medical form. I ran scores of small errands and roamed over the town. I seemed to have thou-sands of friends. Everywhere I went people recognized me and spoke to me. I wondered about the life I would have led if I had stayed in Nashville. Probably I would not have written essays. In New England I have often been alone, and I write, in part, I sometimes think, as a way of filling solitary, gaping hours. In Nashville I would have known so many people and heard so many true stories that I would not have created Vester and Baby Lane, much less recalled that tired voice asking, "Will it never end?"

Unlike love, memories rarely end simply and abruptly. I haven't completely left Nashville. Father's apartment has not sold, and in June, Vicki, the children, and I must go there and pack the furniture. In February, I cleared off some small things: giving away china as mementos to friends and cleaning the medicine cabinets in the bath-room, throwing away all medicines over a year old. Amid Father's Quinidine, Lanoxin, and Synthroid, I found a bottle of Talwin, one of Mother's medicines. Two years ago, Vicki and I purged the bath-room, getting rid of, we thought, all Mother's medicines. Somehow we missed the Talwin, and that, I suppose, is almost reassuring. No matter how time scours the years, something of ours remains behind, be it a memory or a bottle half full of tablets. As I read the label on the bottle I remembered that Mother called Talwin *Tailwind* because it was so strong. Once when Rosie's knee bothered her, Mother gave her two tablets. Almost immediately the wind whipped up and Rosie zoomed aloft before spinning around and out on the living room rug.

I packed four suitcases of Father's clothes and papers for Storrs. In the middle of the suitcases I stuffed oddments and knickknacks, not things that were important to me but simple things that fit. Along the side of one suitcase I put a gray railway spike. Slightly over six inches long and weighing twelve and a half ounces, the spike came from the abandoned line running up the Sewanee Mountain from Cowan to Monteagle, Tennessee. Next I wrapped a fourteen-by-nine-and-a-half-inch oil painting in pajamas and put it in the middle of a bag. The painting was by Henry Pember Smith, a minor nineteenth-century American artist. In the background of the painting an abandoned mill slumped into ruin under dark oaks. In front of the mill a huge grindstone lay tilted on its side; nearby four white ducks wandered through high grass searching for bugs. The picture I really wanted to bring was a portrait painted of me in 1943. Wearing a one-piece pink suit with short pants and white, ruffled sleeves and collar, I sat smiling, a happy blond little boy holding an apple in his right hand. In a large gold frame, measuring some twenty-three by nineteen inches, the portrait was too big for any of the four suitcases. Into another bag I put china, not valuable pieces but knickknacks that sat on coffee and corner tables: a Herend pelican with a gold beak and a Crown Derby pig, this last splotched with pink violets. After filling it with socks and wrapping it about with underpants, I stuck in an old Derby cup. Blue, red, and orange flowers bloomed around the cup. Unlike those on the pig, the colors on the cup had aged deep and rich beyond new, shimmering brightness.

Despite being bookish I brought only one book back to Connecticut, the first edition of William Thackeray's *The Virginians* in twenty-four monthly parts. The parts were published by Bradbury and Evans in London from November 1857 through October 1859. Each part sold for a shilling and resembled a small magazine containing advertisements and illustrations as well as the serialization of Thackeray's novel. I packed *The Virginians* as an afterthought, not because the book was valuable or interested me but because it fitted neatly into a

suitcase, preventing an assortment of Father's shirts and ties from
wrinkling and tumbling over each other into knots. Oddly, once I
hung the painting, put the spike on my desk as a paperweight, and
arranged the china on the mantelpiece, I examined *The Virginians* in
detail. Instead of the story, however, I read advertisements. At 154
Regent Street, T. A. Simpson sold "Gentlemen's Dressing Canes,"
costing from one to fifty pounds. For one shilling "each attendance"
or ten shillings "annual subscription" one could get an "elegant" haircut at Unwin and Albert's shop at 24 Piccadilly. F. Browne of 47
Fenchurch Street advertised "The Gentleman's Real Head of Hair or
Invisible Peruke" for one pound ten shillings. "To Tea Drinkers,"
Strachan and Company, tea merchants, addressed its advertisement:
"War with China is ended, the Treaty of Tien-Tsin is signed, and
open communication with the Chinese Tea-grower is a fact beyond
recall." While the advertisement for W and J Sangster's Silk and Al-
paca Umbrellas depicted a dapper, top-hatted man-about-town standing dry under an umbrella during a cloudburst, the advertisement for
Thorley's Food for Cattle showed a sheep, a horse, a cow, and a pig
bunched together in good gastronomical fellowship. Along with its
famous Macassar oil, Rowlands advertised its Odonto and Kalydor.
While Kalydor was "for visitors to the Sea-Side, and others exposed
to the scorching rays of the sun, and heated particles of dust," Odonto
"bestows on the teeth a pearl-like whiteness, frees them from Tar-
tar, and imparts to the Gums a healthy firmness, and to the breath
a grateful sweetness and purity." On the yellow back cover of each
monthly part, Barry Du Barry advertised his "Delicious REVALENTA
ARABICA Food which restores Health without Purging, Inconve-
nience, or Expense." Du Barry claimed to have received letters from
fifty thousand "former invalids," all praising his food. Each month
Du Barry's advertisement contained selections from the letters. From
Norfolk, Maria Joly sent letter number 49,832. "Fifty years' indescrib-
able agony from dyspepsia, nervousness, asthma, cough, constipation,
flatulency, spasms, sickness at the stomach, and vomiting," she wrote,
"have been removed by Du Barry's excellent Food."

The advertisements amused me, and for a moment I forgot about
the end of my life in Nashville. Of course once Father came to Connecticut more than just a sentimental attachment to place ended.
Soon afterward I turned down the offer to run for Congress. Responsi-

bility binds me to Connecticut. Father cannot move again, and no
longer do I even toy with the possibility of going elsewhere. Last week
I declined to be a candidate for the editorship of a fine, old literary
magazine. Six months ago I would have jumped at the chance. Still, I
am happy. Spring is coming. In the dell between Mrs. Carter's and my
house daffodils are pushing winter aside, their leaves rising toward the
sun like sharp yellow spears. "Daddy," Eliza said to me as we knelt on
the ground looking at the leaves, "forget your old home. You can
write about birds and nature." And in truth not much has ended.
Amid the schedules and responsibilities love goes steadily on, keeping mongrel grumpiness from the door. Baby Lane has just received a
letter from an upset husband living near Sampson's Wells. His wife,
he wrote, had enrolled in an aerobics class and started talking about
eating natural food. "Real natural food," he said, "road pizza—squirrel instead of sausage and possum instead of pepperoni." Josh still
angers folks, and I find myself defending him, or if not him at least
that easier thing, his right to be outspoken. "Look," I said the other
day to a member of the sociology department, "Josh isn't a bad guy.
You just have to know how to take him." "To hell with that," she
answered, "I haven't got any use for people who need to be accompanied by directions like an antibiotic." Writers continue to contact
me, and I say the silly things I have always said. Last Friday a reporter
from the *New York Times* telephoned and asked if I "participated in
any rites associated with spring." "Only one," I answered, "but I can't
describe it. All I can say is that my children appeared nine months
after the first day of spring." "How many children do you have," the
reporter asked. "Three," I said; "a rite should not be overdone, at
least not by someone over forty."

A Fair Advantage

"All I want," Turlow Gutheridge was fond of telling prospective clients, "all I ever want is a fair advantage." Turlow was good with words, and he generally got an advantage, winning countless cases in county seats just south of the Kentucky line: Lafayette, Celina, Byrdstown, and Livingston. Getting the fair part of the advantage, however, took work, and Turlow prowled the ridges and hollows of middle Tennessee speaking at funerals and baptizings and then eating fried chicken and potato salad at lodge and family picnics. Although raised a Methodist, Turlow was ecumenical in his search for friendly, God-fearing jurors and on Sundays always attended two and occasionally three church services. Greed was Turlow's only failing. Despite visiting meetings and often being led by the Spirit to testify, Turlow was frequently able to get off the gospel path and down the highway before the collection plate was passed. One Sunday night, though, Turlow attended a revival in Slubey Garts's Tabernacle of Love in South Carthage. Slubey had just begun to rain fire down on the congregation when Turlow stood and shouted, "At the river—anywhere with Jesus! There's a great day coming and I've got the faith!" "Praise the Lord," Slubey said, "are you going to put aside all sin?" "Amen, just as I am, yes!" Turlow answered; "King Jesus is listening." "Hallelujah, brother, up from the grave He rose!" Slubey said, "are you going to church and to care for poor widows and little children?" "Yes, sir," Turlow shouted, turning to face his potential clients, "I'm going to hitch on my wings and cleave the air. I've got a crown up in the Kingdom." "Glory, glory. Don't let nobody turn you around; just lean on the arms of Jesus," Slubey answered before asking, "Brother, are you going to pay your earthly debts?" "Debts?" Turlow questioned, turning back toward the front of the church and looking hard at Slubey, "Debts? That's not religion. That's business."

Slubey himself wasn't bad with words. After a few months in South Carthage he opened tabernacles in Travis and Thornhill. One day, though, some years later, Slubey decided he needed a will and went to Turlow. After Turlow finished the will and Slubey signed it and paid him, Slubey asked for a receipt. "Receipt," Turlow exclaimed, "I never give receipts. What do you need a receipt for?" "Here in Carthage your word is fine," Slubey answered, "but suppose Jesus calls me home and I fly up to the big gate and, when I knock, Peter answers and says 'Slubey, what do you want?' Of course I'll fall on my knees and shout, 'Praise God, let me in so I can pick up a harp and get fitted for those white robes and golden slippers.' But then suppose old Peter asks, 'Have you paid lawyer Turlow that money for the will?' If I don't have a receipt," Slubey ended, standing up and looking hard at Turlow, "I'll have to hunt all over hell to find you and get one."

Words can shape reality and determine perception. By using words well a person can often obtain a fair advantage or, as in my case, space in the faculty locker room in the gymnasium. The room is small; the men who use it are many, and consequently most people never have any privacy and rarely have much room in which to dress or undress. For years I have brushed against chemists and engineers, historians and sociologists while pulling up my trousers. Collegiality is not a bad thing, but last month when a psychologist stumbled against me while drying his feet, I decided I wanted privacy. "God, this is a boring place," I exclaimed; "nothing exciting ever happens here. For twelve years I have used this locker room, and not once have I seen an erection." The room grew quiet; the psychologist and several other men quickly slipped on their shoes and socks and disappeared. Soon I had all the space I needed.

Knowledge, like the ability to use words, can give one quite an advantage. Perhaps the most useful knowledge is neglected or forgotten lore. All's fair in lore, and long years ago lapsed maidens drowned paper wasps in wine. Afterward they rubbed the wine on their stomachs. The elixir raised a lump, creating the illusion of pregnancy, and ladies used it to transform lovers into husbands. Of course many women preferred lovers to husbands and went to some trouble to avoid the sting of motherhood. If a woman dug a frog out of the ground on New Year's Eve and spat into its mouth three times, she would not conceive a child for the next twelve months. For those men weary of being pursued as lovers or husbands, there were also remedies. If a reluctant swain rubbed the stones of a fighting cock with goose grease and then wore them about his waist in a pouch made from ram's skin, he would not embarrass himself in any locker room, be it for females or males. Lore provides advantages not simply in matters private and intimate but in those social and public as well. A person planning a garden party should study gnats. At sunset if gnats swarm in the open over grass, the next day will be clear and hot. If they hang together in clumps in the shade, the day will start out warm and then end in showers. If gnats bite and are aggressive, the weather will be cold and rainy. The person who dreams of gnats flying into his mouth would be well advised to cancel his party, no matter the weather, for he will soon experience great sorrow, most probably the death of wife or child.

Parents' hopes of giving children a fair advantage ruin many childhoods. Instead of ranging free over hill and across thought, children are bound to desk and book, their lives marked not by sun and rain but by marks themselves—grades, parasitical abstractions that stick in the craw and unlike a simple horseleech cannot be purged from the throat by a wash of bean flies and vinegar. I make my children's meals miserable because I want them to have better manners than their friends. "Daddy," Eliza said just after her fifth birthday and with chocolate cake hanging from her chin like a beard, "that's the way Nature is: mating and then die. Live, live, mate and die—no manners." Resisting ambition for one's self or one's children is practically impossible. Life might be better, though, if people forsook tormenting dreams of bettering themselves, and others, and relaxed into calm, slipshod mediocrity. Of course before such a thing happened this country would have to change. Instead of envying and praising "Number One," people would have to celebrate Number Twenty Thousand: the meek, the merciful, the pure in heart, the peacemakers, all those lasts who in that golden vision of another, better kingdom are destined to become the real firsts. As a gesture toward changing the spirit of the country, the government could, I think, adopt more realistic national symbols.

I have set out bird feeders for eleven years and have yet to see a bald eagle. What I have seen flocks of, though, are starlings. Common, loud, and gregarious, the starling resembles most Americans. Indeed like all of us the starling is an immigrant. In 1890 a huddled mass of starlings was turned loose in Central Park. For five years they nested in New York, becoming acquainted with their adopted homeland and building up nest eggs. Then having gotten their wings over them they flapped westward. In 1955 they reached the Pacific Ocean. Unlike the reclusive, elitist bald eagle, the starling is everywhere: north, south, east, and west; frostbelt and sunbelt; city, suburb, and country. For the starling all America is beautiful for amber waves of bugs. If the starling were national bird, perhaps the spirit of the country would change for the better. No longer would people sacrifice happiness and health trying to soar above their fellows. Instead they would be content, grubbing through the grass, just undistinguished members of the large, speckled flock.

Perhaps a fair advantage comes only with the realization that everything is fleeting: both the sprawling nest of the bald eagle high in the open atop the crown of a giant tree and that of the starling, confined and soiled in a hole ten to twenty-five feet above ground. Instead of behaving like an upholstered chair, maybe one should snap a spring and sag into tattered, threadbare comfort. Rather than worrying about missing tacks, one should follow the loose threads of moment, moving around the frayed edges of things and avoiding being stitched into pattern and identity. Once a person realizes that life itself is a scrap, then bits and pieces of days, and fact, become more enjoyable. I'm forever tinkering, learning, for example, that the Spartan, my favorite apple, is a cross between a McIntosh and a Yellow Newton Pippin. Whenever I plant daffodils in the dell, I keep a list of the names. This past fall I planted a hundred and fifty-eight bulbs, including flower record, double event, orchard place, red hawk, acropolis, birma, belle vista, hilarity, canby, and bit of gold. I spend endless hours watching and listening, and sometimes I stumble across the threads of story. Last month in the Cup of Sun I saw a woman sitting alone at a table and reading a book entitled *Escape from Intimacy.* The woman's face was heavy and frozen. When a man she knew suddenly appeared and spoke to her, saying he would join her as soon as he got a cup of coffee, her eyes budded and her face rippled lightly like spring. Closing the book quietly, she slipped it under her chair, out of sight and conversation.

The mail almost always brings me something enjoyable. Not long ago I received a letter from a public-relations firm, inviting me to Tennessee for the unveiling of "Nashville's Athena Parthenos, the world's only full-scale replica of the 42-foot ancient Greek statue of the patron of civic virtue and wisdom." "Dignitaries from across the country and the world, including King Constantine II of Greece, will be present," the letter explained, adding that Nashville was "proud of its people, especially those like you who have created a place for yourself as a national figure." The public-relations firm must have confused me with some other Pickering. Still, as I sat on a stump out among my daffodils, chewing a Spartan, I was tempted to attend the ceremony, especially since the firm asked me to let them know if I had "any questions about Athena or her unveiling." What effect, I wondered, would such an unveiling have upon faculty in the locker room? Probably not much, I decided, throwing my apple core under the forsythia.

Because I am not ambitious, I rarely attend unveilings or, for that matter, veilings. In truth I don't keep up with contemporary events, preferring old to current newspapers. Last week I bought a copy of the *Federal Gazette & Baltimore Daily Advertiser* for August 31, 1796. Printed on rough paper and measuring twenty by twelve and a half inches, the *Gazette* consisted of only four pages. Nevertheless I spent hours reading it on the stump. What at first interested me were advertisements offering rewards for runaway slaves. For a fourteen-year-old boy named Joe with "remarkably large ears" and the toes missing on one of his feet, John Dorsey offered three pounds. For "a mulatto man named Samuel Matteny," Henry Travers offered twenty dollars. A sailor, Matteny, the advertisement stated, was six feet tall, had a "very bright complexion, and wore his hair queued." When last seen he was wearing a ruffled shirt and nankeen trousers. Because I had just moved Father from Tennessee to Connecticut and was planning to add a room for him onto the house, my attention shifted from slaves to houses. Much as the plan for our house had grown beyond Father's bedroom to include a study and an expanded kitchen and family room, so I rapidly progressed from simple frame houses to farms and then to "A COUNTRY SEAT." The seat was fit for a "national figure" fond of attending unveilings, and for a moment there in the daffodils I owned all three hundred and thirty-six acres of it, a hundred of which were woods, forty a "Timothy meadow," and the rest "corn land." On the grounds were "a small two story Brick House with three rooms on a floor, a large and good kitchen, two plain gardens abounding with fruit, a dairy and a new pump with very good drinking water, about 600 apple trees besides peach, cherry, pear, quince, and plum trees, some of the best kind." The barn was large and contained "stalls calculated for the accommodation of horned cattle and stables for horses." Also on the estate was a limestone quarry and "a lime stone spring remarkably LARGE and COLD."

Amid the peaches and pears and cold, fresh water, I was content and at ease, even though Father seemed to be drifting slowly away from this world. In February, after being helped to his seat on the plane for Hartford, he quoted the English poet Robert Browning. "Grow old along with me! The best is yet to be," he said, stopping before adding, "The bastard who wrote that ought to have been hanged." Father was in the hospital when I went to Nashville to fetch him. He weighed just a hundred and twenty pounds and at some grim times seemed only skin. I hoped coming to Connecticut might put him back on his feet. That didn't happen. Soon after settling in at the nursing home, St. Joseph's Living Center in Windham, nine miles from my house, he lost the use of his legs. A few days later his urinary system started going bad, and he was put on a catheter. While his body collapsed, Father's spirits remained aloft and inflated. On the first of April he told me that he could tell the temperature by looking out his window and watching the nuns walk across the courtyard. If the morning was cold, he said, the nuns took short, quick, almost hopping steps. On warm days their strides lengthened, and they moved more leisurely, "practically ambling." That day I took Father five mysteries from the Mansfield Library, the *Nashville Business News*, a pear, and three dark-chocolate Milky Way bars. He told me to return the books, explaining that his arms were too weak to hold them, but he kept the *Business News* and ate the pear and one of the MilkyWays. For a while we talked about Vicki, the children, and Mother. Then he said he was ready to die. If I could bring him a bottle of vodka and a handful of Valium, he would, he said, "gladly set sail for the sunset." On the way home I stopped at Mansfield Hollow Dam. On the sandy flatlands behind the dam I saw two bluebirds, the first of the season. Amid the scrub, pussy willow bloomed frilly and yellow. In the blossoms solitary bees gathered pollen for their underground nests. Father and spring were traveling in opposite directions, but that, I thought, as I watched the bluebirds dip then pitch over a rise in the ground, was the nature of life, and death. That knowledge, I hoped, would give me some sort of advantage when the days at St. Joseph's grew brighter and grimmer.

Generally, of course, people who live in real communities enjoy fair advantages. Because they belong and have belonged for a long time, they are able to avoid little rules. They deal with neighbors, not that abstraction the public official who often has lost humanity to regulation and precedent. When his legs failed, Father suddenly grew tired, and he asked me to get power of attorney and handle the forms of his daily life. Father signed the papers in his bed, and since St. Joseph's did not have a resident notary public, I carried them to the Mansfield town hall to be notarized. By law the notary was supposed to sign the papers in Father's presence. Unable to walk or even get out of bed, Father could not accompany me to town hall. After I explained the situation to the clerk, I assumed she would notarize the papers. I was mistaken. The town whose hills I wandered and described in my books and for which I labored on the school board disappointed me. A lawyer, I was told, could solve my problem; "the law was the law." Even Turlow would have done better, I said, walking away, but no one understood or cared to understand.

Towns that lack the gentling, comforting virtues exist only as bureaucratic divisions, places where taxes are paid. In such towns matters monetary and material provide identity, and to get an advantage one must spend money. Of course spending money can be satisfying and fun. That night I flew to Chicago and the dubious hospitality of a convention hotel. The following evening I was supposed to read an essay. Not getting Father's papers notarized upset me, in fact bothered me so much that I didn't want to read. To change mood and buck myself up, the next day I ordered lunch from room service, something I had never done before in a hotel. "This is the King Bee," I said, "humming from room 912, and I'd like a big rare sirloin steak, a pot of Colombian coffee, and a sweet hunk of chocolate-chip cheesecake." When the operator said, "Mr. Bee, the honey will buzz up there in twenty minutes," I immediately felt better. That night I gave a dandy reading, and two days later when I returned to Mansfield, I got Father's papers notarized in less than twenty minutes.

In the course of things a fair advantage is usually unfair, at least to some unfortunate or perhaps unknowing person. When Slubey Garts opened the doors to his new tabernacle in Thornhill late one September, he brought "The Happy Days" gospel singers up from Memphis. The show promised to be lively, and much of Smith County, and all the lawyers for fifteen miles around, attended. The summer, however, had been hot and dry, and to work the congregation into a sweating, flowing, shouting mood, Slubey asked folks to thank Jesus for what summer had given them. As might be expected, Turlow was on his feet immediately. Because of the dry weather, he said, he didn't have to replace the tin roof on his house. As soon as Turlow sat down, Ennion Proctor stood. Ennion worked for the state, patching holes in the highways. Since none of the roads twisting through Chestnut Mound had washed out, he was, he said, able to spend time rocking on the back porch, drinking iced tea, and thinking about "dear Jesus." The bottomlands just above the banks of the Caney Fork River didn't flood, and for once Kilty Bryden had a bumper corn crop. The heat kept people so thirsty, Enos Mayfield said, that his "Inn" in South Carthage had never done such a business. With money in the bank there was sunshine in the soul, and the cries of thanksgiving rose almost to God's heaven. At least they rose until old Ben Meadows stood up. Ben owned a rocky, hilltop farm off the dirt road halfway between Many and Less. Even in a good, wet year he was barely able to plow out a living, and this summer the heat and drought had burned his hill bald. Ben was a man of few words. "Jesus," he said, "may have shook the manna tree for you folks. But He's almost ruint me."

Let It Ride

On the Saturday before he died Father thought he was back in Tennessee and that I was Josh Billings, our family doctor. Father talked to Josh first about Mother and then for a long time about me. After visiting for an hour or so, Josh continued his rounds: stopping at St. Joseph's Living Center to say that Father would not return, filling the car with gas at Chucky's, and then going to the Potter Funeral Home in Willimantic to arrange for Father to be sent to Tennessee. "Don't worry about a thing, Mr. Pickering; we are used to this and have," Mr. Parcells told me, "sent the parents of UCONN professors all over the country." Earlier I considered cremating Father. Cremation was cheaper and more convenient, certainly for me. A friend in the history department had his mother cremated in Arizona last year. A month later his great-aunt said to him, "It just makes chills run up and down my spine every time I think of your mother's being cremated."

People do not die, however, for the convenience of the living, and I knew that Father wanted to be buried in Carthage, next to Mother. Still, Father despised flying. "What kind of a son of a bitch would," I thought as I left the funeral home, "force a man who hated planes when he was alive to fly when he was dead?" That afternoon Father recognized me. "Sammy," he said in a slow, pleased voice, "I had a good visit with Josh Billings this morning. Josh, though," he added, pausing for a moment, "didn't look so well." "Daddy," I said, taking

85

his hand and looking off at the gray wall beyond the bed, "Daddy, Josh is getting old." "Oh, that's it," Father answered smiling; "I guess you are right; we are all getting old."

In February, Father fell, and I brought him to Connecticut. Vicki and I planned to add a room on to the house for him. Construction was scheduled to start in May. Until the house was ready, however, Father stayed in St. Joseph's Living Center, a nursing home only twenty minutes from Storrs. Our plan was to visit Father four times a week and bring him to the house and take him on little trips at least twice a week. Although we saw Father four, usually five, times a week, the plan fell through. Father left St. Joseph's only once, and that was to die at the hospital. Shortly after arriving in Connecticut, Father stopped walking. Two weeks later his urinary system collapsed. "Sammy," he told me one afternoon; "it is time for me to die. The nurses here are wonderful and couldn't be kinder, but I find it abhorrent to lie here while three women work on my privates."

On Easter Sunday, Vicki cooked a leg of lamb, and we took Father a meal: lamb, potatoes and onions, spinach, navy beans in a garlic and tomato sauce, rolls, and a huge pink mound of raspberry cream pie. Eliza gave him a small brown and white stuffed rabbit she named Hoppy, while the boys took him an Easter lily and a wicker basket filled with his favorite candy bars: Bountys and dark-chocolate Milky Ways. Two years ago Mother died on Easter, but we didn't talk about that. Instead I described my daffodils and showed him plans for the house. "Don't spare the expense," Father said, "and build for yourself. I won't be there long." After a while the children left the room to visit up and down the corridors. When Vicki went to the gift shop, Father said that Betty Bailey had called from Nashville. The Baileys and Mother and Father had been friends for decades. When Betty moved into the Belle Meade Tower, she and Father occasionally had a drink together. Because of arthritis Betty was unable to walk and was confined to a wheelchair. Sheila, Betty's maid, was helpful, and lively. Once after bringing Betty to Father's apartment and before leaving to cook hamburgers for them, she said, "I hope I'll find you holding hands when I return." After talking to Betty on Easter, Father remembered Sheila's remark. "Can you imagine," he said to me. "Still," he added, "that reminds me of the story about the man with the two monkeys, Wilbur and Alice, I think, were their names." One winter, it seems, Wilbur and Alice caught the influenza and died. An aging bachelor, their owner was so attached to them he couldn't bear to live without them, so he took them to the taxidermist to have them stuffed. "Would you like them mounted?" the taxidermist asked. "That's mighty kind of you," the old man replied; "Wilbur and Alice were close; but I believe I'd just prefer them holding hands."

Three days later Father went to the hospital. Something had eaten through the wall of his stomach or an intestine. Air was under his diaphragm, and infection had spread throughout his body. "Your father is eighty-two," a surgeon told me, "and operating is more a philosophical than a medical matter." "No matter what we found, your father would not live long. He might survive the operation, though," a doctor said, "then he would be sent to Intensive Care and put on machines. And once a person is hooked up to a machine getting him off is difficult." "An operation would satisfy curiosity," another doctor said, "but that's all, and we surgeons are not necessarily curious people—at least," he added, "not when a patient is in the condition of someone like Mr. Pickering." Father had a living will and during his first moments in the hospital told me and the doctors he was ready to die. "Sammy, don't let them keep me alive," he implored; "please don't let them. I have had a full life." On Thursday I told the doctors not to operate. Once I made the decision, I felt relieved and guilty. Although I did what I thought sensible and decent, I wondered if I had merely done the convenient thing. "You followed Sam's wishes and did the right thing," Vicki said that night; "an operation would have cured nothing and made him suffer." Despite antibiotics the infection raged. Friday morning the doctors stopped the antibiotics and put Father on morphine.

On Saturday and Sunday the children accompanied me to see Father. Despite the morphine he recognized them. Eliza climbed into the window and saw robins on the grass outside. The robin, Father told Eliza, was his favorite bird. When Father died, Eliza and Edward cried. Francis seemed indifferent, too involved in a computer manual to think about Baa-Baa. For a moment his not reacting upset me, but then I remembered my childhood. I cried more when Grandma Pickering's cat Scarlet died than I did at the death of Grandpa Pickering. I spent many slow hours with Father over the weekend. I held his hand and sometimes tried to smooth out his hair. At St. Joseph's his hair had grown long and unruly, making him, Edward said, resemble a rock star. At times I, too, looked out the window and watched robins hunt worms. Once I saw a small rabbit. I remember thinking that his chance for a long life in the backyards and streets of Willimantic was slender. Father and I also talked. He told me to urge his first cousin Katherine Ottarson "to be her usual, sensible, composed, solid self." When I said I loved him, saying he had always made me proud and happy, he said simply, "No more accolades." For the children he had one piece of advice. "Tell them," he said, "to be on the facetious side." Once he mentioned two names, neither of which I understood. All I heard was "I wish I could have left them a fortune, but I doubt they are worth it." On Sunday I took volumes of Byron and Tennyson to the hospital and read Father selections from his favorite poems: the description of the dying gladiator from *Childe Harold* and from Tennyson "The Bugle Song" and parts of "Ulysses," "Locksley Hall," "The Palace of Art," and "In Memoriam." The words seeped through the morphine, and Father sometimes recited the poems as I read them. "In the Spring," he said joining me at Locksley Hall, "a livelier iris changes on the burnish'd dove; in the Spring a young man's fancy lightly turns to thoughts of love." Late Sunday afternoon Father thought he was dying, and he asked me to close the door, so he could, he said, "accomplish it with decorum."

Father didn't die until Monday evening. When he died, I was returning to Willimantic after eating dinner at home. Two years ago when Mother died, I was with Father. I had taken him home from the hospital and wanted to return to be with Mother, but he said my leaving would "kill" him, so I sat the night through in the apartment, reading a mystery by P. D. James. Father had been dead for less than ten minutes when I arrived at the hospital. He lay on his back, his head crooked to one side and his mouth open. Little beads of perspiration were on his forehead. I didn't know what to do. Pickerings do not have open-casket funerals, and I had never embraced a corpse. But that was my Daddy lying on the bed, and so I kissed him and brushed his hair back for a last time. I wanted to close his mouth; something stopped me, though, so turning to the bedside table I removed his few things. Then I left the room, stopping at the nurses' station to thank them for being gentle and to use the telephone, to call first Vicki and then Potter's.

I was weary. By Sunday night I reached the point, or at least I thought I had reached it, where I wanted Father to die so my life could return to normal. I had not grieved much. The details of Father's death surrounded me like a cloud, obscuring the man. As I thought about insurance and possessions and organized his funeral, I lost sight of Father. Only when I drove home late at night did I cry. I drove home the back way, along the Mansfield City Road, up Chestnut Hill past Mountain Dairy and Martinhoe Farm. At Pudding Lane I thought of Sawmill Brook. Development had spared a few white pines. Around them the stream turned and ran swiftly, cutting deep banks before spreading out and disappearing in the thick scrub behind East Brook Mall. In places banks had slipped, forming small marshes, green with the broad leaves of skunk cabbage and false hellebore. Just before dusk catbirds pushed through the leaves hunting insects. Yellow warblers jumped about in alders while a flycatcher sat silent on a dead branch over the stream. Along the banks in higher, drier soil celandine and wood anemone bloomed. Near the water were blue patches of violets. Delicate and almost out of sight dwarf ginseng and golden alexanders blossomed. Still higher, on the slope of a hill, lady's slippers nodded slowly toward pink.

On Monday night I telephoned friends and relatives. The death was not a surprise. In general, however, men reacted differently from women. For the women, most all of whom were widows, death was a blessing, sad, but still a blessing, releasing Father and me from a slow, painful, dehumanizing deterioration. The men I telephoned still lived with their wives. For them, in contrast, death brought loss, and two or three interrupted when I started talking, saying, "Oh, no; stop; don't tell me; please don't tell me this." I couldn't sleep after finishing the calls, so I examined the things I brought home from the hospital. There wasn't much: a hearing aid, glasses, a tattersall shirt from L. L. Bean, and a watch presented to Father by the Travelers in 1969 after he worked for the company for forty years. In gold under the twelve on the front of the watch was the Travelers Building in Hartford. From Father's bed I brought back a tract that a nun from St. Joseph's had taped to a support. On the front was a vision of Jesus seen by Sister M. Faustina Kowalski in Poland in 1938. Jesus wore a white robe and stood in a doorway, his right arm raised in a blessing, his left touching his chest. From his breast streamed red and blue rays, the red illuminating the right side of the picture, the blue the left. Last, from the bulletin board in Father's room I removed a drawing the children made for him. On a hillside Easter eggs bloomed blue and yellow at the ends of thick green stalks. Below the hill the children wrote, "We love you Baa-Baa. Love, Francis, Edward, and Eliza." The names were neatly done. Francis wrote in cursive; Edward printed; and the only thing wrong with Eliza's name was that the z was backward.

Early the next morning I called Carthage and arranged Father's burial. Two years ago Mr. Dyer buried Mother, and he remembered me. I told him when Father would arrive, and Mr. Dyer said he would meet the flight in Nashville. In passing I mentioned that Father disliked flying. "He was not the only one," Mr. Dyer said; "this fall a man came in here and prepaid his funeral. He hated flying, and when he died in February, I drove him to Chicago and buried him." After talking to Mr. Dyer, I selected the clothes in which Father would be buried and took them to Potter's. When I returned home, I looked through Father's wallet. Since he would not use them again, I removed the cards and sliced them in half. I cut up eight cards: a Vanderbilt University Medical Center card, an AT&T charge card, a blue and white First American Bank MasterCard, an Exxon card, his Tennessee driver's license, a Texaco card with "Star of the American Road" across the front, a green Gulf and British Petroleum card, and finally a card "In recognition of fifty years of membership in Beta Theta Pi." Father had been initiated on January 16, 1926. He was number two hundred and ninety-nine on the rolls of Beta Lambda at Vanderbilt. "Once a Beta, Always a Beta, Everywhere a Beta," the card stated.

Vicki and the children went to Tennessee with me for the funeral, and in order to catch a seven o'clock flight from Hartford, we got up at four-thirty the next morning. Father was on the same flight and was waiting for us on a baggage truck beside the plane. He was in a light gray box, and if I had not known better, I might have thought him a batch of gladiolas or long-stemmed roses. At two hundred and fifty-two dollars, his ticket cost less than ours. But then, his was not a round-trip. Neither did he get orange juice or read *USAir Magazine* and learn about "Cleveland's Comeback" or how to establish a bed-and-breakfast hotel. We changed planes in Philadelphia. The last time Father traveled through Philadelphia, this past December, he got lost. I spent five hours on the telephone trying to find him. When I finally located him, he told me that not only had his flight been canceled but a substitute flight had been canceled as well. He got on a third flight, but it only flew as far as the end of the runway before returning to the terminal for repairs. This time we hoped he would have better luck. The plane on which we traveled to Philadelphia from Hartford went on to Bermuda, not a place, I thought, someone in Father's condition could appreciate.

Usually after landing in Nashville I rode a shuttle bus to the Holiday Inn on West End Avenue. From there I took a cab to Father's apartment. On this trip Rosie, who worked for Father almost twenty years, insisted that Steve, her husband, meet us. Unfortunately Steve's car broke down, and when he took Father's car out of the apartment garage, it ran poorly. As a result Steve picked us up forty minutes after our plane landed. Before going to the apartment I drove Steve home and then stopped at the liquor store. For callers I bought a jug of California chardonnay and liter bottles of vodka, scotch, and bourbon. For Vicki and myself I bought two bottles of Australian wine, Black Opal cabernet sauvignon. I selected the wine for its label, a black rectangle, the center of which cracked into red, yellow, and blue fragments reflecting light like jewels in sunshine. Friends brought us an icebox of food, and Vicki bought few things in Nashville. Waiting for us in Father's kitchen were a ham, six bundles of sweet rolls, chocolate-chip cookies, a key lime pie, homemade vegetable soup, a pound cake, chicken salad, chocolate and vanilla ice cream, milk, orange juice, jars of coffee both regular and decaffeinated, cheeses, fruit salads, and a plate of seafood sandwiches. The next day a friend sent over an entire meal: a tenderloin of beef, rice pilaf, rolls, pickles, pickled peaches, even mayonnaise and mustard for the beef.

I spent most of that first day on the telephone, talking to well-wishers, checking arrangements for the funeral, and attending to little duties. For example, I canceled Father's subscription to the *Nashville Tennessean*, the morning paper that was being sent to St. Joseph's. Had the paper arrived satisfactorily, a concerned woman asked when I telephoned. "Oh, yes," I answered, "the paper was delivered on schedule." I was not canceling the subscription because Father was dissatisfied. It was just, I explained, that he changed his address, mov-

ing beyond zip codes. When I did not telephone, the telephone rang.
John Brothers said that the nurses at his office knew Mother was happy
now that Father had joined her. They could hear her saying, "Come
on, Sam; hurry up, Sam." From another caller I learned where my
great-grandmother had lived in Nashville—905 Summer Street, now
Fifth Avenue.

That afternoon Vicki, the children, and I walked across Leake
Avenue and roamed through the grounds of Belle Meade Mansion.
Two deer jumped in front of our car early that morning in Storrs, and
Edward was eager to see a zoo of animals. Above Richland Creek
swallows dipped and spun. In the high grass a rabbit raised his ears
then wheeled off under forsythia. Robins nested in the heavy maple
trees; a grackle sat on a rock, while mockingbirds flew from tree to
tree, the white feathers in their tails and wings flashing. A red-bellied
woodpecker dug for insects under the rough, protruding bark of a honey
locust. The creek was low, and we walked in the streambed. Water
had worn the rocks into ripples—footprints, Francis said, made by
people walking on the edges of their feet. In quiet eddies honeysuckle
blossoms papered the water; around them water striders pushed and
darted. Under the water snails clung to algae, looking like black grit
on a cheap green rug. Edward ran ahead, finding first crayfish and
then, wrapped about stones in the shallows, a water snake, its sides
covered with thick reddish brown blotches. We stood quietly and
watched the snake until suddenly it twisted heavily into the current
and rolled away downstream. In bushes above the creek I saw two
pairs of cardinals. Despite what Father told Eliza, the cardinal, not
the robin, I thought, was his favorite bird.

After the snake vanished we climbed the bank toward the Mansion. Richland Creek occasionally flooded, and high under the honeysuckle lay a wash of trash: styrofoam coffee cups with Par Mart, Delta
Express, and Kwik Sak printed on them; plastic bottles of Sprite and
Mellow Yellow; empty white containers of Mobil engine oil; lengths
of orange twine; and then, flattened over a root, a large deflated blue
balloon, a remnant of some bright dance at the Mansion. The trash
brought Father's apartment to mind. On walls and tables and in cabinets and bookcases was the litter of a lifetime. Just after lunch I took
Father's *Poems of Tennyson* out of the library and set it aside to take
back to Storrs. The book had cost a dollar and twenty-five cents. On

the inside front cover father wrote, "Samuel F. Pickering. 359 Kissam Hall. *1925.*" His roommate that freshman year at Vanderbilt came from Anniston, Alabama, and on page 272, Father wrote his name: "L. Huxley Roberts." As I looked at the book I often paused, once "thinking of the days that are no more," a phrase from "Tears, Idle Tears," something Father underlined in 1925.

I could not indulge in melancholy, however, for the afternoon belonged to the children, not to myself or even Father. "Hurry up, Daddy," Edward said, climbing the bank. "Daddy," Francis asked, pointing at spring snowflakes, their white bells tipped with green, "what is the name of that flower?" We wandered the grounds. While Edward turned over rocks hunting for snakes and Francis examined flowers, Eliza and I looked at trees. Her favorites were the big magnolias with their paddlelike leaves and then a tall knobby cedar, its bark shredding but somehow still crisp and neat. Eventually the children pulled us into the gift shop. Many articles there pertained to the Civil War. Along a wall hung a framed selection of Confederate money. On a display shelf near the door were maps, books, tapes, and breakfast mats, all describing aspects of the war. In a jar minié balls were for sale for a dollar each. Scattered about a table were small flags, model cannons, infantry caps, and boxes of soldiers, some in blue but most in gray uniforms. While the children rummaged for presents, I went outside and sat in the boxwood garden. My grandfather Ratcliffe grew boxwood on his farm in Virginia, and along with dogwood and magnolia, box flourished in my memory as indelibly southern. My children, though, were not southern. The central historical event of my childhood was the Civil War. At eight, Francis's age, I could sketch the major battles and name the leading generals on both sides. For my children growing up in Connecticut the war did not occur. Despite the statues of soldiers on village greens throughout New England, my children had never heard of the war, much less Jackson standing like a stonewall and Lee on his gray horse Traveller.

The children would not appreciate the silly stories Father and I enjoyed. Because the population tallies for Smith County changed greatly from one decade to the next, so one tale went, an official from the Census Bureau in Washington came down to Carthage to investigate. The first local dignitary the official called upon was Turlow Gutheridge, sometime acting mayor of Carthage and the most successful lawyer in Smith County. "Counting people in the hollows hereabouts is impossible," Turlow explained to the official as he took him over to the courthouse; "a goodly number of folks don't want anything to do with the government, and then, of course, there is the problem of foreign language." "Foreign language?" repeated the official; "I thought everybody in Tennessee spoke English." "Gracious me, no," Turlow said, "folks in Washington often make that mistake. See that man?" he continued, pointing to an old farmer from Thornhill, sitting on a bench eating his lunch out of a paper sack. "Talk to him and you'll understand about the foreign languages," Turlow said, taking the official by the arm and leading him over to the bench. When Turlow reached the farmer, he stopped and said, "Whar he?" "Whar who?" responded the farmer. Beyond the South being southern made one an outsider, or at least I sometimes thought so. Of course, being an outsider was not necessarily bad, I thought, chewing a boxwood leaf, its taste tangy and woody. Not fitting smoothly into a society forced freedom on a person. In my case, I had become outspoken, at best intolerant of humbug and at worst aggressive and simply intolerant. "Oh, well," I thought, spitting the box out of my mouth as Vicki and children left the gift shop, "all that, like Father, will soon be buried."

The next day went easily. At noon at St. George's Church, there was a memorial service, only fourteen minutes long and just the same as the one held for Mother. Carthage was an hour away, too far to drive, and a twelve o'clock service in Nashville, Father had said at Mother's death, would be convenient for older people and then friends who worked or had engagements. Father, of course, did not attend his memorial service. He was waiting for us under a maple tree in Carthage, not far from his mother and father. Mother died earlier in the month of April. Redbud and dogwood bloomed full behind the cedars along the highway from Nashville, and that funeral day seemed almost celebratory. By Father's burial the last week in April, blossoms had fallen from the redbud and only a few dogwood still held their flowers. The day was peaceful, however; the trees had not hardened into the heavy greens of summer and were softly yellow. The burial was almost fun. The children explored the graveyard, and many people drove up from Nashville. Em and George filled a Rolls-Royce with good friends and Bloody Marys and made an afternoon out of it, something Father would have loved. Before returning to the apartment, Vicki and I stopped at Vandyland and bought the children, and ourselves, double-chocolate sodas. Francis inhaled his, but Edward and Eliza didn't like the fizz, so Vicki and I finished theirs off.

Father liked to drink Bloody Marys more than sodas, and on the Saturday before he died, he turned to me and said happily, "Sammy, didn't I notice a Hospitality Room when they brought me in this hospital—not that it makes any difference to me. But at six o'clock why don't we go downstairs and have a couple of drinks and let it ride." Would that I could let things ride, but I can't. Father has been dead three weeks, and I miss him. I miss the irritations of old age, and I miss the telephone calls. During the past two years rarely did a day pass without my talking to him on the telephone. So that his absence would not gape black in my life, I have busied myself with the minutiae of his death. I have gotten rid of his wardrobe, keeping two pairs of wing-tip shoes and an H. Freeman suit for myself but giving most of his clothes to charity, the Windham Area Interfaith Ministries, or WAIM as it is known. Actually I started disposing of his clothes in Nashville, giving Steve a Haspel jacket, an oxford-cloth suit, and a heavy Mongolian cashmere overcoat. I spent one night figuring the cost of Father's death. As close as I can calculate burying Father—not, of course, counting hospital expenses—cost $7,446.25. To prepare Father for the trip to Nashville and take him to the airport Potter charged $590. The funeral home in Carthage charged $3,833.93. Included among their costs were the coffin at $1,495, the vault at $840, $625 for "Immediate Burial," state sales tax at $138.25, $86.40 for picking Father up in Nashville and driving him to Carthage, and then the $252 for Father's airfare. Airplane tickets were a big expense. The tickets for Vicki, the children, and me cost $1,484. Other fairly large expenses were Father's pall at $353 and then gifts to St. George's Church, to the family friend who conducted the church service and later the burial, and finally to Rosie and Steve. There were also a multitude of little costs, $69.97 for liquor, for example, and $38.56 for "Valet Parking" at Bradley Field in Connecticut. Now I am filling out Medicare forms and filing for Blue Cross payments from Tennessee. When I complete them, I will find something else to do, for I loved my sweet old Daddy. Of course I don't suppose he misses me. No, I expect he is in some heavenly Hospitality Room, far beyond this vale of grief and costs. And I don't expect he's sitting there mildly playing "Whispering Hope" on his harp. No, he is telling stories about monkeys, maybe even elephants, quoting Tennyson, and drinking nectar, good, fermented nectar laced with vermouth and a green olive or two.

After the Daffodils

Not long after Samp Griggs moved to Carthage and opened an accountant's office beside Read's drugstore, he got a sty on his eye and went to Dr. Sollows. "Now Sollows," he said after the sty had been lanced, "what sort of people live in this burg?" "You've just come here from Lebanon," Dr. Sollows answered, "what were folks there like?" "Scoundrels to a man, even the children," Griggs said shaking his head, "mean, narrow, suspicious, you name it." "Oh," Dr. Sollows said, "I am afraid that you are going to find the same people here." Later that afternoon Jeb Buchanan visited Dr. Sollows to have a sore throat swabbed. Like Griggs, Buchanan was new to Carthage, recently having started a small soap and candle manufacturing business on Spring Street. "Dr. Sollows," he said, "you have lived in Carthage for almost fifty years. What are people hereabouts like?" "Well," Dr. Sollows answered, "you have come from Crossville. What did you think of people there?" "Goodness me, I hated to leave them," Buchanan answered, "they were the best folks in the world—always friendly and kind—real neighbors." "Don't worry," Dr. Sollows said smiling, "don't worry, you will find the same folks here."

A person's town is often what he makes it. For twelve years I have lived in Connecticut. Although my children were born in Willimantic and I have been wondrously happy here, I did not really think Storrs home until Father died in April. His death broke my last strong tie to

97

childhood and Tennessee. Often during the past decade I thought about returning to the South. Such thoughts lessened my enjoyment of Storrs. Dreaming of the beauty of other places, I neglected the small hills rolling green outside my window. At Father's death, though, the elsewheres drifted away like a low mist. In the sun I suddenly saw bobolinks pitching white, black, and orange down the side of Horse-barn Hill. In the wet meadow below, redwing blackbirds called, their cries unwinding like brittle twisted springs. Near the chicken houses on Bean Hill kingbirds gathered on the fence, while above the trees buzzards rode the wind, the long feathers at the tips of their wings sweeping upward, dark against the silver light and blue sky. Storrs was home, and suddenly I wanted to know its good places better. Often in the past, in the shank of spring, that time after daffodils and before peonies, I visited Father and Mother in Tennessee, returning to Connecticut only to pack the car for Nova Scotia and our farm in Beaver River. And so in the middle of May I began taking long walks. Although I wandered throughout Storrs, I spent much time on the university farm, roaming the meadows and woods bounded on the south, north, and east by the Gurleyville Road, Old Turnpike, and Fenton River respectively, and then on the west by Route 195, curving over the hills like a flattened ashcan.

Father's death severed a taproot, one that had not, perhaps, sustained me for a long time but one that I, nevertheless, wanted to believe nourishing. Now in the green damp of late May I thrust myself outdoors, hoping the land would pull fibrous roots from me, binding me to dirt and enabling me to absorb place. At first I walked almost aimlessly, my only purpose being to stroll through hours. Observations would inevitably come, I believed, thinking that if I noticed five or so interesting things after walking four hours I might see six or seven after eight. Often I began walking at dawn and stopped at eleven o'clock. Afterward I went to the Cup of Sun for coffee and an apple bran muffin. I carried much gear and wore rough clothes: jeans, rubber boots, a long-sleeved green shirt given to runners who completed a ten-mile race in Norwich six years ago, a sweatshirt with a friendly white husky dog on the front, and then a floppy Tilly sailor hat that I could tie under my chin. In order to drink coffee I took off my backpack. Red and black, the backpack had four separate compartments. In them I stuffed pencils, a ruler, guidebooks, small round plastic containers for insects, rubber bands, and samples of plants—on this particular morning cuttings of white campion and cypress spurge and then twiggy shoots of shadbush and white willow. Atop the pack I set my binoculars, and then, so I could sit comfortably, I spread the contents of my pockets over the table: a four-by-five-inch yellow and blue spiral notebook, a number-two pencil, a hand lens, my wallet, change, house keys, eyeglass case, and a small pocketknife given Father as an advertisement over forty years ago. Under a rectangular window on the side of the knife was the inscription "TO MY FRIEND." When the blade was opened, the inscription slipped out of sight, and "FROM GEORGE HEARN" appeared.

I looked bedraggled, and with my gear spread about me like skirmishers few people approached. On this morning as I examined shadbush with the hand lens, a member of the English department walked over. "Sam," he said looking down at the table, "what have you been doing?" "Research," I said, whereupon he laughed and turned away without another word. For a moment I was angry, ready to damn the study of literature as trivial, having little to do with life, but then I, too, saw the paraphernalia around myself. The very things that taught me about the natural world also separated me from it. In roaming through woods, pencil and pad in hand, I resembled the English teacher who spent days in the library. While I tried to identify trees and flowers, looking at bark and leaves, he examined sheaves of paper, searching for quirks of penmanship and personality. Even worse, I was not able to put the landscape together like a book, binding and words complementing each other and forming a green whole. For me the natural was broken into a series of discrete entities, not articles or even chapters. My vision was narrow, and rarely could I broaden a walk to include, for example, both birds and flowers. Although I made sketches and took samples of plants home, I could manage only one guidebook at a time. After many hours, of course, bits of things stuck together, but they were only bits, the beaver in the Ogushwitz Meadow to alders and willows, the wood thrush to shaded, damp deciduous woods, catbirds to low perches and weathered mossy rocks, and rose-breasted grosbeaks to the tops of trees and bundles of new leaves golden in the high light.

On walks I saw many birds; most were common birds in common places: pigeons and sparrows around barns, finches near houses, war-

blers in alders, and starlings bustling in waves across fields cropped by
sheep and cattle. Occasionally I saw birds that I never noticed before:
a rufous-sided towhee in an oak near the Fenton River, and an indigo
bunting iridescent in the south pasture on Horsebarn Hill. Often I
spent long silent minutes watching birds. At the edge of the woods
under Bean Hill a brown-headed cowbird showed off for females, singing, puffing up, and then toppling forward, making me think of a
dark, lumpy marshmallow falling slowly off a stick into a fire. Behind
the dairy barn swallows gathered mud for their nests in the red barn
on Bean Hill. Sliding and dipping through the air, their tail feathers
streaming behind them, they dropped to the ground near a cattle
trough and after plucking strands of grass picked up lumps of mud
before spinning off blue and orange across the pasture to the barn.
Birds did not provoke deep thought, although I came to think the
mockingbird the writer's bird, imitating the calls of neighbors but
still having a distinct style. In truth the more I walked the more artificial profundity seemed. Even ideas raised upon close observation
seemed false, constructs of people not satisfied with the simple truths
of sight and sound. Sometimes I stopped observing and tried to imagine myself part of the landscape, a flicker bobbing for ants or just a
wing turning through a tree or time. Of course I could not slip into
the land. Not only did the gear I carried set me apart, but I was forever
nervous about deer ticks and Lyme disease. In the dairy barn was a
Holstein with an arthritic knee swollen larger than a soccer ball, and
every day before leaving the house I sprayed my trousers with Per-
manone Tick Repellent and then cinched rubber bands around the
legs just above my ankles.

Although deer trails curved through the woods like interchanges
on a superhighway, I rarely saw deer. When two suddenly rushed away
from me along a slope, I thought their white tails the undersides of
the wings of great birds, turning sideways to get through brush before gathering themselves for flight. Other animals were about. At
the edges of fields were rabbits and squirrels, some of these last red
but most gray. In the fields were groundhogs. Indeed groundhogs
seemed everywhere; Bill reappeared in my backyard, and one evening
Eliza and I watched him eat the stems of dandelions. The next day Eliza
collected a basketful of stems and put them on a rock outside his
burrow. Beavers built a dam in a corner of the Ogushwitz Meadow.

Beavers are wary, and although I brought home a pack full of wood chips for the children, I saw only the beavers' handiwork, not the animals themselves. Below the beaver pond a family of muskrats lived under a low bank along the Fenton River. Often I watched them swimming, their tails curving after them like thin, shiny gray snakes.

Although I can recognize the calls of some birds—robin, mockingbird, oriole, catbird, yellow warbler—birdsong seemed always to run clear but mysterious through the woods. Rarely did I locate birds high in the trees. In exasperation I began paying more attention to the ground and open spaces than to the woods. Down the side of Horsebarn Hill dandelions bloomed like bushy tablespoons of butter. Along the southern slope of Bean Hill winter cress blossomed in yellow bunches. Below the Kessel memorial the field was white with pennycress, shepherd's purse, and star chickweed. Pushing through the grass in the Ogushwitz Meadow were clumps of bluets, buttercups, sedges ragged and tawny, hawkweed, cinquefoil, robin plantain, and blue-eyed grass. In the woods at the edge of the meadow barberry bloomed, bumblebees clasping the small orange blossoms beneath the arching stems. Willows had gone to fluff, but on the road over Horsebarn Hill chokecherry bloomed, its flowers forming small cones of white and yellow. Beside Unnamed Pond and along the stone wall bordering the cemetery autumn olive throbbed with bees. Bunched in thick clusters, its blossoms resembled small horns, blowing sweetness, creamy and fresh, down the hillside.

Toward the end of May, butterflies bloomed like the flowers: whites, bright yellow sulphurs with a band of black bunting around their wings, mourning cloaks, ringlets orange and gray with a black eyespot at the tip of their forewings, and then suddenly swimming through the alders and willows at Unnamed Pond a wave of red admirals. Triangles of yellow and black, dotted with blue and red, swallowtails hung like sugar on cherry trees. I had trouble distinguishing one cherry from another, forever confusing the black with the chokecherry. In truth I have always had difficulty identifying trees. Some trees, of course, stood out: the white pines tall on the hill below the piggery, hemlocks along the Fenton River, and the great white ashes near the sheep barn. Other trees I recognized because I liked them: the hornbeam, for example, its twisted gray trunk rolling smooth and hard like a worn granite ridge. My favorite tree was the beech. Just above Kessel

Pond was a grove of beech. No matter the weather nor the time of day the beech gleamed. Their leaves papered the ground white and almost lacy while their smooth trunks flowed upward in columns, not lifting a heavy roof but reaching open-armed for dappled, fluted light, one moment yellow, the next green, the next pale blue.

Among the trees I longed to be a painter. Only with a brush, I thought, could I capture the chill damp rippling under a hill early in the morning or the sunny wind shaking through a locust, turning new leaves into bunches of yellow grapes. Words were too broad for the melancholy and then the joy behind the light—the lonely sense that everything, including the self, ended, followed by the realization that one was, despite the binoculars and guidebooks, a part of everything: the red lip of a pig-ear mushroom and the white band at the tip of a kingbird's tail, part of biological processes running far beyond the moment. Still, I wanted to capture the textures of my days. I envied the impressionists at Cos Cob and Old Lyme, those painters whose small brushstrokes turned spring's broken colors into lyrics of light and shadow. As I stood among the beeches I knew that such efforts, maybe even truth, lay beyond my skill, and so I turned to metaphor. Instead of describing an object as it really is, metaphor describes it obliquely in relation to something else. As a result metaphoric descriptions are always slightly askew and artificial.

Just south of the beeches Kessel Creek turned through a sharp fold between ridges and fell quickly down to the Fenton River. As I stood on a ledge above the creek, I thought how its course resembled courtship. Much as uncertainty lured the lover, so the broken rocky slope along the creek challenged the walker and seemed almost an invitation to excitement and discovery. Pitching, twisting, then splaying wide for a moment before gathering and tumbling narrowly between two great rocks splattered with lichens, the creek at first seemed to offer an infinite variety of woodland delights, its course a rich green band of false hellebore, skunk cabbage, Solomon's seal, and cinnamon ferns. In places where the light fell through the trees in shutters violets and wild geraniums bloomed purple and pink. Near the top of the ridge was rough purple trillium; farther down gaywings blossomed low and shy, the change from one flower to the other almost an emblem of the transforming power of love. The course of an eastern creek, though, does not run smooth. Despite spicebushes, cool and dry on the air, the way down the ridge was tangled and salty, more tiresome than stimulating. Halfway down I came upon a black racer sunning himself. Too weary to be excited I sat down near him on a rock. For ten or so minutes while I rested, he tolerated me. When I stood to continue downstream, he turned and slowly poured himself through a crack.

I didn't follow the creek all the way to the river. Near the end the going got tough. Sharp shrubs pinched in low over the creek, and then the watercourse itself suddenly flattened out into a small delta of loose black mud. As I turned aside to a path cutting steadily across a hill, I thought of the river as marriage. As the creek finally did not lead me to the river, so I thought, courtship often did not lead to marriage. For two miles from the Gurleyville Road to the Old Turnpike the Nipmuck Trail ran along the river. In pursuit of metaphor I walked the trail. The way was broad and gentle and, unlike the creekbed, seemed to invite one to pause, even to rest. Along the trail hemlocks draped over the water, soft and almost as domestic, I thought, as sofas fat with pillows. On the higher banks near the Old Turnpike lady's slippers bloomed formal in open spaces under laurel. Beside the trail the river flowed solidly. At first glance its bed appeared a joyless reach of drab brown. Much as the vitality of a good marriage, however, is unobtrusive, lying private beneath the surface of home, so the riverbed was muted. For anyone willing to pause and look, the river flowed with color, blue tipping over from the sky, whites and greens falling from trees, silvers and reds hanging from rocks, and browns running off in the light to rust and gold.

As man forever creates unity, be it metaphoric or not, so he analyzes. In doing so, he often destroys, not simply impression or truth but life itself. Like the observations of my walks actual experiences are often random and bundled together only by contrivance. A mydas fly sunning itself on a gray stalk of last fall's goldenrod and comfrey, its creamy pistils pinching the purple flowers inward to form waists, making them resemble small, formal dresses, have little in common—other than the mind of the person observing them. Random impressions, however, make life seem arbitrary, if not meaningless, something people don't like to face. To avoid confronting such a realization people have become addicted to meaning. The longer I walked the less satisfying I found simple observation. I wanted to see complexity and understand links between things. I wanted to explore the unknown and in it perhaps find knowledge or scientific fact.

To this vague end, I borrowed a blacklight trap from the agricultural school. Used for surveying crop parasites, the trap was just over five feet tall. Roughly resembling a weather station it stood on three legs. Made from iron pipe, the legs formed an equilateral triangle on the ground, the distance being a yard from one leg to another. Suspended between the legs was a galvanized tank resembling a shiny bucket in which one put a small pad of poison. Above the bucket a funnel rose up to the base of the bulb; the bulb itself was sixteen inches tall; four metal fins twenty-three inches long and six and a half wide jutted out from the bulb, quartering the space above the funnel and resembling a small paddle wheel stood on end. Despite the name *blacklight trap*, the bulb glowed blue when turned on. At night insects flew into the bulb and fins and, momentarily losing their ways, tumbled down through the funnel into the bucket where they died. I set the trap up in the front yard but used it only one night. Not all insects died immediately. When I opened the trap the next morning, many were still alive, if only barely. Small dark bubbles oozed from the mouths of beetles, while the antennae of moths quivered like minute ferns in a breeze. In wanting to know my place, I destroyed. I felt guilty and remembered the child who once entombed inchworms in clay coffins and then stuck pins through the clay. One careless experimental night, I thought to myself, erased years of gentle living, years in which the only insects I killed were carpenter ants. When Eliza saw the insects, she cried and asked me not to use the trap again. Edward's reaction was worse. He thought the trap "great" and said I should use it until I had boxes full of bugs. What I had was almost astonishing. A dusting of minute gnats, a quarter of an inch thick, covered the bottom of the bucket. Half-buried among them were a bumblebee, small scarabs the size of kernels of corn, two minute tree fungus beetles, ichneumon wasps, and assorted flies: crane, caddis, and may. Appearing toasted brown and almost edible were twenty-three may beetles. Like small light chips of newsprint, moths crumpled together in mounds. Many were the dull gray color of litter, beer cans tossed into a wood fire, burned, and left to age through a season. I identified some moths: the arched hooktip, its orange wings curving out and to the side like the arms of a swimmer using the breaststroke;

the pink-legged tiger; the white-dotted prominent; and the black-
letter dart, a bar on the front edge of its forewing resembling a block
of charred wood, the middle bitten out by fire but the ash gray and
unfallen.

I spent a morning examining the insects. Before lunch, however, I
dumped them out in the yard. Curiosity and remorse, even walking,
occupied only part of my days. The little business of living filled most
of my hours. After dismantling the trap, I wrote and mailed a check to
the Internal Revenue Service. Instead of applying Father's overpay-
ment to next year's tax as instructed, they mailed it to me, forcing
quarterly payments upon me. Unlike comfry and the mydas fly, death
and matters monetary seemed naturally linked. Since Father's death
in April, I had filled out enough forms to set up as an accountant and
put Samp Griggs out of business. Even at Father's burial money was a
concern. "Sammy," an older woman asked, referring to my being the
source of a character in Dead Poets Society, "Sammy, how much money
did you make on that movie?" "Two and a half million," I said, "and I
am still celebrating. This funeral has hardly dampened my spirits."
Father himself enjoyed tales about death and money and would not
have thought the question out of place. When Slubey Garts was dying,
so Father told me, his wife called Turlow Gutheridge to the house
so Turlow could make a list of people who owed Slubey money. "Slubey," Turlow said, "state your affairs briefly." "Ennion Proctor owes
me forty-eight dollars," Slubey answered. "Praise God," Sarey Garts,
the widow-to-be, interrupted; "sensible even at the end." "Kilty Bryden," Slubey continued, "owes me sixteen dollars and twenty-four
cents." "Glory, glory," Sarey interrupted again, "rational to the last."
"To Ben Meadows," Slubey went on, "I owe three hundred dollars."
For a moment the room was silent, then Sarey cried out, "The poor
soul, listen to him rave."

Our car is six years old, and two days after paying Father's taxes I
drove it to Capitol Garage in Willimantic to be tuned up for the trip
to Nova Scotia. While the car was being worked on, I walked to Windham Town Hall and watched swifts flying about the old chimneys.
Repairs to the car cost $162.56. The expense was worthwhile. For the
trip we load the car, even strapping suitcases and my pond net on the
roof. On our return to Storrs we are more heavily laden. The children
bring home rocks and shells, and Vicki always has two boxes of chil-

dren's clothes. In Yarmouth, Frenchy's sells factory rejects and sec-
ondhand clothing. For thirty cents Vicki can buy a shirt that would
cost twelve dollars in Connecticut. My mother disapproved of our
buying used clothes. "My God," she exclaimed when I told her; "the
children will get AIDS." "Mother, we wash the clothes, and besides,"
I said, "you can't get AIDS from clothes." "Well," she said before she
hung up the telephone, "if anybody would know about such things
you would—after all you have done!" As the first week in June swung
to an end and peonies started swelling, I thought about Nova Scotia.
I wondered what Bertha Shifney and Otis Blankinchip, characters
from my essays, had been doing. Bertha, I heard, had a hard case of
shingles. "The hope of dying," she said later, "was the only thing that
kept me alive." For his part Otis erected a sign on Goudey Road just
before it dipped and ran through Crosby Creek. In spring the creek
often overflowed and washed the road out. "WARNING," Otis wrote,
"When this board is out of sight the creek is dangerous."

In May a collection of my essays was published. The first reviews
were good, and in hopes of sales growing luxuriant before the leaf
miners and twig pruners set to work, I agreed to appear on a local
television program called "Profiles." The show was filmed in the living room, and I wore a green sport coat that had belonged to Father.
Two days later a reporter from the New Haven Register interviewed
me. A photographer accompanied her to Storrs, and he took pictures
of me standing on a stump reading my book aloud to grass and scrag-
gly remnants of daffodils. When he finished, I asked where he was
going next. "To Old Lyme," he said, "to take pictures of a woman
who has a nut museum." "Oh," I answered, my vision of fame running all to stalk and gray seed. Family matters also filled days. At six
o'clock twice a week Vicki and I took the boys to Sunny Acres Park
for rag ball. While the boys played, I pushed Eliza and her friend
Lindsey on the swings. On Saturday, Francis had a piano recital; that
Sunday, Eliza was a pink lollipop in a community dance. The previous Sunday I was a marshal for the university graduation and wore a
big, floppy hat that made me resemble a blue mushroom or a giant
hunk of spiderwort. Some days I could not walk because I gave talks.
After messages had been read from the governor of Connecticut and
then the pope, I spoke to participants in a "Peace Games Festival." I
suggested that the starling would be a better symbol for our country

than the bald eagle. If the starling were the symbol, maybe, I said, we would not see ourselves as majestic, lonely, and powerful. Maybe we could come to think of "our nation as just one good country among many good countries." Although I didn't mention it, the starling was more numerous than any other bird in Connecticut, something my walks confirmed. The day after the festival I spoke to a group of school superintendents in Farmington. The following afternoon was the Northwest School picnic. Vicki made tuna-fish sandwiches and choc-olate-chip cookies and carried a bowl of "veggies": sliced tomatoes, celery, and carrot sticks. For a dollar one could buy a huge chocolate sundae. Instead I ate four cookies, after which I went to the soccer field with the first grade and did the bunny hop, the hokeypokey, and the chicken, or at least a dance in which one pretended to be a chick-en, making clucking sounds and flapping his arms. Walking had perked me up, and at the Peace Festival, I wiggled through several African dances with middle-school students. Four days after the pic-nic I delivered the commencement talk at Quinebaug Valley Com-munity College in Danielson. The next night I was speaker at the senior citizens' spring dinner in Mansfield.

When I was not roaming hills, playing with children, or saying in twenty minutes things which, if challenged, I could not have ex-plained in twenty years, I read the mail. A woman who heard me speak thanked me for "sharing your very essence." A man sent a batch of questions ranging from "Have you siblings?" to "How does one expand on truth without causing confusion or moving into untruth?" A girl I dated in college ran across one of my books in Iowa. After reading it she wrote, "You were the only popular boy I ever knew who didn't try to be like everybody else. Remember the weekend at Se-wanee," she continued, "when I had my first purple passion and I started crying? You were a great comfort to me." Any popularity I may have enjoyed had long since slipped from mind. A bomb of grape juice and grain alcohol, purple passion still fermented in recollec-tion, however, fumes rising from the past to turn my stomach even today. Comforting I suppose I was. Indeed until just before I gradu-ated from college, I was always comforting, though I labored, and labored hard and unsuccessfully, to be a great deal less.

Letters led me on walks through the past, and coming home from a long morning of wandering fields and woods, I looked forward to the mail. One day early in June, I received an article written about me by a classmate of Tom Schulman, author of *Dead Poets Society*. The writer, Greenfield Pitts, was a banker, though when I taught him twenty-six years ago he was Wade Pitts, a reddish, freckled, pudgy fifteen year old. Of course all fifteen-year-old boys are either pudgy or skinny, as, for that matter, all fifty-year-old English teachers are paunchy, unless they jog, in which case they are gaunt and bearded. Writing that I had had an "extraordinary effect" upon him and his classmates, Greenfield described the extent to which I was the "inspiration" for John Keating. The me I read about was different from the man who roamed Storrs identifying birds and smelling wildflowers. Did I really stand atop my desk "bemoaning 'Alas, poor Yorick' " to the world globe? Did I hop about in trash cans and run out of the classroom and talk through the window? As I read, I wanted to say, "You bet your sweet ass I did," but alas, poor me, I couldn't remember. One day, Greenfield recalled, when the boys showed up for class, the door was shut. When they knocked, a voice said, "Come in, gentlemen." They entered, but I was not in sight. Only when I said, "Take your seats," did they discover I was under the desk. For the next fifty minutes I read Thoreau with "great gusto." "I will never forget his admonition taken from his day of reading Thoreau from under the desk," Greenfield ended his article: " 'Do not find when you come to die that you have not lived.' "

An article like Greenfield's is dangerous, even for a respectable middle-aged woody Republican. Because I was walking and forgot an organizational meeting, I had recently been "elected" chairman of the committee that recommended promotions within the English department. After putting Greenfield's article down, I wrote a memo to the committee. "So far," I began, "no one has applied to our committee for promotion. It has, however, been suggested to me by a member of the administration, indeed by a member of the inner circle, that our department is so top-heavy with full professors that we are violating the spirit of diversity. To bring us in line with university guidelines this influential maker and shaker has suggested that we consider demotion as well as promotion. 'As promotion is an appropriate reward for some people so,' this person states, 'demotion is an appropriate reward for others.' This unnamed person is not, I rush to add, implying that certain members of our department are layabouts, only that they are undeserving and that we have not apportioned rewards well. To this end I invite you to consider the subject of demotion. For my part I don't believe that people should be demoted through the ranks at one rewarding swoop. No, I believe demotion should be accomplished gracefully in a step-by-step fashion. Thus, for example, the professor would be demoted to associate professor, the associate professor to assistant professor. As for assistant professors, they could be kicked out on their behinds. I look forward to hearing from you on this important and pressing matter. Be prepared to be criticized for even considering this subject. But all our right-thinking colleagues, no matter their new ranks, must applaud our energy and deep, abiding concern for academic integrity."

The next morning the sun was warm and bright. The first of my peonies burst into bloom, red petals wrinkling around yellow centers. I returned the blacklight trap to the agricultural school, on the way dropping the memo off at the English department. That afternoon I took my last walk, strolling along the Fenton River and then pushing up through the woods under Horsebarn Hill. I saw three American toads and two garter snakes. Mayweed and wild madder had suddenly flowered. In a low, open spot blue flag blossomed. Black-winged damselflies perched on spicebushes and fluttered in the sun along Kessel Creek. This time, though, I was not walking for observation but for trash. For four and a half hours I collected trash: plastic cups, a frying pan without a handle, a used disposable diaper, an empty pint of Butterscotch Schnapps, the sharp pieces of a broken bottle of Richards Wild Iris Rose wine, and then cases of beer cans—Budweiser, Keystone, Rolling Rock, Busch, Old Milwaukee, Schaeffer, and Lausthaler. Afterward I felt good walking up Bean Hill, almost as if I atoned for those insects. Waiting for me at home was a letter written by a boy living in Chicago. He wanted to be a teacher; not only that, he said, he collected "autographs of famous people" and "would appreciate it if you could send me an autographed picture of yourself." I was glad he wanted to be a teacher, I answered, adding that I always had fun teaching. Unfortunately I didn't have a photograph of myself, at least not one that wouldn't give a child nightmares, so I drew a picture. Despite admiration for the Connecticut Impressionists, I am not an artist, and I appeared in the drawing as a three-and-a-half-inch thermos bottle with bread-loaf feet, short arms, ears like windmills, and a nose like a lopsided croquet mallet. At the end of the letter I said that I wasn't famous. "I was ordinary," I explained, "a daddy with three small children, a person who spent free hours wandering the hills and fields of his hometown, looking at birds, wondering about the names of trees and flowers, and then sometimes picking up trash."

Again

People in my books repeat themselves. My family and I, even the characters I create, have a light, familiar consistency. In Port Maitland, Nova Scotia, medical matters color Bertha Shifney's conversation like a rash. When Etta Hoskilson's little girls Flora and Rhodena began to recover from the red measles, Bertha told everyone in Gawdry's store. "I'm happy to report," she said, "that the babies are better, although Dr. Pulsifer is still attending them." Two weeks later Dr. Pulsifer himself broke his arm while working on a well cover. The doctor, Bertha told Otis Blankinship, "should have been attending the sick and left the well alone." Otis himself is prone to feverish speech, especially when he visits Bertha. When Bertha informed him that Burle McCallum was studying pharmacy in Halifax, he shook his head. "That may be all right," he said, "but if you ask me the place to study farming is right here in Port Maitland. Old Crosby down Richmond Road would give young Burle some practical experience, something he's not likely to get from those professors in Halifax." On another occasion when Bertha listed the various illnesses and handicaps plaguing the populace of Port Maitland, Otis listened and nodded attentively before he spoke. "Oh, yes, a handicap is terrible, but," he said, "with determination, as Reverend Hupman says, a person can overcome most anything. Why," he added, warming to the subject, "there's Israel Saulnier who hasn't got a tooth in his head, yet he can play a fiddle better than anybody in Salmon River."

Outside of books characters also repeat themselves, and the doings of an early chapter often foreshadow behavior during the middle narrative of life. Twenty-five years ago I went to a formal dinner in Woodstock, Vermont. Sitting next to me was a plump young woman. When soup was served, she looked down at it thoughtfully and then turned to me and said, "I just hate eating soup. My titties are so big that I always knock my spoon against them and spill soup all over my dress." My response was physical not verbal. My hand shook, and a slice of onion curled over my spoon. For a moment it hung on the edge like a question mark. Then, almost as if it realized questions were unnecessary, the onion straightened and letting go fell like an exclamation point, heavy and straight down my necktie. Although the woman disappeared after dinner and I never saw her again, I suspect that for fifteen or so years she tumbled through the rich broth of life, ladles of vichyssoise and gazpacho splashing about her. People, of course, don't repeat the antics of youth forever. Time forces change, not so much mental as physical, and as a person ages body determines behavior more than mind. Recently I've decided to call myself a writer. In the past I denied being a writer. When interviewed, I said that if I were anything, I was a neighbor, son, husband, and father, not a writer. No more—since June, I have been a writer. An afternoon bath precipitated the change. Sitting in the tub, I looked at myself. As round and as hairy as the fruit on a sycamore, I had lost my sex appeal. My bosom had gotten so big that it hung down to my knees, and if I went swimming, anywhere outside the domestic tub, I would have to wear a brassiere. Like a good suit the word *writer* deceives, tailoring perception by tucking fat behind books. And so there in the hot afternoon amid Palmolive, "No Tears" Baby Shampoo, and a small container of bath gel filched from the Drake Hotel in Chicago, I became a writer.

Although the soap moved me in June, I am not sure my conversion can withstand the winter. By December I will probably be a sometime writer and full-time husband and father again. June is the season of school graduations, that time in which platitudes flourish in auditoriums like petunias in window boxes, pink and white and sometimes purple but always bland. My corky appearance did not exasperate me as much as the speeches I read. By changing identity, I must have thought I could alter my relationship to the repetitious world.

"Students Told To Go Extra Mile" read a headline in the local paper. "Jesus," I thought, "if I gave people directions to my house for a dinner party, and the fools went an extra mile, the madrilene would melt before they arrived." At a nearby secondary school a speaker urged students "not to burn their bridges behind them." What was behind was usually over and done with, and burning a back-country bridge or two was meaningless. On the other hand what lies ahead is not only frightening but always fatal. Sensible folks ought to burn bridges ahead of themselves. Eventually, of course, Death finds a ford and crosses the creek to pluck us out of life. Still, a few burned bridges could slow him down, and with smoke billowing through his eye sockets he might err and harvest a neighbor or two before us.

Actually sameness and repetition, even platitude, make people comfortable, and complaint accompanies the slightest change in routine, as naturally as the night, so graduation speakers inevitably put it, follows the day. Twenty-six years ago I studied at Cambridge University in England. Breakfast in my college was always eggs and toast, and marmalade, countless small dishes of stringy, yellow marmalade. I don't like marmalade, and so I suggested putting jam on the breakfast tables along with marmalade. The kitchen staff agreed, and for two mornings a few dishes of strawberry jam were set out. The third morning the man in charge of the kitchen approached me as I entered the dining room. "Mr. Pickering, I have to stop," he said, "the protest was too great." "Protest?" I asked. "Yes," he answered, "about the jellies. The young gentlemen won't have them. They want marmalade." "But I didn't think you decreased the marmalade when you set out the strawberry jam," I said. "No sir, I didn't," he answered; "but the young gentlemen, sir, just won't have those strawberries on the table."

At the time I thought my fellow students silly, but now I am not sure. Routine and repetition may be the sources not simply of composure but of virtue. Never wanting things to change, indeed never expecting anything new, tempers extravagance and leads to moderation. When the forties spin up and the good husbands examine themselves in the tub and find rumpled Osage oranges thriving where soft magnolias used to bloom, those whom routine has made immune to dream will simply give the shampoo bottle an extra shake and after watching the bubbles float about slow and golden will stand and dry themselves and get on with the business of family. Dreaming of beaches round as soup bowls and dinner companions quivering over their plates like coconut palms in a breeze, the others, I am afraid, will spill heartache and sorrow over those nearest them.

Routine contracts vision and focuses interest. At best it creates the expert. At worst it binds people so tightly to the expected that they seem incapable of appreciating the unfamiliar. The familiar, however, is a different matter. Unlike the original and flexible thinker whirling rapidly through idea and place, the person swaddled by routine pauses and amid the dust and mildew of attic and convention finds the ordinary glittering. "Look, Sam," Neil said after pulling into my driveway last week; "look at the treasure I found in the barn this summer." In Neil's hand was a small bottle. Mulligan Brothers Liniment prepared in Willimantic, the label read, "For Man or Beast, One of the best Liniments in the market for RHEUMATISM, SORENESS, STIFF JOINTS & SWELLING." The Mulligans stood foursquare behind their liniment, declaring that if this "does not prove satisfactory after using one-half the bottle return it and get your money." The bottle didn't excite me as much as it did Neil. Family history interests me more than patent medicine, and that morning I received a letter from a woman who attended school in Carthage, Tennessee, with my father. "We had just moved to Carthage and I didn't yet know how to get to town, so I went with Sammy my first day of school (1914)," my correspondent wrote; "we had classes in the old pool hall where the Ford Motor Company was later built at the end of the bridge. The new school on the hill was not finished until the first of the year." "Your great-grandfather Mr. Billy Pickering was Post Master," she continued, "when my father went there as RFD#2 Carrier. Father and your grandfather, Mr. Sam, were friends always." The letter contained nothing I did not know. Nevertheless I read it twice, in part because like Neil's bottle it was a link to the past, an illustration that ordinary life, albeit burdened by chore and routine, is satisfying, indeed not just satisfying but meaningful and enduring.

Repeating something is generally easier than creating something original. In contrast to the original, which can seem strained and forced, the routine often appears natural. Certainly once a statement is repeated enough it digs through the thin topsoil of critical thought and, wrapping itself about a mass of words, grows into sturdy truth. In

June, I wrote people who attended Father's funeral or contacted me
after his death. I wrote one hundred and sixty-seven letters. After just
a few letters I repeated myself. To people in Nashville I said that although life had pulled me away, I would "plant Tennessee stories in
my essays in hopes that their blooming would keep memory green
and the friends of childhood bright." To neighbors in Storrs, I said I
"had grown fond of these small hills and the people who lived among
them. As I watched the creeks tumble over the granite and splay out
into skunk cabbage and false hellebore I felt at peace and at home."
The repetition in the letters shaped truth. Storrs is, I now realize, my
home. Before I began the letters I assumed Tennessee would fade from
my writings; now I am certain that will not happen.

After I completed the letters, Vicki and I ate a celebratory dinner.
Vicki did not serve soup, and the children were present as they are at
all our celebrations. Two weeks earlier I spoke at the spring banquet
of the Mansfield senior citizens. For speaking I received a bottle of
Tott's Champagne. At our celebration Vicki and I drank the champagne. For the main course Vicki served Gorton's "Crunchy" fish
sticks, made with "100% vegetable oil" and containing "No Fillers"
or preservatives. Four sticks contained fifteen grams of fat, something
that bothered me because my friend Pat told me a person ought to eat
no more than eight grams of fat each day. Along with wine and fish
sticks, we had sliced tomatoes, broccoli, and new potatoes. For dessert we had watermelon and one chocolate-chip cookie apiece. Despite the champagne the celebration did not bubble. Still, I was accustomed to flat evenings, and I enjoyed the meal. I even gave Vicki a
present, a bottle of "Chanel No. 5 Eau De Parfum Spray." My presents are not imaginative. When we were first married, I tried to buy
interesting gifts: signed paperweights and "artistic" pottery. Those
presents either traveled swiftly to the attic or after being rewrapped
were doled out, and not to friends either, but to acquaintances. Now-
adays I stick to the conventional: perfume, umbrellas, soap, sweaters,
these last, I always check, containing little wool, for wool irritates
Vicki's skin. Once after a knife rack proved a surprising success, I ran
wild and at Macy's in Atlanta bought Vicki a nightgown. The nightgown was sturdy and matronly ankle length, and I thought Vicki
would like it. Unfortunately the neckline dropped in a square slightly
below Vicki's collarbone, and Vicki wore it only once. Even then she

wrapped a thick brown towel around her chest before putting the nightgown on, so, she explained, she would not get the galloping pneumonia.

When days rasp like trees in a forest pulling against each other in a high wind, I read favorite books. Two that I turn to late at night are Edwin Way Teale's tranquil descriptions of eastern Connecticut, *A Walk through the Year* and *A Naturalist Buys an Old Farm*. Near the end of June when school had been out long enough for the children to change from angels to little devils, as Eliza put it, we drove to Hampton, Connecticut, to visit Teale's farm, Trail Wood. We parked in Mulberry Meadow and after exploring the Insect Garden near the house crossed the road into Firefly Meadow and walked around the Pond. On the far side of Stepping Stone Bridge we turned north through the West Woods and climbed the hill along the Old Colonial Road, passing the Fallen Chestnut and the foundation hole of the Cabin. When we reached the Abandoned Railway and North Boulderfield, we dropped down off the ridge and returned to the house past Beaver Pond and Woodcock Pasture. In reading the landscape afoot, I repeated Teale's wanderings and recognized his landmarks, yet I also changed them, making the land my own. At the Pond I watched bluegill swivel along the shore. In the West Woods I snapped a twig off a black birch and, scraping my thumbnail over it, rubbed its quick fragrance into my hands. On my stepping out of the shadows near the Beaver Pond, a blue heron rose from the water and flew out of sight along Hampton Brook. The Beaver Pond had spread since Teale's death, and the water was still and black. Around the edge water lilies bloomed in shiny green mats while decaying trees jutted up bleached and broken like old teeth. About and in the trees swallows swirled, oily and purple in the sun. Out of sight bullfrogs rumbled, while on a mossy platform under a clump of blue flag a green frog thrummed alone.

Later in the afternoon I went into the house. My mind works by association. An object heard or seen in the present unaccountably evokes the past. For a moment by the Beaver Pond I was a boy on my grandfather's farm in Hanover, Virginia. I stood under a mimosa tree on a warm, damp night, listening not to bull or green frogs, but to tree frogs, their voices ringing through the early dark in a sharp shrill chorus. Over a small desk inside the farmhouse at Trail Wood was a picture of David, Teale's only child, missing in action during the Second World War. As I looked at the photograph, the boy's face changed into that of a haggard man standing by his mailbox on a street near my home in Nashville. Like David Teale, the man's son had vanished during World War II. At his son's death the man's mind broke, and for years every day at noon he could be found standing by the mailbox waiting for a letter from his boy. As the sad images turned through my mind, I pulled Francis and Edward close. My boys, I prayed, would not fight in any nation's war. Suddenly Eliza broke my reverie. "Daddy," she said; "we have been here long enough. Let's go home." "Honey," I answered, a little miffed, "I like this place. Besides," I added, "you get to do everything, and this trip is for me." "Everything!" she exclaimed, looking at me in exasperation, "I haven't gone to Mars. I haven't been president yet." Eliza was right. Mars and the presidency were beyond Willimantic and East Brook Mall, even beyond Santa Claus's big bag, and shortly afterward we left.

The seasons themselves force repetitious activity upon people. When the first deep snow falls in winter, I walk at night, over Horsebarn Hill and then down through the blue woods toward the Fenton River. For me late June is not the beginning of summer but the busy time immediately before going to Nova Scotia. Not only do I race around doing the little errands of closing the house, but I roam nervously about Storrs, almost as if the things I don't see then I will never see. The pain in my back and the weakness in my arms and legs have made me aware of the fleeting nature of life, and at times when change, threatening or not, looms, I clutch at the world, hoping that neither it nor I will slip out of grasp. Near the spillway running out of Mirror Lake I saw a northern water snake twist through moss hunting frogs. I sat beneath a fringe tree, the white flowers hanging over me in shreds. I watched bees swarm across the yellow blossoms on basswood trees. Although iris had disappeared from the banks of Mirror Lake, purple loosestrife was just breaking into flower. Over a green hillside thermopsis or Carolina lupine bloomed in tall yellow spikes. Although the season for transplanting was wrong and the roots reached deep between rocks, I dug a wheelbarrow of thermopsis and planted it beside the driveway.

On June 27, we arrived at our farm in Beaver River, Nova Scotia. The light was silver, and the air buttery. Before unloading the car,

I walked the dirt road that cuts through our property and runs out to the bluff overlooking the Gulf of Maine. The lichens growing on the stone wall beside George's Field made the flat rocks seem round. Where the wall slumped, bay, alder, and winterberry pushed through and up toward the light. Near the wall bloomed sheep laurel and chokeberry, the blossoms of this last white planets circling bushy pink suns. Toward the end of July meadowsweet rose in steeples; beneath it Virginia rose blossomed wholesome and genteel. Knowing the names of plants gives me the illusion of being close to nature. Indeed my walks often seem sweet hours of prayer. Afterward I am refreshed, almost as if I had leaned on an "everlasting arm." For years I thought the rose along the wall to be the pasture rose. After study this summer I decided that it was a Virginia rose. Vicki wondered why I bothered to identify it. Just call it, she said, "a pink country rose." A showy mountain ash grew by the pond; nearby witherod bent under clusters of feathery blossoms. By August the blossoms were pale yellow seeds, shaped like small footballs. At the shoulder of the road blueberry spread low to the ground. In the sun cinnamon ferns rose in coarse fans, their spores dripping rusty on hard shafts. As the road ran down toward the pond and grew shadier and damper, bracken, then New York, crested, and finally interrupted ferns appeared. Across the wall sensitive ferns spread like yellow fans into the wet meadow. Bobolinks nested in the high grass, and some mornings two or three rose singing to the telephone wires. With yellow streaks over their eyes, Savannah sparrows hunted along the wall, their songs slight *tinks,* liquid bells falling softly into buckets. Warblers hopped through the alders searching for worms and bugs. From the spruce around the pond flycatchers darted, flusters of gray and green as they spun about chasing insects. Although I saw redstarts, black-throated greens, and black-and-whites, these last often more blue than black, most warblers were yellow: yellowthroats, yellows, and occasionally a wilson's warbler wearing a black skullcap. By mid-July fledglings and parents seemed everywhere, and some days yellow birds dropped through the spruce and alder along the side meadow like small clumps of snow shaking loose and falling golden in the sun the morning after a storm.

I did not walk to the bluff that first morning. Beyond the pond bunchberry covered the forest floor, making it resemble an old-fashioned kitchen linoleum. Green and white, the flowers appeared waxed, and I turned back toward my chores, wondering for the fifth summer in a row how long cleaning the house would take. We spent much of the next two days inside. Vicki washed the kitchen utensils; I dusted, and the children hunted mothballs and dead mice, finding these latter trapped in pickle and ship's jars, even in a partially opened can of white paint. Last summer I discovered an abandoned Volvo in the spruce woods behind Ma's Property. For the children the car was not trash but the matter of imagination: skeletons wearing iron helmets, treasure chests overflowing with giant emeralds and blood-red rubies, and snakes—a blind snake with a sapphire in his forehead glittering like the sky and then little snakes colored like rainbows and no longer than a hand but wildly poisonous. A single drop turned a man to stone or water, depending on the story. When we finished cleaning the house, Edward and Eliza asked me to go with them to the car. Over winter another door had fallen off; the roof had rusted through, but the car had not changed much. The children were not, however, the only people for whom the car was a source of fantasy. On the ground beside what remained of the front seat was a page from a novel, page 86 in fact. The paper was shredded and damp, and only two sentences were readable. "And," the excerpt began, "drove his spear to the hilt, ejaculating profusely in the exquisite depths of her quaking womb. 'Uh!' he grunted." Unaccountably I recalled that Otis Blankinchip once told Bertha Shifney that "the seed of a good stallion hung together like birdlime." "Well," I said aloud, pausing slightly before crumpling the paper and returning to the search for pearl and jasper, topaz and amethyst.

Francis did not accompany us to the woods. He stayed at home reading, and when I came back from the woods, I found him upstairs in his bed, pillows behind his neck and three books beside him: *The Mutineers*, *The Great Quest*, and *The Dark Frigate*, all by Charles Boardman Hawes. Francis's grandfather read them in Ohio in the 1920s. The covers were orange and black. Across *The Mutineers* a clipper ship sailed for China. From a jungle on the front of *The Great Quest* three scoundrels, one with a bandanna tied over his head and another with a pistol big as a forearm, gazed villainously out into a bay where a brig rode quietly at anchor. I picked up *The Dark Frigate* and thumbed the first pages. "With her great sails spread," I read, *The Rose of Devon* "thrust her nose into the heavy swell that went rolling up the Bristol

Channel, and nodding and curtseying to old Neptune, she entered upon his dominions." Birdlime and wombs be damned. Sails and swells, the Bristol Channel and old Neptune—this was the real stuff.

As books led me to Trail Wood, so they influenced my walks in Nova Scotia. On rocks under the bluff the children found a dead deer. The sun and saltwater had cured the deer, and it had little odor. The children each asked me for a hoof, explaining they could decorate them with limpets and periwinkles. Twisting leg bones out of sockets was easy. The ligaments and muscles, however, had dried into leathery fibrous strings, and I had to cut the hoofs free. The cutting was difficult. When I finished, I was proud of the neat job I did. Vicki did not think highly of my work. "Damnation," she exclaimed when the children showed the hooves to her; "you are not bringing those things into the house." Then turning to me, she said, "Only a ghoul would do what you did. Watch out when you walk at night." Late that night I explored the woody bog. I did not go along the bluff. On the ferry from Portland, I finished reading Susan Cooper's The Dark Is Rising stories to the children. In the last novel, Silver on the Tree, a malevolent skeleton of a huge horse chased two of the main characters through a forest. As I walked, I imagined the bones of the deer clattering together and then the skeleton hunching up over the lip of the bluff and chasing me across the fields, its bones white and maggoty in the moonlight. Throughout the summer I avoided the bluff at night, though now that I think about it, the deer would have had difficulty catching me with three of its hooves hanging in the barn festooned with limpets, painted in Day-Glo pink and green.

Vicki doesn't like cold water, and so I spent much time on the beach with the children. While they raised dikes and dredged spillways to hold the tide at bay, I roamed the shoreline, poking through the trash tossed overboard by fishermen. In past summers I examined the litter and even wrote about it. This summer I wanted to ignore it. For some reason, though, it attracted me. Much as the children dreamed of finding gold in the Volvo, so I imagined discovering diamonds on the beach. I was disappointed. The most exotic items I found were a six-inch aerosol can of what appeared to be a Russian deodorant and then a battered wooden box once containing "Pure Ceylon Tea" shipped by James Findlay from Colombo. All else was ordinary: nests of plastic twine; one- and five-liter containers for motor oil; soft-drink cans; lobster traps, most wooden but two made from coat hanger–like metal and coated with rubber; blue and white cardboard boxes with "Cape Breeze Sea Foods, Port Latour, N.S." stamped on the tops; fan belts; rubber shoes; and then floats and buoys. Edward collected the buoys and by summer's end had thirty-nine. His favorite was a round orange Nokalon Trawlnet float, manufactured in Denmark and twenty-four inches in circumference. One afternoon Francis found an empty pill container, the label still attached to it. On March 31, 1987, Dr. McQuigge prescribed twenty-one capsules of Amoxil for R. Trager and told him to take three a day.

I spent almost as many hours on the rocks above the beach with litter as I did wandering through pools at low tide. The pools sparkled with life: white and yellow barnacles; limpets; shrimp; periwinkles; and seaweeds, red and green and even blue in the sunlight. Under rocks around the pools Eliza caught beach fleas. Often I helped her. Eliza and I were close companions during the summer. I explored the shore with her, and she frequently accompanied me on walks, skipping off her left foot and singing a rhyme she made up: "The green bean went down the stream to sing to the bird of the moonbeam." She told me she wanted to be a ballerina and a veterinarian when she grew up, "a wild animal veterinarian," she emphasized. Together we caught snakes, all garters except a small red-bellied snake she found under driftwood at Salmon River. Eliza named the snake Violet and carried it home to show to Vicki and the boys. In the evening she took it to the headland and turned it loose beside a crumpled stone wall, near a bog rich with cranberries, the sort of damp, lonely place red-bellied snakes like. The children's curiosity about the world pleases me. Whenever one brings a spider or an animal dropping to me to identify, I see myself as a small boy. On grandfather's farm I ran the green hills after insects. Besides being gentle the children are fearless, a state of mind appropriate to cool, venomless Nova Scotia, but perhaps not suitable for the hotter places of copperhead and water moccasin.

In Nova Scotia the small creatures of meadow and woodland seem more curious about us than do their cousins in Connecticut. The day we arrived a one-eared red squirrel, later named Chippy, pushed against the screen door leading from the pantry to the backhouse. When I latched the door, he climbed the screen and chattered at me,

stopping only when I gave him a gingersnap. Chippy lived in a fallen
black spruce across the side meadow. Late every afternoon he visited
us for tea. If he did not get our attention by banging on the screen, he
ran back and forth on the side porch until he received a treat. Treats
varied. Some days I gave him unsalted peanuts; on others a variety of
things: war cake, heavy with raisins; muffins; halves of biscuits spread
with honey or butter; Oreo cookies; granola; shredded wheat; rhubarb pie; and pancakes soaked in both maple and blueberry syrups.
On returning from the grocery one Friday early in July we found two
veery fledglings confused and huddled together under an old stove
in a corner of the backhouse. I caught them in a butterfly net and
set them outside on the well cover. Shortly afterward their mother
arrived and led them off into the roses. There they spent the next four
days growing and demanding food. This was the first time veerys came
close to the house, and at late dusk throughout July, a veery sat atop a
tamarack at the end of the side meadow, its song turning like a doorknob to let the night slip in.

Many years ago Vicki's father planted a willow beside the roses
behind the well. Each summer caterpillars of the mourning cloak butterfly feed upon the tree, and dutifully I get out ladder and shears and
slice off the infested branches. This summer I let the caterpillars eat
themselves into chrysalises. On July 18, they started leaving the tree,
and at various times during the next three days they crawled off in
different directions. Not all became chrysalises. Big robins hunted
through the meadow. Fat and spiky with hard black bristles, the caterpillars were difficult to eat. Watching the robins I imagined myself
eating a lobster. The birds first stabbed with their beaks, and then
seizing the caterpillars shook them back and forth, sometimes throwing them into the air, almost it seemed in exasperation. Still, despite
not having a bowl of melted butter in which to dip the flesh, the birds
must have found the caterpillars tasty. Content to let dinner come to
them, most robins ate caterpillars only when they happened upon
them humping through the grass. One bird, though, was greedier and
more ingenious. Flying into the willow, she shook the small branches
on which the caterpillars rested and fed. When a caterpillar lost its
grip and tumbled to the ground, the bird dropped down for lunch.
Leaving the willow over a period of three days and at various times
during those days insured that at least a few caterpillars would escape

the robins. At first I saw a guiding mechanism behind the dispersal, but later I was not sure. Perhaps the caterpillars left the tree simply when they had eaten enough to strengthen them for pupation. Like children some probably gobbled their leaves, while others, picking at mesophyll and parenchyma, dallied, dreaming of flowery adulthood when all their meals would be sweet dessert.

That aside, though, the caterpillars were determined to crawl some distance from the willow before molting. Probably molting would not start until the caterpillars crawled for an hour or two. Several times I found caterpillars in the open middle of the meadow and moved them to shelter. Despite being close to places that their brothers and sisters seized as appropriate for molting, the caterpillars did not slow down. Often I put them on the side of the barn where they restlessly crawled up and down, back and forth, not, it seemed, searching for a place to molt, for they often molted near spots where I placed them initially, but simply to use energy sufficient or stir enough heat to trigger pupation. To molt, the caterpillars hung upside down in dark, mottled js, their tails attached by a pad of silk to a stem or clapboard above and their heads curving around and up. After hanging quietly for two days they turned out of their skins, corkscrewing them up toward their tails. For a moment the skins clung like battered baggage to the chrysalises. Then abruptly the chrysalises twisted, and the skins fell to the ground in nondescript bundles. I found twelve chrysalises: one on the house, one under a gutter, three on the backhouse, one beneath a leaf on a lilac, and six hanging on the barn. Although all resembled battered leaves caught in spiderwebs or small plops of mud flung up by a storm or dropped by a swallow building a nest, the colors of the chrysalises were different. The one on the house was light gray like the house itself; that under the lilac had a green tinge; while those on the barn and backhouse were dark and speckled and resembled the moldy grain of shakes long weathered and damp in the shade. Camouflage was important for the caterpillars. Of the twelve chrysalises six were parasitized, most probably by ichneumon wasps. Named after the ichneumon or pharaoh's rat, which supposedly ate not simply crocodile eggs but young crocodiles themselves, the wasps relentlessly hunted for prey about the house and meadow. The insect that parasitized the mourning cloaks inserted an egg into the chrysalis. After feeding on the pupa for eight or so days, the parasite bored out of the chrysalis, leaving a small hole behind. As the remaining flesh of the caterpillar rotted, the chrysalis became home to other insects, often earwigs. I watched the chrysalises carefully. At the end of two weeks those that were not parasitized changed and seemed to swell with life. When I accidentally touched a chrysalis, it wrinkled and bucked. On the morning of the sixteenth day, the first chrysalis split, and a mourning cloak pulled itself into the sun, its wings blue and cream and brown. We gathered around it in a semicircle touching each other and feeling close not simply to family but to a familial natural world.

No matter the weather I walked every day in Nova Scotia. Despite long intentions and a good grip on my walking stick, I sometimes got no farther from the house than the wrinkled roses behind the well. The roses were an insect garden and on a sunny July day bloomed with life. While a two-spotted ladybug hurried between thorns, bumblebees lumbered from blossom to blossom, their hind legs heavy with clumps of pollen. Sitting warily on leaves were midges, flesh flies, and then, resembling flakes of polished metal, small gold flies with minute dark stripes crossing their abdomens. While an ichneumon wasp, its wings purple in the sun, blinked into sight momentarily, a lacewing fluttered slowly by, looking like a loose tuft of greenish cotton. Unlike the lacewing, whose fragile appearance belies a ferocious predator, the hover fly, most varieties of which feed on plants, usually resembles an angry bee, beating its wings rapidly in the air. Even when it rests on a leaf, its abdomen shakes threateningly. In contrast to the hover fly, the crane fly is still, its translucent wings spread, veins breaking brown through them like copper between panes of Tiffany glass.

Some walks began with purpose, to watch birds or to find small wildflowers. Under the willow fragrant bedstraw and forget-me-not bloomed early in July. Through the grass moneywort spread, its blossoms a soft yellow and its leaves in pairs resembling pudgy green spades. Low along the bluff were minute sandwort, three-toothed cinquefoil, and sundrops, moneywort's bright cousin in the primrose family. Near the wall at the edge of Ma's Property speedwell crept over the ground; in the woody bog behind bloomed wood sorrel and the last of the starflowers. In the middle of the road to the bluff stood small blue beacons of self-heal. In late July eyebright appeared, the white blossoms streaked with purple. Uncultured people often furnish writers with character and provide the stuff of tale. When Hinds Jasperson met Otis Blankinchip coming out of the Gate of Heaven Cemetery in Digby, he exclaimed, "Lordy, Otis, it's strange meeting you here. Is anyone dead?" "Yes," Otis said, stopping and nodding, "yes, all of them." Unlike people, uncultivated flowers are silent; sometimes nodules of lore are attached to them. Usually, however, the lore is forgotten, out of sight and mind like nitrogen fixed to the roots of alder. According to an old tale if a person puts mugwort in his shoes, he can walk forty miles without becoming weary. To purge one's self of a pesky worm, a person, Bertha Shifney advised, should crush mouse-ear and drink the juice in dark ale. Uprooting a plant is occasionally more difficult than getting rid of a worm. At the south end of our property where the bluff smooths out flat and Beaver River drains into the Gulf of Maine, hedge bindweed has spread in a heavy mat over the ground, choking most other growth. Pigs like the plant's roots, and aside from using a bulldozer or strong herbicide, perhaps the only way to get rid of the bindweed is to fence the land and turn pigs loose in the enclosure. I like bindweed. A morning glory, its pink and white trumpets quicken the slow heat of July. Moreover the larvae of tortoise beetles eat the plant's leaves. Flat and milky, the larvae themselves appear dull. At the end of a larva's body, however, are two prongs. On them the larva deposits droppings, forming a protective shield. When a potential predator disturbs it, the larva thrusts the shield into the predator's face. Among humans, of course, an unusual use of dung provokes, not discourages, curiosity, and for a night the larvae and their shields enriched the mulch of dinner-table conversation.

My writing reflects my life. Much as I have just strayed from small wildflowers, so I was easily distracted on walks. Like a mourning cloak caterpillar twisting out of its skin, I shed purpose with a turn of the head. One afternoon while watching warblers in the alders around the pond, I noticed the empty shells or exoskeletons of dragonflies. Clinging to burweed and water horsetail, the shells reminded me of the halves of seeds from big maples—sycamore or Norway maples. The shell's long tapering abdomen resembled the wing of the seed, while the seed's thick embryo looked like the upper end of the shell, the head with its bulging eyes and then the wings folded compactly behind. After looking at the shells, I forgot the warblers. Instead I watched dragonflies, small red ones resting on rushes and then, with yellow stripes across their thoraxes, big blue adders, cutting back and forth over the pond.

Insects often influenced my walks. Each spring the road to the bluff is mowed. This year the mower cut deep into the dirt along one shoulder, leaving behind a dusty brown scar the size of a small coffee table. By mid-July the table was a grasshopper maternity ward. On hot days six or seven grasshoppers were there laying eggs, the bottom halves of their abdomens curved downward into the soft dirt. Often Francis and I stretched out on the road and watched. Once we lay down, we usually did not get up quickly, for inevitably something else captured our attention, a large black ant struggling with three small red ants or a dead toad under which two tomentose burying beetles were busy digging a pit. Once when I set out briskly for Beaver River, a white admiral butterfly lit on me. White admirals eat carrion, and as I watched him breakfasting up my arm, I remembered one of Mother's sayings. "The butterfly," she remarked of an inappropriate marriage, "flies all around the butterfly bush and lands on a dog turd."

In truth I suspect that purpose and ambition only influence the lives of young people. By middle age the word *ambition* may elicit mechanical lip service, but it doesn't determine the tenor of days. As for purpose, it is suspect, associated with the zealous and the intolerant. The best that can be hoped for is distraction, distraction from one's darkening journey through life. No matter my intention, almost all my walks turned into ambles, brightened by summery distraction. Plants and creatures I had seen before I saw anew. Once while hunting wild raspberries along an overgrown wall I noticed fireweed, its spikes rising purple around me. At the top of fireweed the last flowers to bloom clung demurely to the stalk. Below them other buds freshened and, sticking out from the stalk on stems, began to swell. Just before blooming the buds curved slightly up at the ends, looking like minute red velvet slippers, shoes for a fairy, not a mischievous fairy either but a sentimental Victorian fairy with tinkling glass wings and a sugarcoated wand. In contrast the flowers themselves were racy and strident. Four big purple petals round as soupspoons loomed upward; beneath them dangled a narrow petal resembling a long tongue. From the center of the blossom the female part, the pistil, hung out thick and white. At the end farthest from the stalk it split into four parts, each part curving back on itself like a white worm startled and suddenly rearing upward. About the pistil were the stamens, male parts, each furry with pollen. The blossoms smacked of dumplings and dinner parties more than they did gothic spires and sleeping princesses. A Sunday school picnic of small stinkbugs agreed with me. The plant was their trysting spot, and below the flowers twoscore of them were misbehaving tail to tail.

Youth takes health for granted and in the fast, muscular pursuit of power or position rarely thinks about sickness and decay. For me position and power have faded into delusion. In contrast, health has become real and preoccupying, and only on those walks I took for exercise did I hold fast to purpose. For my weak leg I often walked north from our farm along the shore past Bartlett's Beach out to Black Point, just south of Salmon River. A rocky arrowhead of land jutting out into the sea, Black Point consists of high pasture cut off from Route 1, the shore highway, by a thin line of spruce and then by a deep, broad neck of open bog. After climbing down the bluff I strode quickly along the beach, only noticing the shoreline when willets pitched crying overhead to distract me from their young. Occasionally the willets succeeded, though not in the way they hoped, and I stopped and examined the plants growing above high water: purple beach pea, oysterleaf, and tall, yellow goatsbeard. Once or twice at the end of July when plovers and sandpipers began to gather for the migration south, I paused and watched them feed along the shore. Usually, however, I maintained a swinging pace until I reached Black Point.

The language of the essayist is homespun, the sturdy twill of workaday sentences. Unlike the essayist the poet is a tippler, reveling in the figurative and raising the ordinary to the visionary and inspirational. On Black Point I longed to be a poet, and I spent hours crossing and recrossing the pasture in hopes that somehow I could draw the colors about me into speech. When friends return from exotic vacations and describe apricot days on green islands, I will not speak. Have you, I will think, sat in a wheel of daisies, hawkweed spinning off in yellow lines like comets? Have you ever seen devil's paintbrush burn over a hillside, orange and red and smelling faintly of strawberry shortcake and frothy, light cream? Have you bathed in a pool of blue flag, yellow vetchling stretching beyond like a deserted beach. Across the headland grasses waved purple and red, and then orange. Through the grass cow vetch rose shaggy and blue. Along the ground lady's-mantle bloomed green. In sunlight its broad leaves lie still under the currents of color flowing over them. At night, though, they gather the mist, and when the high blooms above them become black, the leaves leap to the eye, silver and alive. Along the north face of the Point a ribbon of black spruce frayed into root and bleached trunk. On big rocks in the sea cormorants sunned themselves; in the waves eiders paddled about while loons fished, diving then reappearing then diving again. Back from the water at the edge of the bog, robins perched atop trees, from a distance looking like small hawks. On a branch a phoebe sang, its tail bobbing. Rushing like paper caught in wind, a flock of cedar waxwings forged through the spruce, disturbing warblers and goldfinches.

A house and barn once stood on Black Point. Animal paths twisted through the foundation, and meadowsweet grew between the stones. As I looked down into the foundation hole, I thought about the small scars that mark a man's passing. Each summer I cut paths and sometimes imagine, I'm ashamed to say, readers of my books following them as I followed the paths at Trail Wood. That vanity aside, I make paths because cutting them satisfies me. This summer I chopped paths from the brush behind the pond out to the edge of the quaking bog and from the spruce woods behind Ma's Property to the dirt road running to the bluff. The paths were long, but the work was easy, aside from cutting through twenty-three yards of alder, withe-rod, and winterberry near the quaking bog and twenty-four yards of highbush blackberry and winterberry near the spruce woods. Although paths ease the going from one place to another, they can narrow vision. Paths attract walkers. Once the path existed, I took it whenever I went to the quaking bog. No longer did I push sweaty and alert through underbrush. For convenience I sacrificed excitement and the possibility of stumbling upon something new. Still, I was proud of the paths, and Francis said they were not paths but highways. In the afternoon I often stood in the middle of the path to the bog and watched warblers search for insects. I stood still, and frequently the birds came within two feet of me.

Since walking on the paths was easy, I paid less attention to my immediate surroundings than when I struggled through brush. Sometimes I even forgot about Nova Scotia and the actual and, recalling the letters I wrote after Father's death, shaped tales about Tennessee.

Like other characters of mine the people in the stories lived in the small towns of Smith and Jackson counties, towns with names like Burncoat, Alanna, Union Corner, Bible Hill, Nineveh, Conquerall, and Rising Tide. The name of this last town has always puzzled me. Along the banks of the Cumberland River the moon influences the course of love more than the flow of water. That mystery aside, however, a simple and almost appealing penuriousness ruled these hill folk. Always a spendthrift and a ne'er-do-well, Tiddy Preeper went to Nashville for a weekend and quickly ran out of money. Having reached too often into the pockets of his Nashville acquaintances, Tiddy was forced to fall back upon his drinking companions in Bible Hill. Googoo Hooberry was the first person he called. "Hello, Googoo, is that you?" Tiddy said when Googoo answered the telephone. "Yes," Googoo answered; "this is Googoo." "It doesn't sound like Googoo," Tiddy said. "Well this is me speaking," Googoo said. "Are you sure that's you, Googoo?" Tiddy replied. "Yes," Googoo shouted, "it's me. Who the hell do you think it is—the Pope of Rome?" "Oh, that's good," Tiddy said; "listen Googoo. This is your old buddy Tiddy. I have run into a little embarrassment down here in Nashville. Could you lend me fifty dollars?" There was a long, thoughtful pause; then a cold voice said, "All right Tiddy, I'll give the message to Googoo when he comes in." One morning, not long afterward, Googoo knocked at Hoben Donkin's front door. "Is Hoben in?" he asked when Hoben's wife, Clulee, opened the door. "Oh, Googoo," Clulee sobbed, throwing herself into his arms, "Hoben died last night." "Oh, no, what terrible news!" Googoo exclaimed, gently extracting himself from the grasp of the grieving widow, "that's a great loss to me. But did he, Clulee," he added, "say anything about a bucket of yellow paint before he died?" Over the summer I grew fond of Googoo and sent him to Nashville for the Elks' convention. After he bearded a Moose and plucked the feathers from a couple of earthbound Eagles in Nashville, Googoo felt assertive and confident. "My good man," he said to the conductor as the train from Nashville approached Bible Hill, "I want to be procrastinated at the next town." "You want to be what?" the conductor answered. "Procrastinated," Googoo said puffing and rubbing his hands over his stomach grandiloquently; "don't be ashamed of your ignorance. Why even I had to look in the dictionary to find out procrastinate means 'put off.'"

In making the path to the quaking bog I chopped down witherod.

I tossed the bushes over alders beside the path. Instead of drying into brittleness, the leaves turned black and, becoming supple, exuded a heavy oily fragrance. The aroma attracted moths, and at night they clung to the leaves in swarms. Like years on Chinese calendars, each summer in Nova Scotia has a particular identity. Three years ago was the summer of the mushroom, as mushrooms turned the spruce woods into a garden, great fairy wheels and then mounds of blossoms, color-ful as beds of perennials: white, green, blue, and ocher. This year was the summer of the moth. The first time I walked through Ma's Prop-erty webworm moths rose from the grasses in white streams. That night polyphemus moths beat against the bedroom windows. Cling-ing to the side of the house the next morning were two polyphemus moths, their antennae resembling the downy inner feathers of birds and their bodies hairy and orange. On each hind wing was an eye, almost as large, it seemed, as a knot in a pine board. Ringed about with yellow, blue, and black, the center of the eye was transparent and in the moonlight must have shone silver and coolly disturbing. On the backhouse I found three blind sphinxes, wings folded up be-hind them and looking like leaves gnawed by the wind. Under the roof over the entrance to the front door was a false crocus geom-eter, yellow and splotched with red. Sharp-angled carpets and white-banded blacks flattened themselves against window frames. Between spiderwebs over the door pale beauties clung, looking fragile and drained by the night.

Most moths were small and to me at least resembled neglected wildflowers. As I walked about the farm looking for flowers, so I de-cided to hunt moths. Instead, though, of searching hard for them, I let them come to me, attracted by the lights in the house. Instead of snipping them out of life and the air, I only caught them, using round clear plastic containers three and a half inches in diameter and five-eighths of an inch tall, the kind of laboratory dish in which ento-mologists keep insects. For large moths I used a square spice container with a yellow top. After identifying moths I freed them. Never did I catch moths after one o'clock at night. I also decided not to remove moths from spiderwebs, no matter how interesting the moth appeared. Scores of foliate and gray cross spiders hung webs about the house—evening glories, Edward called them. The biggest spiders seemed tame and tolerated Eliza's and my stroking the backs of their abdomens. I

caught moths at the front door and at windows looking out of the
kitchen, pantry, study, and front and back parlors. In the front parlor
are two large bay windows, and for a while they were good hunting
grounds. Vicki set up the card table in the parlor, and for ten or so
nights in July she sipped Baileys Irish Cream and worked on a seven-
hundred-and-fifty-piece jigsaw puzzle depicting three green totem poles
in British Columbia. Many moths were beautiful: yellow slantline;
lettered Habrosyne; virgin tiger, creamy channels slicing the forewings into deltas of dark islands, and the hind wings pink fields strewn
with black boulders; Ferguson's scallop shell, rippled like a sandbar
and almost smelling like the ocean; Canadian owlet; yellow-headed
cutworm; and then even prettier than its name the rose hooktip, the
ends of its forewings beaches curving around inlets red and gold in a
soft sunset. I caught several darts: bent-line gray, knee-joint, dappled,
clandestine, pink-spotted, and flame-shouldered. I liked the names of
many moths: cloudy arches, honest pero, and pale metanema. Some
moths, like the American ear moth, needed new names, and at times
when I could not identify a moth, I imagined turning it loose on
lepidopterists as Pickering's beauty.

As the light fell dappled across the moths, soft poetry came easily.
True observation, though, was beyond me. Those moths like some of
the inchworm moths which depended upon salt-and-pepper camouflage for their safety seemed more alert in the day than the thicker,
heavier sphinxes and loopers. While the large moths went limp and
seemed to play dead, inchworm moths flew off at my approach, recognizing, it appeared, that their disguises had not deceived me. That
small observation aside, despite the rigor with which I caught and
identified moths, I saw comparatively little. Although the children
found moths for me, they never named a moth, as Eliza did our first
mourning cloak butterfly, calling it Katy. At the end of July, I had a
notebook of names, not observations. Perhaps I would have seen more
if moths had been less a study and more a distraction.

We left Beaver River the first week in August. Another group of
mourning cloak caterpillars fed on the poplars by the front gate. They
dispersed in August, and while I packed the car, the children searched
for chrysalises along the house and backhouse, finding eight and then
four dead caterpillars parasitized before they molted. This summer
may have been our last on the farm. Francis and Edward are nine and

seven respectively and need to learn to swim, something that can't be accomplished in the Gulf of Maine. Although I think recognizing wildflowers and insects more important than being able to play tennis or paddle a canoe, I am not sure an old daddy is a fit companion for children. Next summer I will probably send them to camp so they can learn to do the things their friends do. Should a five year old, I sometimes wonder, carry spiders about in little boxes and let snakes wrap through her hands like twine? And then, of course, I don't have income enough for two houses. Accounts of my meanderings don't attract readers like huckleberries do ants, and me, in late July. Still, my books might sell, and maybe we could go to Nova Scotia after camp. In September the light breaks low through the spruce in long white slats. Along the dirt road asters straggle into bloom, flat-topped asters and then, almost under the ferns, small blue asters. By September mosquitoes will have died down, and I could cut a path to and then around the pond, on the far side joining the path to the quaking bog. Maybe I could make a shelter like Edwin Way Teale's Brushpile. From it I could watch hummingbirds feeding on pickerelweed and study dragonflies. The smaller brownish dragonflies of ripened summer are almost tame. If a person approaches one from the front and slowly slips a finger under its front legs, the dragonfly will likely climb on his finger and perch there, even if the person raises his hand and walks away.

I have trouble letting go of Nova Scotia. The last five summers have been fine, and I dream of returning in September, although I know both the children and I are bound to be in school. At the exhibition this July, Eliza rode the merry-go-round by herself. In past summers I stood beside her, the horses flowing up and down and my joy brighter than water. This summer time spun me off, and like a castoff dragonfly shell I stood unneeded and empty in the dry gravel. "Daddy, I love you," Eliza said as we boarded the ferry for Maine; "I wish whenever you were too old and going to die you would become a baby in your mommy's tummy again." Yes, yes, I would relive the foolishness of all the dinner parties just for a summer in Nova Scotia, my little peanut beside me, skipping off her left foot and singing, "The green bean went down the stream to sing to the bird of the moonbeam."

Traveling, but Not Alone

Aside from the afternoon's drive to Portland and the overnight ferry to Yarmouth and then quick flights from Hartford to Nashville to visit my parents, not until this August had Vicki and I taken a trip with the children. Despite having spent many summers in Nova Scotia, in Vicki's case over thirty, neither of us had been to Halifax. Although the two hundred miles from the farm in Beaver River to Halifax was no longer than the drive from Storrs to Portland, the trip stretched arduous through my imagination, draining energy and clogging curiosity. This summer, however, was likely to be my last away from Connecticut, and I decided that we ought to travel about Nova Scotia. To this end I collected maps and guidebooks. At nine, seven, and five, the children were small, not little, and the days of potty-chairs lay behind us. Moreover, in our car we were not liable to upset or be upset by other travelers. Once on a crowded December flight to Nashville, Edward sneezed, washing the head of a bald man sitting in front of us. The man was considerably exercised, and he refused both the offer of a handkerchief and the suggestion that he loosen up and get in the Christmas spirit. Indeed, he was so vociferous that he drove away all thoughts of angels bending near and the sweet notes of "peace on the earth good will toward men." In strong, unseasonable language I urged him to behave, adding that if a little moisture so upset him he ought to get a hair transplant, one of the waterproof ones, I said, made from

133

cat piss and acrylic. The man was a business traveler, and remembering that IBM and Aetna frowned upon employees who got into fist-fights on airplanes, particularly at Christmas, he turned around and, putting a pillow on his head, did not say another word.

Early August is very different from late December. Instead of gray and damp, the light was soothing and yellow. Low in the fields purple orchis shone through the grass like bright church candelabra. At the pond hummingbirds circled blue spikes of pickerelweed. In the bog bunchberries were red. By the road pearly everlasting bloomed in clusters, small white jugs with bands of orange about their mouths. Along the stone wall bay slid, then swirled through the breeze, natural and green, not forced like the paper-whites and often the moods and flights of December. To book places to stay on the trip I went to the tourist bureau in Yarmouth. I had a list of inns with names like Hillsdale, Queen Anne, Bread and Roses, Blomidon, Tattingstone, Boscawen, and Halliburton. Although some, I suspected, would not take children and others would be full throughout August, the season made me serene. To reach Yarmouth I drove down Richmond Road in Port Maitland. Coming over a rise, I saw a turtle in the middle of the road. A truck just missed it, and the turtle pulled into its shell. I stopped and darting out of the car scooped up the turtle. With red and yellow stripes running across its legs and head, it was a painted turtle. I crossed the road and after clambering down a steep bank ducked under a barbed-wire fence. I walked along a field until I reached wetlands at the edge of Churchill Lake. Water lilies were blooming; beyond them glided a pair of loons. I set the turtle down in a clump of rushes and went back to the car. My shoes were muddy and my socks soaked, but I felt good and was certain booking rooms would be easy.

I was right. Some inns were filled; others did not take children; nevertheless, I found rooms in places on my list. Only in Halifax did I not book an inn. A little chlorine does wonders for tired children, and I decided that after a day of wandering the hills of the city a hotel with a pool suited the children better than an inn, even, alas, one serving afternoon tea in a garden. Since this would probably be our only trip around Nova Scotia and since earlier in the summer I earned fifteen hundred dollars speaking to a teachers' convention, cost did not matter much. I refused to stay, as Googoo Hooberry, a character in my essays, put it, in "one of those places what keeps a dog to wash the dishes." Not only that, I was too old to count nickels and dollars. Years ago I bargained for rooms. Once I paid $2.50 for a motel in New Hampshire. The room crawled with bedbugs, and when I saw the owner the next morning, I mentioned them. "Oh, yes, I feel bad about those bugs," he said shaking his head sympathetically; "tell you what; I'm going to let you stay a second night free." For the eight nights we spent on the trip, rooms cost $959.18 in Canadian money or $834.49 in American.

After reserving the rooms I walked to Main Street and treated myself to a bottle of wine at the Liquor Commission, a liter-and-a-half jug of L'Entre Côte, a "Dry Red" produced by Brights Wines in Dartmouth. I put the wine in a paper sack and feeling in high, hungry spirits hurried down Main to the Tim Horton doughnut shop. "I must," I said when the salesgirl waited on me, "have a doughnut to go with this wine." "What kind," she asked, looking behind her at the trays of doughnuts. "Why, red, of course," I exclaimed, "do I look like the sort of person who would drink white wine?"

I bought an "old-fashioned" chocolate-covered doughnut, and for a moment ambling up Alma Street I forgot the trip. Once I reached the car, though, I remembered it. The right rear tire looked low. Before leaving Storrs I took the car to Capitol Garage in Willimantic for a tune-up. Because the tires had forty-two thousand miles on them, I wanted to buy a new set, but the garage manager insisted I did not need them. The car itself was six years old, and that also bothered me. My grandfather believed cars dangerous after a year and said that only fools kept cars longer than twelve months. Each spring he traded in his car, as well as Grandmother's and Mother's. Grandfather worried excessively, or so I thought when I was younger. Now I am not sure. For years Grandfather refused to let Grandmother drive by herself and insisted that a farm worker ride with her in case her car broke down. Despite my fears the car and tires lasted the trip. Of course I drove slowly, never faster than fifty-six miles an hour, and the trip itself turned out to be shorter than it seemed on the map and in my anxiety, only five hundred and forty-six miles.

When traveling alone a person usually has the leisure to be curious. With a family, worry, not observation, dominates a trip. Instead of wandering through odd corners and talking to dusty strangers, I herded the children through clear fields of conventional sights, making sure no stranger talked to them. Always watching the children I had no time for other people, and I passed unseeing and unhearing through crowds. In contrast, when I travel by myself, I hear collections of stories. On the way back to Yarmouth after speaking to the schoolteachers, I bought a chocolate croissant and a cup of coffee at Logan Airport in Boston. As I sipped the coffee, a man sat beside me. He was, he told me, a millionaire. "Do you know why?" he asked. "Because," he said before I could respond, "it's because I am as serious as cancer." Later, after the man left, a woman and her little girl, two and a half or three years old, sat beside me. The girl ate a butter pecan ice-cream cone. When the ice cream melted and ran down her chin, I wiped her face with a napkin. The woman was an American living in London. In December her husband died suddenly, and sadly, she recounted, she did not think she could continue living abroad. While we talked, her flight was called. Getting up, she took her daughter's arm and started toward the gate. Six or so feet away from the table the little girl pulled loose and turning back stared at me with a puzzled expression on her face. Slowly she extended her hand toward me, her small, round fingers opening like flower petals in the sunshine. "Daddy?" she said softly, both a question and a catch in her voice, "Daddy?"

When I travel alone, I often amuse myself by creating characters. With children practicalities fill days. After forcing a crying child to eat two hard rolls and drink a pint of milk to dislodge a fish bone from his throat, I have little appetite for fiction. All I long for is a firm bed and sheets flowing over me, cool as milk, sweeping me out to the soft, dreamless depths where the whales don't call and the salmon never run. While on my way to address the teachers, in contrast, I flopped about in the shallows of anecdote. Loppie Groat lived in Little Dover, a small hill town on a white ridge not far from Carthage, Tennessee. Although simple, Loppie made do by growing tobacco and then hiring out to work on the highway with Jeddry, his big, black mule. One day Jeddry wandered off into the woods behind Cow Cove. As soon as he discovered Jeddry was missing, Loppie searched for him. When he met someone on the road, he said, "Jeddry has disappeared. Praise God! Have you seen him?" "Why are you praising God when your mule has vanished," Turlow Gutheridge asked after Loppie approached him. "Turlow, I don't want to lose Jeddry," Loppie explained, "but I'm thanking the Lord because if I'd been on Jeddry's back when he disappeared I would have been lost too."

The trip around Nova Scotia wore me out. Twice I woke up thinking I was in Connecticut, and once I thought Vicki was Mother. Like me Loppie was not a great traveler, and when he did travel, he was cautious. Going to Nashville for a convention of the Elks frightened him, and so he would be recognizable and not get lost, he fastened three pieces of okra and a big Smith County turnip to his belt. One night while Loppie was asleep, Googoo Hooberry removed the vegetables and tied them to his own waist. As soon as he woke the next morning, Loppie ran his hands over his belt. When he didn't find the vegetables, he was upset, and he looked quickly around the room. When he saw Googoo asleep, the turnip rising and falling on his stomach like a purple jellyfish in a heavy surf, he was relieved, at least for the moment. Then as he reached for his trousers, he sat up straight, concern wrinkling his brow. "If that's me over there with the nice produce," he said pointing to Googoo, "and surely it is, then who am I here?"

People who invite me to speak take me to good restaurants. Slightly foreign and sometimes a little exotic, the names of the restaurants are usually Christian names, Mario's or Julian's, for example. At home Vicki and I do not eat veal. When I travel, I always eat veal. Often I do not know exactly what sort of veal I am eating because the menus are in French or Italian, not English. At dessert I don't order from the trolley or look at the menu. I simply say, "Bring me the sweet with the ladyfingers and the liqueur." For a person traveling by himself mystery adds spice to a meal. With children one must avoid not only mystery and spices but most foods. Edward and Eliza do not like vegetables, and their favorite meal consists of a hamburger and french-fried potatoes, both covered with an eiderdown of ketchup, and then a Pepsi and ice cream. Francis, on the other hand, likes vegetables and will eat almost anything except a hamburger, french fries, and ketchup. He also refuses to drink soda, and only rarely will he touch dessert. Of the twenty-five meals the family ate on the road, Vicki and I ate twenty-four with the children. In Wolfville not only did our room have a television, but it was in an annex across the drive from the dining room. Because the inn was known for its food, Vicki and I took the children downtown for spaghetti. Afterward we returned to the inn where they stretched out in front of the television while we went to dinner. At one end of the dining room behind twin fluted columns was a dark-chocolate, bittersweet Federal sideboard. Over the mantel at the other end was an eighteenth-century copy of a Murillo painting, the colors aged out of brightness into shadowy creams. On either side of the fireplace were glassed-in display cabinets savory with Worcester and Rose Medallion. During the meal Vicki and I drank red wine from great round glasses, and romance rose to the mind glazed and lemony. At ten-thirty we left, thinking to stroll over the grounds and nibble at the moon. As soon as we stepped outside, I heard a shout. Racing over the lawn in their pajamas were our little french fries. Because we had been gone two hours, they worried about us. Edward told Eliza that robbers had probably stolen us. After agreeing that we could have been stolen, Francis said that it was more probable that we were drunk. Whatever had happened, however, the children thought we needed help and they came looking for us. As we pulled them close and looked up at the moon, all thoughts of romance vanished. In our arms we held the main course of our lives, not delicate and quick on the tongue, but hearty, peppered with fear and hope, a rack of years thick with growth and sometimes loss.

Despite the plain food, meals with the children were frequently full-bodied. "What is kissing for?" Edward asked over salmon. "What does it mean to be in heat?" Eliza said across a long table in a "family" restaurant. The second day of the trip Edward asked if I knew any "cool dudes." When I replied that I was a cool dude, he scoffed. I did not, he pointed out, drive a motorcycle, have a tattoo, a mohawk haircut, or even a pigtail, or wear an earring or blue jeans with patches and holes in them. At dinner that night I asked Edward if he enjoyed eating with the "coolest dude in Nova Scotia." Before he replied Eliza shouted, "You are not a cool dude. You are an old fart." Much as the speech so the habits of home accompany a family on a trip. On the farm the children don't kill insects. Whenever they find a moth, beetle, or even a hornet in the house, they catch it and turn it loose outside. At lunch in Annapolis Royal the first day, Edward noticed a green and yellow grasshopper trapped behind a curtain in the restaurant. "Daddy," Edward began, and I knew what he wanted. I caught the grasshopper and, carrying it across the street, turned it loose in a graveyard. At dinner Eliza found an earwig in the flower arrangement on our table. Before coffee I took the earwig outside and dropped it over a fence into a rose garden. The next morning at breakfast two ants accompanied our pancakes and syrup. These I put on an oak tree.

This summer Vicki planted a row of marigolds around the porch at the farm. Slugs soon attacked them. Knowing that slugs liked to eat mushrooms, Edward and Eliza took their beach buckets into the woody bog and picked several pounds of mushrooms. They piled the mushrooms around the marigolds, forming what they hoped would be delectable, distracting earthworks. Shrewder and maybe lazier, Francis refused to help, arguing that mushrooms would attract, not distract, slugs. The next morning proved Francis right; great battering rams of slugs beat paths through both the mushrooms and the marigolds. By the end of the week the marigolds were stalks. From their roots, however, grew "Slugamania" as Edward and Eliza started collecting slugs. Edward got up early the second morning in Annapolis Royal. When Vicki and I came into the breakfast room, he was waiting for us, in his hand his beach bucket filled with slugs, so many they resembled a bowl of shiny orange popcorn, a hundred and eight, he told us after he returned from dumping them behind the inn. In Wolfville he brought spiders to breakfast rather than slugs. He found them, he explained, on the porches and under the windows of the inn. Somebody, he said with disgust, had sprayed them with insecticide, and he wondered if the spiders would revive if he washed them in cold water. They didn't. Spiders and slugs were not our only small companions. A cloud of fruit flies accompanied us around the province. Concerned about Eliza's diet, we stopped at roadside stands and bought raspberries, cherries, blueberries, and peaches. Every morning after breakfast and each night before bed we ate fruit. The fruit probably did Vicki and me more good that it did the children. We also ate ice-cream cones whenever our energy ran low, at least two or three times a day. To elevate indulgence to science I studied the family's likes and dislikes. The favorite ice cream was Chocolate Supreme, a black blend of nuts and soft gobs of chocolate. Following close behind on the palate was Raspberry Cheesecake, black or red. Finishing at the other end of the table were Bubblegum and Gooey Chewy Candy Bar, this last damned as much by name as texture.

Like an invisible but heavy suitcase I carried the summer's doings with me on the trip. As soon as we reached an inn and unpacked the car, I tried to take a walk, much as I had done every day in Beaver River. Rarely does change of place alter vision. Accustomed to looking for birds and flowers, I saw birds and flowers. Although I visited forts and museums, I didn't really see them, their cannons smokeless in my imagination and their ships sinking through my consciousness without a ripple. At Fort Anne in Annapolis Royal I followed butterflies over the earthworks to butter-and-eggs, yarrow, knapweed, and Canada thistle. Behind a dike at the edge of the Allains River I saw a willet chase a marsh hawk. On top of the dike fireweed shredded into silky arches of white seed. Twice I wandered among the roses in the old gardens at Annapolis Royal. At midday the sunlight fell flat and hard, melting and thinning the colors. In the green of the evening the light stretched and cooled. Shadows spotted the roses, and colors and fragrances flowed about the plants, kinking and turning as the sun sank lower. At low tide in Wolfville I walked along the edge of the Minas Basin. Below the dike the mud was light brown, the small harbor itself a deep tub of buttercream. On the dike swallowtails hung on Queen Anne's lace, shaking in the wind like scraps of blue and black paper.

For me old graveyards resemble gardens, the weathered inscriptions flowers gone to stalk and seed, the fallen stones marking paths through feelings. In Annapolis Royal and Wolfville I roamed graveyards, plucking inscriptions. Hannah the "Relict of the late Rev. John Millidge" lived long, dying at ninety in 1869, and her tombstone declared simply, "The weary are at rest." Francis Lecain was eighty-four when he died in 1806. "He Liv'd Respected," the stone stated, "and Died Lemented." That, I thought, as I looked at the stone, a crack breaking across it like a root, is the inscription I'd like Vicki to put above me. "Farewell dear friends a short farewell," read George Johnson's stone in Wolfville, "We shall meet again above; / Where endless joys and pleasures dwell, / and trees of life bear fruits of love." In 1819 Armanilla Dewolf died at fifteen, and the carving on her marker stated a conventional warning: "Behold you youth's as you pass by, / As you are now so once was I; / As I am now soon you must be, / Prepare for death and follow me."

Graveyards are peaceful and reassuring, even happy, places. I like simple poetry and the signs of lives well spent. Under the great elms in Wolfville death was not frightening, and the warnings, despite being trite, made me think. Like a spiderweb, silver threads against the night, a child's life is fragile. Why, I wondered, as I bent over reading Armanilla's inscription, did parents ruin a child's present for a vague, improbable future. In pounding the little facts of manners and education into children parents often crushed joy. Would it not be better, I thought, to spend the money I saved for the children's futures on their nows. I did not linger in the graveyard in Wolfville. The elms and my ponderings were not the only things rising. From the grass mosquitoes swept upward in a ravenous fog, and I fled across Main Street to Acadia University and the lower, ephemeral world of pride. I went into Vaughan Library and looked through the card catalog to see how many of my books the university owned. Not one. Despite the boutiques, the restaurants, and the university itself, Wolfville, I quickly decided, was not so sophisticated as it first appeared. The Nova Scotia Liquor Commission was near the bay by the Dominion Atlantic Railway tracks. I walked there quickly and asked a question. Did they, I inquired, sell more wine or liquor. "Liquor," the clerk answered, "without a doubt." "Ah," I thought to myself, "one should not expect simple people to have literary taste. When Wolfville becomes truly cultured and wine outsells whiskey, then the university will own my books, probably even," I thought walking back to the inn, "probably even making them required reading."

Unlike small towns, which cling to recollection as moods, green and blue like the grassy battlements of Fort Anne against the sky, cities flatten out into streets. In a small town one rarely needs a map. In a city a map is a close companion, and for me Halifax is now a grid of names: Lower Water, Sackville, Argyle, Grafton, Market, Barrington, Morris, Dresden, and Spring Garden. Up from the grid rise buildings; in front of them cars jerk like knots in twine. The buildings are gray or red, and few have distinctive fronts. In one or two are restaurants. Because a small town has few restaurants to choose from, one does not spend time looking for a place to eat. In a city one searches almost, it seems, forever, reading menus and price lists in windows. During our three days in Halifax, a buskers festival took place. Small parks and street corners became one-ring circuses, featuring dancers, jugglers, puppeteers, and magicians. For the children the performers were, as Edward put it, "totally awesome." For me the entertainment

was at first fun then wearying. Of course hovering over the children I
had little time for awe. In fact *awe* is not a word I use any more.
Instead of helping one see things clearly, awe obscures, cloaking objects with distracting, often packaged, feeling. The ballets and operas
that years ago left me muttering about sublimity have drained from
memory, in part, I suspect, because I never looked at them closely or
critically. What I recall now are not high entertainments but low, the
buskers I saw perform when I traveled alone. In Fort Stockton, Texas,
I once went to a country-music show at the local high school. The
star was Ernie Ashworth. His most successful recording was a song
entitled "Trembling Lips." Ashworth appeared onstage in a yellow
cowboy outfit; on it were stitched luscious red lips outlined in se-
quins. For a moment Ashworth was still; then he grabbed the micro-
phone and began to sing, the lips on his clothes quivering like scarlet
pools.

   Our trip unsettled me slightly. Property in Nova Scotia is inexpen-
sive, and life in the province seems sensibly slow and decent, just the
place for a middle-aged man fond of flowers and worried about children. In Annapolis Royal the children would not grow wise too fast.
As I climbed the hills of Lunenburg and looked back over the harbor
to Kaulback Head, I imagined leaving Connecticut and moving to
Nova Scotia. That I was happy and comfortable in Storrs mattered
little. Every once in a while desire for difference surfaces in a man.
Usually it slips quietly by unnoticed, like a fox across a meadow at
dusk. Occasionally, though, it barks, breaking the still evening, bringing moving vans to a door and divorce to a family. In my case, though,
I didn't think long about moving to Nova Scotia. Almost like an
antidote Eliza took my hand as I turned to look at the Blue Rocks and
blurted, "I don't want you to go make those talks and speeches and
interviews because you go away lots of times, and I love you and we
have fun together." In Carthage, Turlow Gutheridge owned a nice
white house on Main Street. One hot summer, though, he dreamed
of moving, not to Nova Scotia, only to Alma Cave in the hills above
Carthage. When he told Boat Reddick, the local real-estate sales-
man, that he was thinking about selling his house, Boat advised him
to put a notice in the *Carthage Courier*. Explaining that he had experience with such things, Boat said he would write the advertisement. In
truth, Ceatrice, Boat's wife, the secretary of the Ladies' Home Book
Club, wrote all the advertisements. That night thunderstorms rolled

wet and cooling through Middle Tennessee, and the next morning, when Boat showed Turlow the ad, the air was light and full of the green smell of new rain. "Eight-room house," Boat read, "modern plumbing, good well, new tin roof, sidewalk to school and bank, ice company delivers, quiet neighbors, undertaker next door, well-manured strawberry patch, shady maples in yard, porch with hanging swing, beds of iris, trellis for morning glories, tobacco barn, pasture for horse, and carriage house." "Carriage house," Turlow said getting up to close the parlor window; "read that again." When Boat finished the second reading, Turlow looked thoughtful for a moment then said, "I've always wanted a carriage house, and here I've had one all along. Only I called it a shed. Boat," he continued, rubbing his jaw, "all my life I've dreamed of owning a house like that one. Strawberries and maples and swings, even a new tin roof. If I read that ad in the paper, I'd have to buy this house, and so to keep things simple, I guess I just won't sell."

From Lunenburg I drove to Yarmouth and we took the ferry back to Maine. The eight-day trip cost $1,717.42 American. We arrived home on August 16, the shoulder of the summer, that restful time after trips and before schools started. The grass had been mowed before we returned, and for a day or two I did little except answer mail and catch up on reading. Then I began to roam a bit. I discovered a toad in the garage and found skunk droppings near the back door—these last were half the length of my little finger and so black they seemed blue in the sunlight. I poked through them, pulling out wings and the hard shells of beetles. Early one morning I strolled down Hillside to the university and near the library picked a basket of crabapples. One Sunday I walked to the silverbell tree below the sheep barn. A young rabbit let me approach to within three feet. When he hopped away, he frightened grasshoppers, and two flew into the web of a black and yellow argiope. Over the hilltop goldenrod bloomed bold and yellow, so thick that it seemed a hedge. That Monday I bought Edward a bigger bicycle and put new tires on his old one for Eliza. After dinner the children rode about the campus. While they raced around Mirror Lake, Vicki and I sat on a bench feeding the ducks. Beneath loosestrife in the shallows a heron hunted carp. Overhead a kingfisher rattled, noisy and almost cross. On the small island near the spillway were cormorants and a pair of bitterns.

That night Eliza turned the upstairs hall into a sand dune. She put

on a pair of sunglasses from Pizza Hut, the frames triangles over each
eye, one yellow, the other red. Then she wrapped herself in an assortment of colorful silk scarves and, stretching out on a towel, looked
fruity and Brazilian, or so we said. While Francis hung scallop-shaped
earrings on her, Edward arranged seashells around the towel. What
floated ashore in the lazy hours of late August, however, were not only
crabapples and a little girl's dream of a bikini on a white beach, but
things that busier seasons washed out of mind. Not long before he
died Father reminded me that I had pets when I was young. "You
should," he said, "get those children a dog." In the bustle following
his death pets were far from my mind. Now, though, in the soft hours
of August, I thought about a dog. Out of curiosity and boredom I read
advertisements for dogs in the *Hartford Courant*. I had never heard of
some of the dogs: Shih Tzu, vizsla, and keeshond, for example. Much
as I rated the flavors of ice cream the children ate on the trip, so I
studied the popularity of dogs. In the *Hartford* the three most popular
breeds were rottweiler, German shepherd, and springer spaniel, not
dogs suitable for our family. Living in a small house with a modest
yard, we had to have a small dog. Moreover, because Edward and Eliza
suffer from asthma, our small dog had to be short-haired, probably, I
told Vicki, a dachshund, coincidentally the breed I had been raised
with.

Before taking the trip this summer Vicki and I talked about driving around Nova Scotia for five years. Vicki is deliberate, not impul-
sive, and when I began reading advertisements in the newspapers,
I assumed buying a dog would involve much discussion, probably
stretching through another five years. Still, I had August hours to fill,
and when Vicki went to the grocery or mall, I answered advertisements. The prices of dogs astonished me, six hundred dollars for a pet
and eight hundred and up for a show dog, one breeder said. For a
down payment of a hundred and fifty dollars, a man in Massachusetts
told me, I could reserve a puppy in a litter to be born in September.
The day before school started, Vicki took the children to Willimantic
to buy Edward soccer shoes, and I made my last telephone call. At
five-thirty that afternoon I was washing Georgie in a good strong flea
soap by the back door. The children chose the name; the spelling,
however, has not been settled. Vicki, as might be expected, prefers
Georgi. Although friends from childhood call me Sammy with a *y*, I

prefer Georgie with an *ie*. At five o'clock the next morning I walked Georgie. Ten minutes later the children joined me. At five-thirty Vicki appeared. At seven our next-door neighbor telephoned. "You have," she said, "a new dog."

Georgie is six weeks old and weighs four pounds four ounces. His coat is fawn, and a black streak runs from the back of his head to the tip of his tail, making him resemble an improbable, one-striped, low-slung zebra. He has sharp teeth and a busy, happy tail. He is a good country dachshund, raised far from coop and cage. I bought him twelve miles away in Lebanon. When I drove in the owner's driveway, she was waiting, smoking a cigarette. "Let them out," she shouted, and Georgie suddenly rolled up in a tumble of dogs and children and one poor, confused toad. Georgie thinks I am his littermate, and now, as I write, he lies sleeping in my lap. Puppyhood comes easier to George than it does to me. I suffer from the walking staggers and have my first fever blister in eight years. In a week Georgie has changed not only my writing habits but also my correspondence. Yesterday I received a letter from a noted student of early American furniture. Accompanying the letter was a newspaper clipping describing a food that supposedly renders dog droppings practically odorless. "Charles," I wrote back last night, "without the sweet aroma I'd never find the little fellows on the oriental rugs." Along with letters Georgie has affected my conversation, making it, I am afraid, more canine than usual. "If you will bring a stool sample," the veterinarian said when I made an appointment for Georgie's shots, "we will check it for parasites." "What," I yelped, "you want me to bring a handful of dog shit down there?"

After Georgie is housebroken, fragrances less domestic, those of skunks and flowers, will attract me once more. Then my conversation will lose its bark, and turning smoothly lavender will bumble with bees. Still, some things have changed. Dog days are not travel days. Vicki, the children, and I enjoyed the trip around Nova Scotia, so much so that we talked about spending a weekend on Cape Cod in October. Although I have lived in New England for over twenty years, I have never been to Cape Cod. In October, I am told, crowds are smaller and rates lower. I'd like to walk the beach and wander through old graveyards. Two days before Georgie appeared, I explored the grave-yard in Mansfield Center. In 1813 William Sheldon died just after his tenth birthday. "Stop blooming youth and mark how soon," the inscription on his tombstone read, "My voyage of life was oer. / Your sun, like mine, before tis noon / May set to rise no more."

Pets are less welcome at inns than children, and Georgie has put a sudden end to my voyages. Even if we found a place that would take all of us, Georgie has cost so much that we cannot afford a trip. I paid two hundred and fifty dollars for Georgie. On the way home we stopped at the pet store in East Brook Mall and spent $27.92 for food, a collar, a leash, a clear plastic bone, and a book called *Dachshunds*. Two days later Vicki bought a different dog food for $12.42. At Caldor she spent $7.64 for Georgie's toys: a pink rubber bone containing a bell, a small blue and red football, and a little rubber jogging shoe that squeaks when gnawed. For $5.00 at a tag sale she bought a used baby gate for the entry between the kitchen and dining room. Country dachshunds have strong jaws, and the gate lasted one night. Georgie's visit to the veterinarian cost $49.00: seven dollars for the "parasite examination," eighteen for a six months' supply of heartworm pills, and then twenty-four dollars for a distemper and parvo virus shot, the first of three batches of shots. Just now Vicki came home with a blue puppy basket covered with pink flowers and costing $21.99 and then for $4.26 a sixteen-ounce bottle of Four Paws "Stain and Odor Remover" guaranteed to clean fabrics, carpeting, tile, and linoleum. In a week I have spent $378.23 on Georgie: a long weekend on Cape Cod. By Christmas he will probably have cost a honeymoon in Acapulco or, more fittingly, since I don't plan to divorce Vicki and move to Nova Scotia, a trip to Disney World.

What Next

"Daddy," Edward asked at dinner, "have you ever seen a protomag?" "A what?" I answered, carefully spreading whipped cream over the last bit of plum cake on my plate, "a protomag? No, I don't think so." "I knew it. That's what I told Randy," Edward answered; "protomags aren't nice. They have pictures of naked people." You mean pornography, I thought, but before I could swallow the cake and answer Edward, Eliza spoke. "Daddy," she said, "I met a nice girl on the school bus today; she's just moved to Mansfield and is a little sad." "I'm sorry," I said, slicing another piece of Vicki's cake, "did she leave her friends behind?" "No, not her friends," Eliza answered, "her daddy. He's in jail, he robbed a bank, by accident." "Good Lord!" Vicki exclaimed, "what next"—a plum as big as a moon rolling off her fork and landing in the whipped cream with a soft, purple splat.

September had arrived. The long summer in which time eddied silently, rippling the hours like a breeze, was over. The year had narrowed, forcing life into a quick channel of clutter and event, attention hooking momentarily on school and soccer, ballet, piano, magazine, even telephone before being pulled loose to whirl rapidly on. "I'll eat that plum," I said to Vicki, reaching for the bowl of whipped cream. "By the way I read something amazing today. According to an article in *Connecticut Environment*, a skunk cabbage," I continued, spooning up the plum, "can live for more than a hundred years. How,

I wondered, could anyone be sure about a fact like that, so I called the author of the piece. 'If that is true,' I said to her, 'then I am going to stop washing, so I will stink and live forever.'" "What did she say?" Vicki asked. "Oh," I said, "only that my wife might object. But I fixed her. I told her." "That's enough cake," Vicki suddenly interrupted, getting up from the table and picking up the whipped cream, "you are all excused. And," she said, opening the icebox, "don't forget this is bath night."

I washed the children, and myself. The next morning I drove to Four Corners and bought a Stanley Wonder Bar at Willard's for $8.99. A foot long and shaped like an L, the bar was made from "forged tool steel" and with "beveled nail slots" was supposedly "ideal for pulling nails, prying, lifting, and scraping." Nine miles away in Hampton the Brewster House was for sale. Built in 1755 by John Brewster, a descendant of Elder Brewster who arrived on the *Mayflower*, the house exuded style and history. With wide floorboards, a beehive oven in the living room, five bedrooms upstairs, and a big rambling barn in back, the house appealed to me, and I considered buying it until my friend Josh said, "The house might suit your view of yourself, but Dr. Dardick's office is at Four Corners, and at fifty you have reached that happy age at which the sane man dares not live more than a mile from his doctor." Josh was right, and so instead of moving to Hampton and becoming Lord of the Manor, I bought the Wonder Bar and began ripping up wall-to-wall carpeting.

The carpeting was on the floors when we bought our house: green in the dining room, gray in the hall, and scarlet in the living room. Every September, Vicki and I discussed removing it. The snarls of the month, however, always snagged us, and I did not take out the carpet. Although the dining room was small, only twelve feet wide and thirteen feet long, the living room measured fourteen by twenty-five feet, and the hall snaked through the downstairs forming what was, in effect, four small rooms. Tearing up the carpet was difficult. Nailed to the floors along the walls was Roberts Smoothedge Carpet Gripper, thin strips of wood spiny with lines of upturned tacks. Pressed down upon the tacks, the carpet clung to the floor.

Once I pulled the carpet off the tacks, I pried the grippers from the floor. Almost always the grippers buckled and splintered, forcing me to wedge them up inch by inch. Stapled to the floor beneath the carpet were rubber mats. Tearing the mats up was easy. The staples, though, were a different matter. Some I pulled with pliers; others had to be wedged loose with a screwdriver. Scores snapped off in the floor and had to be coaxed up and then muscled free. After the carpets, mats, grippers, and staples were gone, I cleaned the floors, washing and sanding, then sanding and washing.

The chore took days. When I finished, cuts ran sharp like wire across my hands, and infections rose in mounds. Bits of wood and metal lay in the centers of the infections, turning the flesh red and proud like small volcanoes. Removing carpet is not a job for a Lord of the Manor. Along with hands my temper frayed. So that I would not, "by accident," say something regrettable to the children, I took walks before they arrived home from school. I did not go far, only through the backyard and then south along the cut under the power lines to the baseball field behind the high school. At the edge of the cut coral fungus grew in narrow orange clubs. Beside a tree was an old-man-of-the-woods mushroom, dingy white channels slicing through the brown cap like the teeth of a saw. Above the field sweet fern tattered and blew through the light like a wild salad. Beyond the outfield flowers bloomed in thick leggy bunches: Queen Anne's lace, butter-and-eggs; asters, blue, white, and pink; boneset, arrow-leaved tearthumb; evening primrose, bull thistle, and yellow sneezeweed. Near the creek south of the field were cattails, bullrushes, purple gerardia, wood sorrel, and nodding lady's tresses, these last delicately sweet like a mysterious dessert in an Indian restaurant. In the damp shade stood heavy shafts of white turtlehead, the petals tinged with pink and the stamens arched, making the inside of each blossom resemble a cathedral, marbled and white.

Behind third base goldenrod rose chest high, the blooms heavy and falling over each other, forming tall, airy, yellow pools. Around the edges of the pools individual plants slipped outward, their blossoms tumbling and rolling downward in bright streams. Over and through the goldenrod bees fell like leaves, mostly honey and bumblebees, though occasionally paper and golden digger wasps, even black-and-yellow mud daubers appeared. Above the flowers churned butterflies: sulphurs running in yellow streaks, whites twining upward in clotted pairs, and then monarchs, busy orange hands flapping in the wind. Through the grass behind the drainage ditch slipped a garter snake, its greens and yellows bright ribbons, binding the flowers into bouquets.

Although the goldenrod sang with life, summer was ending. The light had stretched and thinned, gliding pale through the woods and across the field. Color had leached out of the days, and leaves had begun curling. Suddenly insects were apparent, a small dung beetle, elegantly black, its back a ridged morning coat and its antennae rounded like tiny dark monocles. As leaves dried and sap began to run downward, spiders became visible, their nests conspicuously thick. Dragonflies slowed and stooping with the season flew sluggish and low to the ground. On goldenrod small purple blotches stood out like liver spots. Although the blotches first appeared flat, they were rounded. Inside each was a minute yellow egg. Under a leaf hid a marbled orb weaver, its orange and brown abdomen resembling a small wormy peach. A foot above the ground hung the white webs of black and yellow argiopes, garden spiders I called them as a boy. One day I found fourteen webs. Caught in three webs were red dragonflies. Suspended on the chain fence enclosing the outfield were eleven egg sacs, brown and as big as acorns, weathered like foul balls lost in high grass.

I roamed the field until classes started at the university. Often I sat longer than I walked. One day I popped the seeds of jewelweed. At a touch the pods exploded, thrusting out seeds with a snap. The insides of the pods then rolled quickly up and around like "Blowouts," the curled paper favors children puff at birthday parties. What I saw around the field stripped the musty carpeting from my mind, and after a walk, I felt clean. Always I took something home to show the children: the chocolate seeds of blue flag, or a thin green caterpillar, so marked with black that it resembled a splotched, parasitized blade of lance-leaved goldenrod.

After classes started, I continued walking, in part to avoid Josh and the impatient cynicism of middle age. The morning before classes began Josh dropped by my office to ask about the rugs. "By the by," he said, "I have seen the sunshine. No longer do I refer to religious affiliations or national and ethnic backgrounds. If I go to a restaurant and find it filled with one of those groups, I say, 'My goodness, aren't there a lot of trees in here.'" "What?" I said. "Trees," Josh explained, "don't you understand: walnut, cedar, cottonwood, chinquapin. Of course," he continued, "like a good forest ranger I know the land. All eastern Europeans, for example, belong to the same family." "Sure, the Slavs," I said. "No, you damn fool," he shouted, "the hickory: shagbark, pignut, butternut, shellbark, and mockernut. Despite sharing a common taproot the trees have uprooted each other's saplings for years." Then he slapped his knee and before I could interrupt rushed ahead, "I have a forest of hornbeam and hackberry jokes. Do you know how many hornbeams it takes to change a light bulb? Of course," he went rapidly on, "no one wants to be thought prejudiced and so I have advised the pinyons and mesquites not to call anyone a beech. One of the limp-twigged weeping willows around campus might mistake the horticultural for the canine." "Josh," I broke in, beginning to perspire and thinking to change the subject, "how was your vacation at Disney World?" "Blighted," he practically shouted, slapping his leg again, "too damn many papayas and palmettos."

"Josh, calm down," I said, getting up to shut the door, "aren't there any people, rather trees, that you like?" "Of course," he answered, "maples, elms, and oaks, though even with them you have to be careful. Never turn your back on a blackjack oak or lend money or a sister to a slippery elm. Most maples," he said, pausing and looking thoughtful for a moment, "are heartwood, though to tell the truth I am tired of bigtooth maples with their queens and princes, their nasal accents and wooden ha-ha smiles. Look Sam," he continued, staring at the closed door, "you don't have to be ashamed of me. Talking to me isn't going to compromise your reputation as a sweet nature boy, lover of people and brambles. I'm not biased. Some of my best friends are ginkgoes, and I have nothing against the average mulberry, though I wouldn't want any planted in the vacant lot down the street. Doesn't it sometimes," he asked, "get under your bark when soapberries knock at your door and try to sell *The Firetower*? What do you think about madders rolling around and chucking rattlesnakes at each other? Or the loblollies with all those elders and their Grove Choir? Even a low-church magnolia like you must occasionally think about clearing away the scrub and brush so that hardwood can thrive."

Josh doesn't talk; he harangues and rarely gives me a chance to speak, which, considering the thickets he chops into, is probably for the better. "Well, Sam," he forged on, "shed your leaves and look beyond the hedge. Can you name a sassafras who makes house calls?

Don't most fringe trees drive old Volkswagen beetles with bumper stickers saying 'Save the Sequoias'? What do you think about ambulance-chasing smoke trees and those fat cashews at the Bank of New England? For my part I would like to slash and burn through the Pentagon, felling all those dahoons and thick mahoganies who went to West Point. On their stumps I'd graft apple and peach, olive and silverbell. Don't you get tired of old possumhaw forever rocking on his front porch in the Blue Ridge or hunkering down in the cotton and boring everybody's limbs off with his stories about Cousin Jethro and Aunt Maybelle and then cretinous drupes named Googoo and Loppie? Well, enough," he said, suddenly standing up and opening the door; "time to go. I am having lunch with a budding little redbud. She is a bit of a conehead, but what the hell. I'm not taking her out to talk about phellem and cambium, am I? Anyway old trunk, avoid grass willows, and," he added, stepping out into the hall, "don't take any wooden nickels."

Josh's visits are strenuous and disturbing, more so than tearing up carpeting. Rarely does Josh appear, however, when school is not in session, and so I have learned to avoid him. He does not bother me if I take walks, and this fall I scheduled my classes in the agricultural school. Because one class ended at twelve-thirty and the next began at two o'clock, I had an hour and a half for walking. I wore a coat and tie to the first class. After class I changed clothes in the men's bathroom in the Ratcliffe Hicks building, putting on blue jeans, a sweatshirt, and boots. I did not change until after twelve-thirty classes began and the bathroom was empty. Josh was right. I care about my reputation, and if a student found me naked in the bathroom, a misunderstanding could have occurred. Indeed I undressed and then dressed in great haste because earlier this fall I called the men's locker room in the gymnasium "The Greater Storrs Bathhouse," a label which, I later heard, raised not only eyebrows but an untoward speculation or two.

All my noonday walks were similar. I followed the dirt road up the south side of Horsebarn Hill. At the top I turned north and walked beside the corn to Bean Hill. I crossed the paved road behind the chicken houses and then circled the field on the eastern slope of Bean Hill before returning to Ratcliffe Hicks. On the way back to class I usually climbed the fence surrounding the low pasture behind the dairy barn and poked about in the marsh. I spent much time on Horsebarn Hill itself. Resembling slivers of green Lifesavers, northern corn rootworm beetles fed on corn tassels early in September. Later in the month the beetles left the corn, moving to goldenrod by the fence. On the southeast side of the hill smut infected much corn. Resembling brown, partially burned torches, the smuts were homes to earwigs, and in damper, bigger smuts, I often counted more than twenty. Because the upper surface of corn leaves is hairy and roughly abrasive, I usually walked along the edge of the field, not between the rows of corn. In fact the corn turned my attention to other leaves, and often I examined the leaves of wildflowers more carefully than I did the blossoms. Despite having written about the seed disks of velvetleaf, I had never noticed the smooth, cool texture of the plant's leaves. In the past jimsonweed's pink trumpet-shaped flowers made me imagine warm music. Thick and coldly moist, the leaves smack not of high, cottony notes, but of wet dells and deep, dank coughs.

Around the borders of the fields—beside fences and ditches and at the edge of the woods—life was more various than in the fields themselves. In corn furrows only velvetleaf and green amaranth thrived. Along the fence grew gardens of wildflowers: yellow mustard, deptford pink, fall dandelion, fleabane, and chicory, the blossoms of these last blue fall curtains, rippled and running. Above a drainage ditch smooth bromegrass rustled silver in the wind. Near a pile of barn soil, pale smartweed stood seven feet tall, the nodes from which leaves branched out of the stem swollen and resembling small beets, the flowers at the top of the plant clustering and then tumbling downward in a fall of pink locks. Over a pasture a flock of starlings rose and fell, black ashes caught in a swirl of sunlight. At the edge of the marsh crows hunted through the grass; overhead a sharp-shinned hawk rode the air, flapping its wings rapidly then swooping to glide, then flapping aloft. On the south side of Horsebarn Hill a groundhog ate alfalfa, the wind pushing gray waves through his fur. Disturbed while dozing in the sun, a red fox bounded down the path behind Bean Hill.

On the edge of things life was richer and better than in the center or in cities. I enjoyed seeing thrushes and sparrows more than I did listening to Josh's arguments. Although my observations were soft, indeed sentimental, they were not brittle like Josh's strength. In fact as I walked, I often thought of possumhaw's country characters.

Although not intelligent, they were gentle folks, and a visit with them, unlike a conversation with Josh, turned me into a conservationist, a cultivator of all trees: sumac and buckthorn as well as sweet gum and ash. When Turlow Gutheridge met Loppie Groat in Read's Drugstore in Carthage, he asked about Loppie's neighbor Hoben Donkin. Hoben had caught the influenza and lost flesh. "Loppie," Turlow said, "how is Hoben doing?" "Poor Hoben," Loppie answered, "I'm afraid he is heading for the sheltering rock." "What! Is he dying?" Turlow said; "I thought Dr. Sollows fixed him up." "Oh the flu is gone, but Hoben is so skinny," Loppie said, shaking his head, then adding in explanation, "you're skinny, and I'm skinny, but Hoben is skinnier than both of us put together." Hoben had wasted away, and two weeks later at his funeral, the small talk naturally ran to weight. "Yes," Goo-goo Hooberry said to Loppie, "Hoben was monstrously thin, but that ain't nothing much. Lots of folks are thin when they die. What's really amazing is that my father, Mr. G.G., only weighed three and a half pounds when he was born." "Great God Almighty! I never heard of such a thing," Loppie exclaimed; "did he live?"

In August, five months after Hoben's death, the Democrats gathered at Red Boiling Springs for their annual convention. Coker Knox came over from Nashville, and despite not being nominated for lieutenant governor, Squirrel Tomkins took the train up from Hardeman County. Although the Grand was still dirty and the conventioneers were the same in character, if not always in name, as in years past, some delegates thought they, personally, had changed. During the winter Coker Knox took a course in poetry at the YMCA Night School on Church Street, and now considered himself sensitive and poetic. Disappointed at not being chosen to run for high office, Squirrel Tomkins had gone on the wagon. Early the first morning of the convention, Coker and Squirrel met in the bathroom on the second floor of the Grand. "Ah, Nature is a real artist," Coker said, shooing the flies away with his right hand and then waxing poetic. "The sunrise obstetric," he hymned; "the lambent flame of life skipping odalisque over the bosom of the world, the wild wood grape gleaming through the grove dappled with waves of dew, the azure breeze soothing the slumber of the weary marsupial, the velveted reveler murmuring above the festal dainties of the woodland board, our feathered friends warbling their sonorous notes vermilion and crepuscular, the bosky tortoise munching the ruddy nightshade, the brown cow letting down her milk, the downy chicks hopping from under the incubator to seek a better worm. Squirrel, my dear, dear Squirrel," Coker said, "have you never stood bareheaded before the rising sun and had such thoughts?" "Not," Squirrel said, turning back from the wall and fastening a last button or two, "not since I stopped drinking."

Not only does walking make my days brighter and gentler, but it also makes me more observant. On the nightshade by the side door I found a tobacco hornworm. Fatter than my index finger, the worm was three and three-quarter inches long and five-eighths of an inch "tall." For days the children and I watched it eat through the tomatoes. Then one Sunday it was gone, probably to spin a cocoon and spend the cold winter safely out of sight. That afternoon we went to a christening in Manchester. Several children were baptized, and while the priest sprinkled their brows with holy water, I read the church bulletin. Local businesses paid the printing costs, and the last page of the bulletin contained their advertisements. Both businesses and advertisements were commonplace, urging parishioners to patronize video stores, florists, plumbers, pizza restaurants, service stations, and barbershops. One advertisement, however, caught my eye. At 219 West Center Street, the John F. Tierney Funeral Home was, the advertisement stated, "conveniently located." Convenient for whom, I thought—God, the deceased, his family? Convenience was not something dead people usually thought much about. Generally, or so I have been told, thoughts about the temperature of their new abodes, whether or not they would need electric blankets, occupied their minds. Maybe, I pondered, the funeral home was near a golf course, and between visiting hours and the burying, sad widows could nip out and squeeze in a quick back nine. For corpses who had lost so much weight that their best clothes didn't fit, a haberdasher would be convenient. Perhaps a lawyer was around the corner. Certainly the wills of dearly beloveds often needed tidying up. The advertisement intrigued me, and the christening rushed by quickly. Not able to read so well as I do, Edward, in contrast, found the ceremony boring. "Edward," I said to Vicki when we were outside the church, "had the wiggle warts." Before Vicki answered, Eliza spoke. "So did I," she said; "I was just damn tired of the whole thing."

Although I usually walked alone, walking brought me closer to

people and community, real people, too, neighbors, not fictional country characters. After learning that Neil bought a red pickup truck in
Maine this summer, I telephoned him. Neil bought the truck from a
carpenter. "I rescued it from a life of toil," he said, "turning it into a
gentleman's truck." "Gentleman!" I exclaimed, "With those two old
cars of yours and now this truck, all you need is a case of beer cans
scattered around the front yard and a couple of flat chickens out front
on the road." On my asking if he had bought big tires and hung a gun
rack in the back window, Neil said that he wanted to knock a hole in
the muffler first, adding that for Christmas he'd like me to give him a
license plate with "I Love My Truck" stamped across a big red heart.
Presents should be surprises. In the church bulletin was an advertisement for a shop selling accessories for cars. Deciding to obey ecclesiastical instruction and "Patronize Our Advertisers," I drove to East
Hartford and bought Neil a bumper sticker, reading "Guns, God, and
Glory. Let's Keep All Three."

The immediate future or what next is usually a continuation of
the past and present. In August, I bought a dachshund puppy for the
children. Although the children romp about the yard with Georgie
after school, I am his littermate, in charge of food, scratching, and
housebreaking. After I bought Georgie, Eliza told me she preferred
poodles. "Poodles," she explained, "just walk around and be elegant,"
adding that she wanted two, a gray and purple one and a pink and
white one. From hindsight Georgie's becoming my dog appears to
have been almost inevitable. In fact I ought to give Neil a puppy for
Christmas. Dogs are good companions for middle-aged men. Unlike
wives and children, dogs need us. Rarely are they ashamed of us, and
they like us around the house. Even better they don't find our affec-
tions inconvenient. Of course a dachshund would not do for Neil. He
needs a truck dog, a big-jawed, black mongrel, maybe a cross between
a doberman and a German shepherd, a dog that can wear a "Forget
Hell" Confederate license plate with impunity.

Much as it was inevitable that Georgie would become my dog, so it
was certain I would buy a dachshund. For me Georgie was not unique.
He was another dog in a pack of dachshunds, to be sure a pack scattered by a twenty-year gap, but a pack nonetheless. For that matter
the doings of twenty or thirty years ago seem but yesterday, or at least
such doings as I remember seem more in the present than in the past:

Mother's sticking her tongue out at Heinzie, then Heinzie's getting up and trotting out of the room, a disgusted expression on her face. When Pup Pup ate spoiled meat, the veterinarian pumped his stomach and sent him home, telling Father he would be fine. That night I dreamed about the dogs. When I called, Heinzie came running. Although I searched for Pup Pup, I could not find him. Early the next morning Father came into my bedroom. "Sammy," he began. "Daddy," I interrupted; "you don't have to tell me. Pup Pup is dead." Fritzie was born in the garage and for eighteen years was my dog. Strangely I don't remember much about him; perhaps I recall little because he was with me so much. What I do remember is the odd occurrence, the time, for example, when Fritzie and I wrestled on the floor in the living room. Somehow Fritzie became excited, and when he tried to bound over my head, his penis jammed into my ear. Fritzie's jump collapsed in midair. Yelping, he rolled to the floor and then gathering himself, tail and nothing else noticeable between his legs, scurried away to his box in the pantry.

Once school began this fall, I received mail from teachers. A woman wrote that she was intrigued by my being the source of the Keating character in *Dead Poets Society*, adding, "If you are at all interested in corresponding with a purported dead poet and teacher of the semi-living, you can reach me at the address at the top of this page." My children, I replied, drained excess words from me. Besides, I added, I lived a simple life, one cluttered with small niceties, things that made days bloom but that blighted letters. From Atlanta the editor of an educational magazine wrote, asking me to write an essay on "what and why you read to your children." For the past four and a half years I have read to the children for at least thirty minutes and, more often than not, an hour a day. I have read through libraries: shelves of fairy tales, Homer, Tolkein, C. S. Lewis, and George MacDonald. I am not, however, sure why I read. In part I do it because I like stories. Also I am conventional, and can rarely think of anything besides reading to do with the children. Since I have a bad back, I cannot play athletics with them. And, of course, I read to keep the children from fighting. When I read, they don't quarrel, and the house is peaceful. Lastly, since Vicki and I rarely go out at night, my evenings are free. Because I know that I will say foolish things that I will later regret, I refuse invitations to dinner. At a word, conversation can

suddenly wash through restraint and become unpredictable and disturbing, even frightening. In contrast the rigid page and shaped tale
are relaxing and consoling. A book provides not only the illusion of
ordering chaos but actual order itself. With attention focused on the
printed word, I have both conversation and thought under control.

The truth is often too mundane for an article. I knew the editor
wanted an instructive or inspirational essay. Behind her request lay
the assumption that reading to children is educationally, probably
spiritually, beneficial. Georgie is the only purebred in my house. Vicki
and I are mongrels. Yet, like many parents, we once wanted registered
offspring. Whatever effects reading has, if it has effects, are mysterious, and vary from person to person. A mulch of books will not
produce seedless blackberries or gifted children. If the goal of education is to rear better, sweeter people, grafting the enjoyment of reading on a child may weaken rather than strengthen the stock. Books
are fun, so much so they are opiates. For me love of people is more
important than love of books. Could reading someday, I wondered,
appeal to my children more than people? When the boys become
men, I want wives, not books, to fill their arms. Around Eliza, I hope
children will bloom like flowers, not cultivated flowers either, but the
ordinary wildflowers of baseball field and Horsebarn Hill, milkweed
and fleabane, thistle and boneset, amaranth and velvetleaf.

Unable to justify my reading to the children, I did not write the
essay. Explaining the reasons for my refusal would have taken much
time, and so instead I included a short tale in my letter to the editor.
Except for entertaining, the tale had nothing to do with childhood
reading. I thought the tale, though, would make the editor smile.
Humor disarms criticism, and once she smiled, she probably would
not dismiss me as an educational or philosophic lightweight. After
deciding to build a brass foundry in Red Boiling Springs, Venican
Quickfall, I wrote, stayed twelve days in the Grand Hotel. To impress
local people he traveled over from Memphis in a private railway car.
During the twelve days he entertained and spent lavishly. One Sunday he attended Slubey Garts's Tabernacle of Love in South Carthage.
At the end of the service he strode conspicuously up to the pulpit and
shook Slubey's hand. "Reverend," he said loudly, "you preached a
damn fine sermon." Venican's lordly manner and patronizing tone
irritated Slubey. "I don't know who you are or where you come from,"

Slubey said, "but I want to tell you right now we don't take kindly to cussing in this church." "Don't get your blood pressure up, Reverend," Venican answered, patting Slubey familiarly on the back, "you preached such a good sermon that I put a hundred dollar bill in the collection plate." "The hell you did!" Slubey exclaimed, grabbing the plate and looking in and seeing the bill, "Damn if you didn't!"

I soon forgot the essay on reading. Something else came up. In a family something else always comes up. While cleaning the boys' room, I found a torn strip of cardboard. On it Francis wrote, "I was crying at the piano because I thought I was too fat and thought that I would get too, too, too, too, too, too fat and thought I would get so fat so fast I would never be able to get thinner." From the battered condition of the cardboard, the faded writing, and the poor sentence structure, I could tell Francis wrote the statement two years ago, back, alas, when he was pudgy and Vicki and I playfully dubbed him "Portly." As I read the cardboard, I wondered what we had accidentally wrought. Now Francis is too thin. In the town library he studies health magazines and reads articles on diet. He won't drink sodas or eat fried foods and sugary desserts. Rarely does he touch meat. When he walks, he sucks in his stomach so that his trousers hang loosely on his hips. At night he examines himself in the mirror and pulls at his hips, checking for fat. I am thankful that Francis is healthy, but I know that a nine year old should not be so concerned about weight. If lighthearted, indeed loving, playfulness can be so misunderstood, how could anyone, much less me, presume to know how reading affects children?

Of course Francis's eating is just one of the things bothering me. I also worry about money. When my father came to Connecticut in February, I put his condominium up for sale. Father paid one hundred and eighty-five thousand dollars for it three and a half years ago. I asked one hundred and thirty-five thousand. Eight months have passed, and the condominium has not sold. Each month I pay $616.35 in fees and taxes, money that I would rather spend on the children. Despite their not being up to American Kennel Club standards, I want the children to have blue-ribbon opportunities. To earn show fees I lecture. Two weeks ago in Pittsburgh I earned a year of piano lessons for both Vicki and Francis. Despite the work the trips often exhilarate me. On arriving in Pittsburgh I went to the public radio station to be interviewed about my books. The interviewer was Fred

Rogers. I would not cross Hillside Circle to meet the president of the United States. For Mr. Rogers not only would I cross the street but I would write an essay on reading to children. Almost every afternoon and many mornings for nine years, he and his neighbors have been guests in my house. Being in his real neighborhood in Pittsburgh flustered me, and during the interview I was practically incoherent. For Mr. Rogers the interview must have been a failure. For me it was a great success. At the end of the interview I asked Mr. Rogers to introduce me to King Friday. Not only did King Friday grant me an audience, but Lady Elaine Fairchild deigned to greet me. Later I shook paws with Daniel Tiger and Mr. McFeely gave me a Speedy Delivery bag for Eliza to take to show-and-tell. Eliza was not the only Pickering to receive a present. I left the station with a rack of T-shirts for Vicki and the boys. Some depicted the neighborhood trolley in red, yellow, and blue; the others, Mr. Rogers wearing a striped red tie and a blue cardigan sweater. Under him is written "You Are Special."

One year several Republicans were elected to office in Carthage and Red Boiling Springs. As might be expected the state legislature then decided not to appropriate money to repair roads in Smith County. For years Loppie Groat worked summers on the highway with Jeddry, his mule. Out of work because of the elections, Loppie went to see Turlow Gutheridge in hopes that Turlow could find him a job. "Loppie, this ought not to be difficult," Turlow began; "can you read writing?" "Read writing," Loppie answered, shaking his head, "I can't even read reading." Occasionally I wish I could not read reading. Reporters often attend my lectures and interview me. Sometimes what appears in a newspaper differs greatly from what I said. In Pittsburgh a reporter asked me if there was a practical reason for studying poetry in college. "No," I answered, "poetry isn't a practical subject. A person doesn't study poetry to learn how to build bridges. Poetry is above the merely practical," I continued; "it can change lives." Two days later the reporter's account appeared under the headline "Dead Poets Inspirer Hits Poetry." I said, the article stated, that poetry was impractical and as a result colleges should not teach courses in poetry. Actually most reporting is fairly accurate. The next week in Fayetteville, Arkansas, my comments were reported correctly. "The University of Arkansas," I said, "has a fine English department, and the press has become distinguished. Despite having a big-time athletic program, the university is good."

Whether one is quoted correctly or incorrectly is, of course, unimportant. What matters is the clutter of life, the what next of which newspaper articles are a small part. Yesterday I planted sixty-three daffodils: three palmyras and then a dozen each of five other varieties, confection, chamois, snow gem, bookmark, and Sacramento. At eight-thirty this morning Neil came over, and we filled his truck with carpeting and drove it to the dump. On Friday I fly to Tennessee to earn ballet, swimming, and ice hockey lessons. This past Sunday I talked to a seventy-three-year-old woman who takes care of her ninety-six-year-old mother. "How are you getting along?" I asked, knowing that her mother was failing and that she herself had recently been ill. For a moment the line was silent. Then the woman said, "The walls move in." Occasionally the insignificant what next of my days tires me. But, oh, how thankful I am for the clutter. Under the strain of family and tale the walls about me bow outward, bulge obstetric as Coker Knox would put it in a poem—or, as I might think on a walk, swell green and yellow like Horsebarn Hill, the corn thick on the top, the goldenrod tumbling over the fence, and my happiness soaring, a hawk light in the blue wind.

Shopping

In October, I spoke at a book festival in Tennessee. Although speeches oil the Plymouth and send the boys to camp, leaving home makes me feel guilty, and so whenever I travel, I buy presents for Vicki and the children. Satisfied by sweatshirts decorated with pudgy sailors or razorback hogs, the children are easy to please. Vicki is difficult. Little I buy appeals to her, and when I shop for her, gloom rumples about me like a rain cloud. Occasionally, though, sunlight falls unexpectedly upon a store; the cloud blows away, and mockingbirds rise from the grass singing. In Tennessee, I suddenly found myself outside Victoria's Secret. "Your Favorite Panties—Four Dollars" declared a sign in the window. For a moment I hesitated by the door. If I bought underpants for Vicki, would people in the store, I wondered, think I was buying for myself? "What the hell," I finally muttered, stepping inside, "so what if I treat myself to a lacy little present." My panties were boring, boxer shorts in the morning, boxer shorts in the evening, boxer shorts on Christmas, boxer shorts even on my birthday. "The real man," I decided, "buys whatever he wants and wears it when he damn well pleases."

The store resembled a hothouse. Potpourri curled through the air, one moment jasmine, the next lavender. On the wallpaper bouquets of small pastel flowers bloomed in furrows, while on the rug roses pouted, red but thornless. Despite my brief hankering for foundation

162

garments frilly, I am a conventional, daffodil-bulb sort of guy. Once inside the store I forgot my underpants and began rooting through panties for Vicki. The petals on some were furry; on others they were tattered, full of holes, almost as if they had bloomed too early and been shredded by a March wind. On others beads circled the stems looking like white drops of dew. Plucking pair after pair from the drawers, I became indecisive and would have left without a present if another customer had not helped me. "I just love these things," a forty year old woman said, stepping in front of me and picking up a minute red and purple handkerchief sort of arrangement. "They really look good on the floor," she said, handing them to me; "they are you." I, they might have been. Vicki, alas, they were not. That night at home Vicki declined to model them. Eliza, however, thought they were dashing, and after putting them on and looking at herself in the mirror asked if she could take them to kindergarten for show-and-tell. What a wonderful idea, I thought. The gap between words and thought is often vast, however. "No, Eliza," I said frowning, "young ladies do not show people their underpants." In a few years, I suspect, Eliza will buy wardrobes at Victoria's Secret. One afternoon when she was three, she said, "Daddy, I'm not going to marry one man. One is not enough. I'm going to marry six hundred."

Shopping resembles exploring. Although a trip is often mapped out beforehand, one is never sure what he will discover, or, for that matter, what will discover him. When I walked out of Victoria's Secret, a policeman approached me. He heard me speak at the festival and said he had just finished his autobiography. Would I, he asked, look at the letter that he planned to send to publishers asking if they would be interested in reading the manuscript. Of course, I answered, taking the letter from him. "I joined the Highway Patrol," the first sentence read, "to help God in his fight against Satan." Although God has always needed help against the Devil, the battle may be over. Perhaps the best our God can hope for is a dusty shelf in the basement of the Smithsonian or a quiet retirement in Florida: shuffleboard, martinis at sunset, and the memory of better days. I almost told the policeman that I admired him for fighting the good fight, but I am one of those people who cannot rise up, as the hymn puts it, and have done with lesser things. Instead, I thought, "Jesus, I'd hate for this man to stop me for speeding."

After revising the policeman's letter, I drifted into a shoe store. Bostonians, which usually cost one hundred and twenty dollars, were on sale for ninety-six dollars a pair. I didn't buy any. In the store I met a boyhood friend, now a criminal lawyer. We sat in a still corner far from the fret of commerce and chatted, first remembering sunny school days of football and debate team, then discussing our children, the conversation clouding and becoming slightly threatening but still remaining warm and optimistic. Finally dark mortality lowered over us, and we talked about the deaths of our fathers. "Lionel," I asked, "did many of your clients write when your daddy died?" "Sam," he said, "I got letters from every prison in the South. The most memorable," he continued, pausing and shaking his head, "came from Bushy Mountain right here in Tennessee. 'Dear Mr. Browning,' the letter began, 'I read in the newspaper about the death of your father, and I write to say how sorry I am for your bereavement. Having recently lost a parent of my own, I can sympathize.'" Lionel rubbed his hands across his knees, gathered himself, then continued, "Lost a parent of his own! Lord God, yes! The man was in prison for killing his mother. Shot her three times in the back with a hunting rifle."

Shopping gives one an excuse to roam. Late last Friday, Vicki rushed out to buy an eight-pound bag of Eukanuba dog food costing eleven and a half dollars. Two hours later she returned with a VCR that cost $248.39. "Waldbaum's was out of Eukanuba," she explained, "so I wandered around the mall. The VCR was on sale, and I bought it." That night the children watched *The Black Stallion*; Saturday they watched *The Black Stallion Returns*, and then on Sunday a film about a talking Volkswagen named Herbie. Movies do not appeal to me, but wandering does. In November, I spent two days in Portsmouth, New Hampshire. To find Vicki a present, I got up early the second morning and explored the town. It was a stainless-steel day, polished and sharp. The light was glazed, falling in hard tines through a rack of thin, high clouds. Along the shore the Piscataqua River ran in icy slivers toward the land. In contrast the town seemed warm. Having aged out of edges into softness, bricks on old buildings resembled bits of orange taffy, and the names of streets seemed domestic and familiar: Ceres, Bow, Daniel, Market, and Pleasant. At Market Square a steeplejack painted the tower of the North Church. Beside the river were red hills of scrap iron, individual bundles looking like rusty suitcases. Docked at Granite State Minerals was the *Bright Evelyn*, a freighter flying the Cypriot flag but coming from Mexico, its hold loaded with salt for winter roads. Tied to a wharf were three tugboats, the heavy tires on their bows making them seem children's toys, pug-nosed and friendly. I roamed the streets for two and a half hours, ambling through stores with names like Salamandra, Jester's, Gallery 33, The Doll Connection, Moods, Cobblestones, Wholly Macrol, and The Paper Patch. Outside The Tub Shop I paused. "Hot tubs for rent," a sign on the door stated. What people, I wondered, rented hot tubs? Probably people who slept on waterbeds, I decided, not my kind in any case. After walking for an hour, I stopped for a snack, not a homey sandwich at Woody's Restaurant, Goldi's Deli, or Emilio's Foods, but a chocolate croissant at the Café Brioche. Eventually I found Vicki a present, a small basket made from spruce and cedar roots, birchbark, and sweet grass. The basket cost sixty dollars, and when Vicki discovered the price in the checkbook, she exclaimed, "They've got some nerve charging that. Twenty-four would have been highway robbery."

A really different gift might have pleased Vicki. Buying some-thing unique in a tourist town, even a nice one like Portsmouth, is almost impossible. If Mother Noon still operated Noonday, a store in Beaver River, less than a mile from our farm in Nova Scotia, find-ing an extraordinary present would be easy—maybe too easy, how-ever, now that I think about Mother Noon's stock of herbs and nos-trums. Baskets swung from rafters, and pots, boxes, and jars jumbled together throughout the store. On the counter was a flat box contain-ing necklaces of amber beads. If a baby slept in one of the necklaces, fairies, Mother Noon assured new parents, could not steal him and substitute a changeling in his place. Atop the box was a pot of dried moles' feet. To prevent teething pains Mother Noon recommended tying a mole's foot around a child's neck. For nosebleed she suggested snuffing the spores from puffballs, and on the counter kept a jar of them. At first glance they resembled big chocolate truffles, and mis-taking them for candy Otis Blankinchip bought one as a present for Bertha Shifney. In a blue cabinet stood a line of bottles, each contain-ing a salve: red mud for freckles, milkweed juice for warts, and for piles leaves from jimsonweed crushed in lard. On a hook behind the back door hung red onions, useful in bringing on labor. For palsy

Mother Noon sold nerve-root, roots of lady's slippers washed in stump water. Beside the door was a basket of cat tails, all supposedly from black cats. Tied around the waist they cured shingles. Bertha Shifney bought two, but they did not help her much, in part, Otis Blankinchip said, because one of the tails was dyed, originally coming from a yellow, not a black, cat. "A green winter," Mother Noon said, "brings a fat graveyard," and she carried several preventatives for spring fever: the juice of fireweed, strings of buzzard feathers, and grasshoppers dried, then powdered and stirred into Flower Honey. For that other spring fever, the one effecting heart not body, she kept snails in damp moss. She told girls who wanted to know the names of their next sweethearts to sprinkle meal on the kitchen floor and to turn a handful of snails loose in the kitchen. As high wasps' nests were a sure sign of a wet summer, so the snails, Mother Noon assured young customers, would always trace lovers' initials in the meal. The more I think about it, though, the less certain I am that Mother Noon's exotica would please Vicki. For medicines Vicki shops at Storrs Drugs, taking the advice of Dr. Dardick, not a country herbalist. Moreover, the only cattails in our house were plucked from the marsh behind the high school baseball field, not from the bottoms of cats. Insofar as spring fever is concerned, Vicki is a well-mannered matron with three children—beyond, I trust, curiosity about either love or sweethearts.

Every day, of course, is potentially a department store of event. For a browser the commodities of daily living are endlessly various. "Ethnicity is canceled for today, November 14" stated a notice in the Humanities Building at the University of Connecticut. Would that ethnicity could be canceled forever, I thought as I read the notice, then we could be people instead of races and nationalities. Three weeks ago Vicki cooked rabbit for dinner, the only time she has ever cooked rabbit. Basted with a sauce made from orange and rosemary, the meat was fragrant and buttery. Unfortunately Vicki did not know I was reading Richard Adams's rabbit epic *Watership Down* to the children at bedtime. With Holly and Hazel, Fivver, Bigwig, and Strawberry hopping through our dreams, neither the children nor I had an appetite for rabbit.

On Thursday nights I attend school-board meetings at town hall. Although not so various as the goods in Noonday, discussions at the meeting are almost as entertaining and certainly as quirky. Because tax revenues have decreased and expenses for oil and then benefits for teachers have increased, the board must cut the budget. To save money we have talked about jettisoning programs for "gifted" children. At the board meeting last week a parent urged us to keep the programs, arguing that gifted children needed to be challenged. If they were not, she said, their creativity would be stifled and they could become bored and lose interest in school. "My dear woman," Josh said when she finished speaking, "don't you realize that coping with boredom is the greatest challenge of life. Boredom doesn't stifle; it fosters creativity. If we were really committed to challenging students, we would stop entertaining them and start boring the hell out of them. If we did so, in a few years perhaps we would have schools full of Einsteins and Shakespeares. At the least we would have prepared students for life, most of which is unendingly, reassuringly boring." More startling than pleasant, Josh is not a comfortable acquaintance. Occasionally, though, he is almost original. "Sam," he said rushing into my office four days ago, "recently I have thought a lot about basketball." Josh holds athletics in great contempt, and for a moment I thought he had lost his mind. "With goals at the opposite ends of the playing arena," he continued, seeing he had caught my attention, "the game is ludicrously inefficient. The goals should be side by side. That way contestants would not have to jog about so much. Scoring would be faster and higher, and coliseums could contain more seats." I liked Josh's idea. Early in November, I spent a day making a propaganda film for the university. To be shown during halftime of televised basketball games, the film depicted the university as a "caring" and intellectual place. When asked to appear in the film, I protested at first, declaring that "peddling learning at a basketball game resembles advertising a vegetarian dinner at a barbecue." Still, I appeared in the film. Not to have done so would have been churlish. I feel responsible for my community, and when asked to help community, I almost always do so. Filming took a day. I got up at six in the morning and was out of the house by seven. I returned home at four that afternoon. For my trouble I received a can of Coca-Cola, some noodle salad, a ham sandwich, two chocolate-chip cookies, and as many ripple potato chips as my cholesterol could stand. The "payment" seemed fair until I read in the newspaper that the university paid the basketball coach eighty-five thousand dollars for "public relations," this in addition to a salary of one hundred and twenty-thousand dollars and another fifty thousand paid annually into an annuity. "And I got potato chips," I told Josh. "But," I added, falling back on platitude for support, "but I suppose it's the thought that counts." "True," Josh said, leaning forward and looking at me, "but what exactly was that thought?"

Although the day's little doings furnish my life with interest and pleasure, I still shop. Often I search for story, probing the pasts not of self or family as I did when I began writing but of characters I have created. I want to know what shaped them. I want to hear the old tales that lie neglected in the attic. Long before he founded the Tabernacle of Love in South Carthage, Slubey Garts was religious. "Little Slubey was born with his hands strapped to the Gospel Plough," Zeolla, his mother, told friends. "When Slubey was still just a precious baby, Brother Methodist Gaskins," she recounted, "placed a Bible, a whiskey bottle, a pink pair of woman's drawers, and a silver dollar on the floor in front of him. Slubey didn't hesitate," Zeolla said proudly, "he grabbed the Bible and started sucking on it, and we all commenced to praying, thanking Jesus our baby won't going to be a drunkard, a miser, or some sort of pervert or sex fiend." Although not greedy or lusty like many pentecostal preachers, Slubey enjoyed eating, so much so his sermons often resembled advertisements for Barrow's Grocery. In fact on Easter and Christmas, Lowry Barrow sent Slubey a groaning board of food—little enough payment, Turlow Gutheridge said, for turning modest, temperate pagans into starving Christians and doubling the grocery business in Smith County.

Slubey was especially fond of describing Paradise, where catfish and shad, spot and mullet splashed about in the River of Life, searching for hooks to bite. "A man don't need no hunk of horse head or rotten meat to catch crabs neither, no sir," Slubey preached, "all he's got to do is set his bucket on the shore, and the crabs will crawl into it, already deviled." For Slubey the long fields of heaven didn't run to milk and honey, but to sweet potatoes, black-eyed peas, okra, and greens: kale, turnip, collard, mustard, and poke sallat. Chickens roosted low; corn pone and chowchow, pepper jelly, peach preserves, and blackberry jam grew on brambles. Creeks flowed with pot likker. Brunswick stew bubbled in wells. Chitlins smelled sweet, and outhouse doors were made from half-moon pie. From the sky Dr Pepper and iced tea rained down, and grits and buttermilk biscuits fell like snow. When a man got his mule out to plow, he didn't turn over stumps and rocks, "praise God, no siree bobtail, he turned up pot roast and spiced round, and if he sweated, he didn't sweat no water, he sweated gravy: gizzard, liver, and heart gravy." "There ain't no pearls cast before hogs in heaven," Slubey often said, "just watermelons, stewed tomatoes, cheese pie, and egg bread—brothers and sisters can you smell the glory, can you taste it, the wonderful glory of God?"

If Slubey had a failing, it was love of language. Sometimes his words pitched wildly and swamped the frail bark of thought. Still, Slubey thought words important and in the Tabernacle of Love did not tolerate profanity. No man is perfect, however, and once or twice Slubey himself cursed. When first built, the Tabernacle only had a front door, the back door being added later, the day after Adair Trull's funeral. Adair died after eating a big dinner of carp and buttermilk. Luburl Haskew prepared the body at his funeral home, and when he and his boys loaded Adair on the "Glory Wagon" for a final leave-taking at the Tabernacle, everything seemed normal. Unfortunately, Pearline Haskew's big black tomcat Salvation had been shut up in the coffin with Adair. Salvation often napped in empty coffins. Always in the past, however, he scampered out when a body was stuffed in, Pearline explaining that he just couldn't stand cold feet. This time, evidently, all he did was stretch then wrap himself around Adair's toes. Later, of course, people speculated about his staying. Turlow Gutheridge blamed his behavior on the carp, but Lowry Barrow attributed it to the buttermilk, saying that a cat couldn't resist good buttermilk, especially the kind he sold at the store, which Adair, "Lord rest his soul," drank every chance he got. The road to the Tabernacle was bumpy, and the trip irritated Salvation. When the coffin was brought to the front of the church and Slubey lifted the lid, saying "Brethren let us bid farewell to our dear departed brother," Salvation leaped from the casket hissing and scratching—his eyes, Clevanna Farquarharson swore later, burning like coals. "Jesus," Vardis Grawling shrieked, and almost as one the mourners rose from the pews whooping and hollering and stampeded for the door. Alas, the path was straight and narrow, and what with the umbrellas, hats, white gloves, and good Christians longing, as Turlow Gutheridge put it, "for the wings of a dove," the door was soon jammed. "You could hear the lambs bleating all over God's heaven, but above it all," Turlow recounted, "you could hear Slubey shouting, 'Damn a church what ain't got but one door.'"

"Daddy," Eliza said on my birthday this fall, "I understand now. You go to high school then college. Then you marry and have babies and get very, very old. Then you die. Then you have your funeral and go up to heaven and see God, and then there's nothing else." Eliza's words were autumnal, fit for late October and November, that season of empty trees and open woods in which ridges distant and hazy in high summer suddenly pull close in hard, granite strips. For a moment the walker is deluded into thinking he sees clearly and deeply. Fallen trees resemble rails and slice the woods and vision into small, comfortable lots, as distinct and seemingly as graspable as a child's divisions of age. People divide and separate in order to understand. Seeing unity is difficult, perhaps impossible. Because one must dissect in order to approach understanding, a person rarely appreciates the grand weave of nature, that tapestry of relationships which knots fiber and mystery together into life. Seeing only strands or at best imagining a thin patch of the fabric, man seems condemned to tug wrong conclusions from effects. Not understanding how one thread colors the tapestry, he exploits and destroys, all the while reassuring himself with fact and statistic.

Besides story and gift I shop for season. Throughout late October and early November, I browsed field and wood. I did not search for or think about unity. I am only capable of seeing particular objects. But, oh, how appealing those objects are, the stuff of mood, if not thought, of appreciation and of awe, that blest tie, as Slubey would put it, that binds our hearts together in fellowship. One afternoon while cold flapped like a sheet on a line, rising up swollen then deflating then rising again, I watched starlings in an oak. Facing the wind they were as still as periods at the ends of declarative sentences. Occasionally, however, one dropped from the oak to a pin cherry and started feeding, the cherries shaking orange and red and the bird itself a dark smudge, almost an erasure. In the distance crows called; overhead Canada geese passed on their way to glean across Horsebarn and Bean hills. I did not watch the geese. Common winter residents, they travel in yelping packs, not flocks. Before they stopped migrating south, they were majestic, even frightening. High in the air their cries seemed barks, not those of mongrels begging bread, but those of Gabriel hounds, fierce dogs with human heads who ranged the skies pursuing the souls of sinners.

Although I saw a red-shouldered hawk hunched in a white pine near Tift Pond and then watched a downy woodpecker spiral jerkily around a beech, I did not spend much time looking up through trees. Whenever I did, the openness of the woods pulled my vision beyond the immediate toward the distant, the trees' bare, crooked branches framing the sky into bits of stained glass, blue and gray and silver, then sometimes yellow cooling into red, purple, and night. Instead of riding a tall wind, I generally scratched through brambles and low bushes watching nuthatches, titmice, chickadees, brown creepers, and Carolina wrens. One afternoon a small flock of bluebirds picked its way along the cut for the power line behind the house. Through thorn and goldenrod, kinglets hunted for insects. Toward the end of October juncos or snowbirds arrived. To me the name *snowbird* seemed apt, not because the bird was a harbinger of cold but because its gray back and white breast resembled deep winter in my Connecticut, round soft hills with dark clouds heavy over the snow, blocking out the horizon.

Much as I saw small birds, so I noticed little things: a chipmunk red against brown leaves and a blue jay sharper and brighter than he would have been in spring. Over a stone wall lichens rippled blotched and dark in the center then sandy and light green along the edges. At the top of a gully hay-scented ferns crumpled. Down the slope icy blades of Christmas fern shone like silver vertebrae in the sunlight. From a log grew common polypody, the fruit dots under its leaflets resembling small red puddings. Near Unnamed Pond bittersweet curled orange around staghorn sumac. Below, brambles curved in thin lathes, a fungus turning them blue. Nearby were stalks of peppergrass and fuzzy yellow spikes of foxtail.

Despite being bare and seemingly clean and almost well lit, the woods became dangerous in November. In the cut behind my house I found a dead deer, swollen and with hair scattered about it like seed from cattails. Raccoons discovered the deer before I did and tore a passage through its backside up into its chest cavity. The raccoons pushed the back legs wide, springing the bones loose so the pelvis

seemed to hang off-jamb like a rusty door falling off its hinges. In
November deer-jackers scour the woods. On walks I find places where
deer have been gutted, brown mounds of frozen entrails marking the
spots like low milestones. Along with deer-jackers, November brings
out gunners. One afternoon under the hill below Kessel Creek, at the
west side of Ogushwitz Meadow, I picked up handfuls of shell casings,
not simply those for shotguns—12, 16, 20, and 410 gauge—but also
for rifles—.22, .30 caliber, .30–06—and then pistols, 357 magnums,
and 9 and 10 millimeter, the 9 millimeter being a Luger.

In November rain gusts heavy and cold, sweeping across sidewalks
in shiny half circles, resembling scales from massive fish. The rain
keeps me safely out of the woods. Not only does the water make walking uncomfortable, but it reminds me of chores. I am afraid to climb
a ladder and clean the gutters, so I call Brian Gamache. What I do myself, however, is rake. Indeed November sometimes seems the month
of the rake. On clear days I pile leaves into a burlap carryall and dump
them into the woods behind the house. This year raking took three
days and sixty trips with the carryall; last year raking took five days
and seventy-four trips. While I rake and dump, Vicki cleans the
garage. When a storm stopped me from working for four days and Vicki
moaned she "had never seen anything like it," I told her Turlow Gutheridge's story about Chalkey Varnell. Chalkey was a talker, his main
subject being himself. After he drowned in the Buffalo Valley flood
and went to heaven, he described the flood to every angel he met,
explaining how the Gospel Tavern had been swept off its foundation
and how he had seen Alonzo, Casper Higgerty's mule, floating down
Fox Creek on its back, all four legs in the air kicking "to beat the
band." Even though they were busy trimming lamps and counting
fallen sparrows, the angels, with just one exception, put their work
aside and listened politely to Chalkey's descriptions. "Are the guys
treating you all right," Peter asked Chalkey when he saw him sometime later. "Yes," Chalkey answered, "everybody except one fellow.
When I started telling him about the disaster in Buffalo Valley, he just
walked away without so much as a how-do-you-do." "Did he have a
bushy beard with yellow tobacco streaks in it," Peter asked, "a cast in
one eye, white spots in the other, and thin, kind of knotted shanks?"
"Yes," Chalkey said. "Shucks," Peter said, shaking his head, "that
was old man Noah. You can't tell him nothing about no flood."

Along with wood and field, holidays make a season. For children Halloween is a harvest celebration. This year Francis was a wizard, Eliza a princess, and Edward a gorilla businessman. Edward wore a shaggy mask, horn-rimmed glasses, the coat to one of my gray suits, and was, he said, "a good businessman and a good gorilla." Whatever the influence of Edward's appearance, the reaping was good, and sweet. Neighbors filled the children's baskets with candy: Twizzlers, Charleston Chews, Dum-Dums, York Peppermint Patties, Mounds, Reese's Peanut Butter Cups, Tootsie Rolls, Milky Ways, and then toothbrushes, two Oral-B Ultras and a blue Reach with "We Love Your Smile" stamped on it in gold letters. Because the middle of November is often overcast, Northwest School celebrated Veteran's Day earlier in the month. One sunny afternoon not long after Halloween the children tumbled out to the soccer field. While parents smiled and took pictures, the children sang patriotic songs: "America," "America the Beautiful," "Yankee Doodle," "Columbia, the Gem of the Ocean," "The Battle Hymn of the Republic," and "The Star-Spangled Banner." At the end of the program Edward exchanged "high-fives" with his friend Sean. That night at dinner I told Edward that he was the first member of our family ever to exchange a high-five in public. "I trust," I said, "you will never do so again. Your grandfather must be rolling in his grave."

Despite my cautioning Edward against display, I am not retiring. Unaccountably, however, ordinary doings sometimes make me nervous. Election day followed five days after the Veteran's Day celebration. When the curtain of the voting booth closes behind me, I become tense, worried that I will break the machine or that the curtain will not release when I finish voting. Occasionally I consider not voting. If I did not vote, elections would certainly be more relaxing. Whenever Slubey Garts became nervous, he went fishing. One morning as he was climbing Bible Hill to visit a client, Turlow Gutheridge saw Slubey fishing in Dunphy's Pond. "What sort of luck have you had?" Turlow asked three hours later on his way home. When Slubey replied that he could not have enjoyed better luck, Turlow stopped. "Let me see your catch," Turlow said. "Catch," Slubey answered, "I haven't got any catch." "What," Turlow began but then stopped, noticing that Slubey's line was lying slack and curled on the surface of the pond. "Slubey," he said looking closer, "you don't have any bait or even a hook on that line. No wonder you haven't got a catch. You've got to fix the line." "Turlow," Slubey said, turning slowly around and looking up in exasperation, "Turlow, if I tie a hook on this line and stick a worm or two on it, the fishes in this pond are going to start worrying me, and I didn't come out here to be worried. I came here to fish."

Josh snorted when I told him voting made me tense. "Hell," he said, "that's easily taken care of. As soon as the curtain closes behind you, yell out at the top of your lungs, 'I'm not voting for you, you crooked bastard, nor you either you rotten shitass.' Then open the curtain, walk out, smile your best honeysuckle smile, shake your head, and say, 'The bottom rail is on top, and I'm just so worried about the country.' If you do this," Josh concluded, "I guarantee voting will never make you nervous again." Although Josh's medicine would probably work, it's too strong for my constitution. Vicki and I avoid using purgative language. Of course the children hear it at school. "Nathaniel said the F-word at recess today," Francis said at dinner ten days ago. "What!" Eliza exclaimed. "Did he," she continued almost in a whisper, "did he say fanny?"

Thanksgiving did not give me indigestion but depression, Park Avenue Depression. That morning Vicki, the children, and I drove to New York City and ate lunch with her brother Alex and his family. Afterward we returned to Storrs, the driving taking three hours each way and covering a total of two hundred and seventy-seven miles. For twenty years Alex has haunted art galleries, and his apartment glittered. No matter what I pawned, the turkey carcass was about the only thing in the apartment not beyond my bargain-basement pocketbook. That night as I snacked on Vicki's mincemeat pie I felt dissatisfied. The kitchen is my dining room, and the table is not mahogany but pressed wood, imported from Yugoslavia and sold by Unclaimed Freight. Instead of art peering down from walls, magnets stare out from the icebox, the stove, the dishwasher, even the handles to drawers. Cheap magnets too, first a zoo then a dreary highway strip of signs: ladybugs, a dancing pink dinosaur, a yellow cat holding a red heart, bees, mice, a frog with goggle eyes, a purple rhinoceros wearing gray tennis shoes with black stripes, then a blue and white rectangle reading "Jonathan Pelto Mansfield State Representative," another rectangle, this one white and red saying "CVS Today's Neighborhood Drugstore," and finally a yellow square in the middle of which is printed "Wawa Food Market" and the declaration, "We do it just a little bit better."

My dissatisfaction did not last longer than Vicki's pie. Living furnishes my mind with so many knickknacks that I don't have room in my thoughts for envy. On Friday my friend Pat gave me a magnet advertising his real estate business, "Ferrigno Storrs," and I put it on the icebox. The magnet was strong, and I stuck business cards behind it, first that of Tony Hulme, owner of the Piano and Organ Warehouse in Bloomfield, and then that of Paula Gladue, veterinarian at the East Brook Animal Hospital in Mansfield Center. The following Wednesday I flew to Ohio to speak at the College of Wooster. That night as I dressed for a faculty dinner the telephone rang. For a moment I considered not answering. Whenever I am in a hotel room, I turn on the television and watch programs that I would not look at in Connecticut. On the television in Wooster was a show about male bosom implants, not, so far as I could tell, for men who envied the soft endowments of the fair sex, but for men who thought hard landfills below the collarbone masculine and fetching in both boudoir and weight room. Thinking that Vicki might be calling about something at home, I answered the telephone, at the same time shimmying and pulling up my boxer shorts, in truth a nifty pair, a birthday present from the children decorated with wide bands of black, red, green, and white. On the telephone was a reporter from *Newsweek Magazine* eager to discuss college teaching. "Teaching!" I exclaimed; "I am sitting here in my underpants looking at men's nipples. Still," I said, pausing, "a person probably couldn't have better surroundings in which to pontificate about education." For fifteen minutes we talked, and the television show shifted from bosom to calf implants, these last designed, someone said, for people whose calves had been rustled by heredity. Suddenly a man appeared on the screen modeling a chest wig, for, I suppose, ecologically inclined males hopeful that brambles would attract chickadees and titmice. Like the show the interviewer and I ranged over a body, not a human body, though, but an educational body, one moment delving into the prickly relationship between research and teaching, the next snickering at literary and pedagogical theories, themselves implants, puffery designed to confuse and awe the unobservant.

Finally, to end the conversation I told the interviewer a story. Slubey Garts and Turlow Gutheridge often swam together at Dunphy's
Pond. One Sunday, Slubey preached a sermon based on John, chapter
three, verse sixteen, "For God so loved the world, that he gave his
only begotten Son, that whosoever believeth in him should not per-
ish but have everlasting life." "Come to the Cross," Slubey shouted.
"Trust in the Lord, and He'll send Jesus to bear your burden." The
next morning at Dunphy's Pond, Slubey almost swam into a water
moccasin. Both Slubey and the snake were startled and terrified. Unfortunately they turned in the same direction to escape, and Slubey
thought the snake was chasing him. Although the snake quickly
changed direction again and started for the opposite shore, Slubey
did not know it. "Swim, Slubey, swim," Turlow shouted from a bank;
"he's right behind you and gaining. Swim, Slubey, he is as thick
around as a cow's neck." At this point, according to Turlow, not necessarily the most reliable of witnesses, Slubey began to moan and kick
up more water than a steamboat. "Pray, Slubey, pray," Turlow yelled;
"I can see his white mouth. He's almost got you." Then, Turlow recounted, Slubey prayed and prayed as clearly as a church bell on a
cold, smoky morning. "Lord," he said; "I know you got a habit of
sending your son down here to take care of folks, but I want to tell you
right now, don't you come sending no son down here. You come yourself because saving me from this snake is a man's job."

The day after returning from Ohio, I drove Vicki and the children
to Buckland Hills, the new mall in Manchester. The mall contained
over one hundred shops, and in it we expected to find Christmas
presents for relatives. We were not successful. We browsed through
several stores. At G. Fox we examined champagne glasses on sale for
twenty-one dollars apiece. Afterward Eliza dragged us into Victoria's
Secret. "Why are they so fancy?" Francis said, looking at a display of
panties; "nobody can see them when they are on." At Sears we made
our only big purchase, rubber sheets for the children's beds. Flu season had begun at school, and nighttime throw-ups were sure to follow.
For a while I watched people. Although the flak over Tolland and
Vernon has never been heavy, many people wore brown leather flying
jackets, the sort worn by the crews of B-29s in movies about World
War II. At the Original Cookie Company I bought two chocolate-
chip cookies, while Vicki bought a large cup of Swedish coffee at

Gloria Jean's Coffee Bean. For dinner Edward and Eliza ate hamburgers, while Francis and Vicki ate egg rolls from Panda Express. Wanting something different, I tried a roli boli, a tube of dough wrapped about assorted fillings. For my fillings, I chose the group labeled "Yuppie"—lobster, artichoke hearts, eggplant, asparagus, and mozzarella cheese. The sandwich gave me indigestion, and if the mall had contained a franchise of Noonday, I would have hurried there and purchased earthworms dissolved in marigold juice, according to Mother Noon a certain remedy for "all grippings of the gut." Early the next morning Vicki went catalog shopping. By lunch, $461.45 later, she finished buying presents. She did not order gifts for the children. For them she shopped throughout the year, buying toys and clothes at sales. They are stored in the basement, and on Christmas Eve, Mrs. Claus and her husband bring them upstairs and wrap them. This year we must drink less eggnog and be more observant. "Daddy," Edward said to me just yesterday, "if Santa Claus is real, why does he put price tags on his toys?"